Jingle Bell Rock

Jingle Bell Rock

Lori Foster

Janelle Denison

Susan Donovan

Donna Kauffman

Alison Kent

Nancy Warren

KENSINGTON PUBLISHING CORP.

http://www.kensingtonbooks.com

BRAVA BOOKS are published by

Kensington Publishing Corp.
850 Third Avenue
New York, NY 10022

All Kensington titles, imprints and distributed lines are available at special quantity discounts for bulk purchases for sales promotion, premi-
ums, fund raising, educational or institutional use.

Special book excerpts or customized printings can also be created to fit
specific needs. For details, write or phone the office of the Kensington
Special Sales Manager: Kensington Publishing Corp., 850 Third Avenue,
New York, NY, 10022. Attn. Special Sales Department. Phone: 1-800-
221-2647.

Brava and the B logo Reg. U.S. Pat. & TM Off.

ISBN 0-7582-0569-4

First Kensington Trade Paperback Printing: October 2003
10 9 8 7 6 5 4 3 2 1

Printed in the United States of America

CONTENTS

He Sees You When You're Sleeping
by Lori Foster
1

All She Wants for Christmas
by Janelle Denison
45

Turning Up the Heat
by Susan Donovan
99

Baby, It's Cold Outside
by Donna Kauffman
145

A Blue Christmas
by Alison Kent
209

The Nutcracker Sweet
by Nancy Warren
261

He Sees You When You're Sleeping

Lori Foster

Chapter One

Booker Dean stood in front of his six-foot Christmas tree, gazing at the brightly lighted star atop and thinking of things that should be, but weren't. Yet.

The drive home had shown so many beautiful sights: laughing people laden with packages, store windows lavishly decorated, wreaths and lights and song. It was a magical time of the year, a time when anything seemed possible, a time when love became clearer, and he hoped, more attainable.

He'd only come in moments ago, had just hung his snow-dusted coat in the closet before going to the tree to think about her, to consider the task ahead of him. Resisting her was never easy, but in his present mood, it would be doubly hard. He was a man, and he wanted her, right now, this very instant. He wanted to share the magic of the holidays with her, today, tomorrow, for the rest of his life.

Did he dare approach her now, or should he wait until he was in better control?

Those thoughts got interrupted when his apartment door flew open without a knock. Booker strode to the entryway, saw his visitors and cursed. Damn it, he was too tired and edgy to have to put up with company from his brother tonight.

Axel hadn't come alone. He had his best friend Cary Rupert with him, and they both looked too serious.

Booker cocked one brow high. "Forgotten how to knock?"

"On my own brother's door?" Axel snorted, then shook himself like a mongrel dog, sending snow and ice around the foyer. It would be a white Christmas this year for sure, given the present weather and next week's forecast. "Besides," Axel continued, "I figured if you were doing anything private, you'd have the good sense to lock it."

"I just got in." Booker propped his hands on his hips and surveyed them both. Axel's dark brown eyes, much like his own, were strangely evasive. Cary unbuttoned his coat while casting worried glances toward Booker. Given the combined behavior of them both, misgivings surfaced. "All right. What's going on?"

Cary forestalled him by shivering and slapping at his arms. "You got anything hot to drink?"

Seeing no hope for it, Booker nodded. "Yeah sure." The apartment was dark except for the multicolored lights on the tree, blinking in random patterns. The scent of evergreen filled the air. When he walked through the living room, the musical mistletoe triggered on, playing a tinny "Jingle Bells." Frances had bought him the whimsical gift only last week—an early Christmas present she told him. More than anything, Booker had wanted to hold her under the mistletoe and give her the killer kiss of a lifetime.

But Frances was a friend and only a friend and he had commitments he hadn't quite ended. Yet. But he was working on that, and then he'd see to Frances. *Soon,* he promised himself. *Very soon.*

Cary pulled a wooden chair away from the table and straddled it, crossing his arms over the back, his gaze still watchful. Axel went to stand by the sink. He rubbed his face tiredly and Booker realized he hadn't shaved.

At thirty, Axel was one year older than Booker, but ten times more outrageous. Where Booker had always wanted to settle down, buy a nice house and start a family, Axel seemed hell-bent on sowing wild oats till the day he croaked. He took his residency as a gynecologist seriously—despite all the teasing he got from male friends and family. But other than that, other than his chosen profession, Axel was a complete hedonist intent only on having fun and indulging desires.

Booker opened the cabinet door and pulled out a strong coffee blend; it looked like he was going to need it. "While I fix this, why don't you tell me why you look so glum."

Appearing more morose by the second, Axel groaned. "That's why I'm here, so I suppose I should. But God knows I hate to be the bearer of bad news. It's just that I figured you should hear it from me, not anyone else."

Booker paused. "Mom and Dad—"

Cary made a sound of exasperation. "Your family is fine and no one died. Jesus, Axel, just spit it out."

Axel pointed a finger at his friend. "You're here for moral support, so how about showing a little?"

Cary just rolled his eyes.

"Out with it, Axel." Booker threw in an extra scoop of coffee for good measure. "What did you do now?"

"I said no, that's what I did."

"No to what?"

"Not what, who."

"All right. Who?"

Visibly pained, Axel blurted, "Judith."

"Judith?" And then, with confusion, "My Judith?" Even as he said it, Booker winced. He didn't want her to be *his* Judith anymore. She was a sweet woman, very nice and innocent, but he wanted Frances. Hell, he'd been with Judith for five months now and . . . there was nothing. Just fizzle. Once Frances had moved in next door two months ago, he'd figured out what he really wanted in a woman, and Judith wasn't it.

But Frances was.

Axel pushed away from the sink. "Swear to God, Booker, I was just there minding my own business, burning off a little tension after a really long week."

Because Axel had raised his voice, and because Cary was busy nodding hard in agreement, Booker's suspicions grew. "You were just where?"

"At the bar. Hell, I was hitting on a redhead two seats down.

She was hitting back, things were looking good, then suddenly Judith was there."

"Judith was at a bar?" That didn't sound like the Judith he knew.

"I think she was drunk, Booker," Cary explained in a rush. "She, uh, wasn't acting like herself. Said something about being tired of pretending."

Axel's Adam's apple bobbed and he said in agonized tones, "She grabbed my equipment, Booker. She just . . . grabbed it. I know you've been seeing her for a while now, but she's not who you think she is."

"She grabbed his equipment," Cary reiterated, still nodding.

"It was like . . ." Axel opened his hand over his fly and held himself firmly, making sure Booker understood. "Then she pressed up real close and breathed in my damn ear that she wanted me. *Me*, Booker." He shook his head in apology. "Not you."

Booker was so stunned, he reached back for a chair. Cary acted quickly, sliding one underneath his ass so he didn't hit the floor. "She grabbed you?"

"Like this." Still holding himself, Axel gave his crotch a small shake. "I damn near swallowed my tongue and, well, hell, Booker. You can't hang onto a guy's equipment without getting a rise. I didn't mean to react. I even told her to let go. But she held on real tenacious like, even when I backed up. And backing up wasn't easy, I can tell you that. The place was jammed and that girl has a grip."

"He did say no," Cary assured him. "I was there, Booker. It was sort of a strangled whisper, a little garbled, but he said it. Only Judith didn't want to take no for an answer."

Booker looked between them. Scenarios played out in his mind in rapid succession. "Did you sleep with her then?"

"No!" Axel pulled back, horrified by the mere suggestion.

"Booker!" In his friend's defense, Cary was equally affronted. "You know your brother better than that."

It was all Booker could do not to laugh at the two of them, squawking like hens. He rubbed his jaw, bit back a grin, and said, "Axel, you can let go of yourself now."

"Oh. Yeah." Axel released his crotch and shoved his hands into his pockets. He hesitated, his frustration bubbling up until he started squawking again. "You had to know, Booker. I didn't want to be the one to tell you, but you had to know."

"Yep. I had to know."

Cary leaned toward him, filled with masculine concern. He clapped Booker on the back of the neck, gave him a too-tight squeeze. "You okay, Booker?"

"I'm fine actually." He shrugged off Cary's stranglehold, glanced up and saw the coffeemaker give one final hiss and spit. "Good, the coffee is done. You can each have one cup. I'll even let you have a Christmas cookie. Then I want you gone."

Axel and Cary looked at each other helplessly. "You upset?"

"Not really." Surprised. Exhilarated. But not upset. Booker filled three mugs to the top. None of them used sugar or cream, though Booker kept it on hand because Frances liked her coffee with plenty of both, and there were many a lazy Sunday morning where they shared a cup and talked about upcoming sports, work, or just sat together, doing nothing.

Well, Frances did nothing. Booker spent his time surreptitiously watching her, thinking about getting her out of her clothes, basically doing all the fantasizing men indulge when with a woman they want. Bad.

He opened his cookie jar, took out a handful of the delicious, decorated cookies Frances had made for him, and set them on the table.

"What are you going to do, Booker?"

Booker shook off his musings. He noticed that Cary's brown hair was still damp from the sleet and snow. He pushed it back from his face while watching Booker with sympathy and concern. Hell, did they expect him to go ballistic? To be furious with Axel? To sit around and mope with a broken heart?

This time he did laugh.

Cary leaned forward, and as a doctor, gave his professional opinion. "Damn, he's hysterical."

Axel's eyes widened. "Booker. Man, I swear I'm sorry. Judith is sweet on the eyes, no way around that. But I would never go behind your back—"

Knowing he had to put them at ease before they started trying to hug him or something equally unsavory, Booker set down his coffee. "You want to know what I'm going to do? Okay, I'll tell you. First, I'm going to shower and change into clean clothes. Then I'm going to go next door to see Frances. And then . . ." He savored the moment, his voice dropping to a husky drawl without him even realizing it. "Then, I'm going to make up for lost time."

Silence filled the kitchen until Axel fell back against the counter. "Frances?" he asked with some confusion.

Cary drew an incredulous face. "Your neighbor?"

"Yeah." In extreme anticipation, Booker rubbed his hands together. Frances might think of herself as just a friend for now, but that was about to change. The sooner the better.

When he got her naked and kissed her from head to toe, she'd understand he wanted more than friendship. A lot more—like everything.

"You're talking about that tall girl next door?" Cary asked, apparently needing clarification. "The one who likes football and runs all the time?"

"She jogs, and yeah, she's the one." She'd been *The One* almost from the day he'd met her.

"I kinda thought she was gay," Cary confided.

Booker laughed. "No. She just doesn't date much because she's always working." Frances was a very talented artist, though so far most of her work centered around commissions for commercial outlets, like window paintings and murals in pediatrician and dentist offices. Recently, however, the local galleries had started showing her work—with much success.

"You got a thing for her?" Axel asked.

"Yeah. A thing. A big thing. Like a hard case of *gotta have her.*"

"No shit?" Axel grinned and for the first time that night, he relaxed. "Well, hell, that's great news, Booker." Then he thought to ask, "Does this girl feel the same about you?"

"Woman, and no. At least, not yet she doesn't. But then, we've done that damned disgusting platonic thing because she thought I was permanently tied to Judith and I was waiting until I could figure out how to end things with Judith without breaking her heart."

Cary choked. "I think her heart will be safe."

"It seems so." Booker was so relieved to have that particular problem solved that he couldn't wait to get to Frances. He turned to his brother. "I suppose I owe you a thank-you, for helping things along."

Axel fell into a thoughtful silence while sipping his coffee. "So let me get this straight. You're not even the smallest bit upset that Judith was pawing me and licking on me?"

"Pawing you *and* licking you?"

Axel shrugged. "My ear and neck and stuff. She's got a hot little tongue on her, too. I thought for a minute there she was going to take a bite. And I had a helluva time getting her fingers off my zipper, but with the way she used that tongue, no way did I want my zipper down. She'd backed me damn near into the men's room and I swear, I thought the girl would molest me."

When Booker smiled, Cary added, "I've never seen your brother in such a panic, Booker. If I hadn't been worried about how you'd take it, I'd have been laughing my ass off."

"I'm not upset, Axel. This gives me the perfect out and I won't even have to be the bad guy."

Axel nodded, did some more thinking, then plunked down his coffee cup. "You know, Booker, I really wish you'd have let me in on all this *before* I told Judith no."

Cary snickered. "She was plenty pissed when you turned her down."

"Probably because she knows my brother never turns women down."

"Almost never," Axel specified. "But even I have to draw the line at women involved with my baby brother." He tipped his head at Booker. "Say, I don't suppose you'd care to give me her number?"

"God, Axel." Cary shook his head in disgust. "You're unbelievable."

Axel just smiled. "The way that girl held me was unbelievable. And since Booker doesn't mind, I figure why not?"

"I don't mind at all." Booker wrote down her number and handed it to Axel with his best wishes. "Good luck, and get out. I have things to do and they don't include the two of you."

"Given that look in your eyes, I should hope not," Cary said with a laugh.

Axel slung his arm around Booker on the way to the front door. He was twenty-five pounds heavier and an inch shorter than Booker, but other than that, the similarity in their appearance was uncanny. "So you think you'll be bringing Frances to Christmas dinner?"

With all his most immediate plans centered on getting her into bed, preferably tonight, he hadn't yet thought that far ahead. But it sounded like a hell of an idea. Frances was friendly, open, easy to talk to. If things worked out as he hoped, they'd be spending a lot of time together, especially during the holidays—and especially in bed. "I'll work on it."

Frances had paused in front of her tree to straighten a plump Santa ornament. The delicate glass reflected the white twinkly lights, looking almost magical. But there'd be no magic for her this year. What she wanted most, Santa couldn't put under her tree.

After working all day, she was hot and tired, and so when What-She-Wanted-Most knocked on her door, she almost jumped out of her skin. She knew it was Booker, because she knew his knock, just as she knew his laugh, his tone of voice when he was excited, and his scent. God, she loved his scent.

With her heart swelling painfully, she opened the door with a false smile. As usual, he looked dark and sexy and so appealing, her pulse leaped at the sight of him.

Hands snug in his pockets, his flannel shirt open over a white thermal and nicely worn jeans, he leaned in her doorway. His silky black hair was still damp from a shower and his jaw was freshly shaved. He had a rakish "just won the lottery" look about him and the way he murmured, "Hi" had her blinking in surprise.

Somehow, he was different. There was a glimmer in his dark eyes, a special kind of attentiveness that hadn't been there only the day before. His gaze was direct and almost . . . intimate. Yeah, that was it. And he wore a funny little half smile of expectation.

Expectation of *what?*

Uncertainly, Frances managed a reply. "Hey, Booker. What's up?"

He stepped inside without an invite, but then, they were *friends* and Booker visited with her a lot. Whenever he wasn't working—or with Judith—he came by to play cards, watch sports, or just shoot the bull. Like he would with a pal.

Maybe it was the holidays making her nostalgic, but when she thought of being Booker's pal for the rest of her life, she wanted to curl up and cry.

A stray lock of hair had escaped her big clip and hung near her eyes. Taking his time and stopping her heart in the process, Booker smoothed it behind her ear.

No way in hell did he do that with his guy friends. She gulped.

In a voice low and gentle and seductive, he said, "What have you been doing that has you all warm on such a cold snowy day?"

Unnerved, Frances backed up out of reach. Booker stepped close again. "I, ah . . ." She gestured behind her. "I'm moving my room."

"Yeah?" He looked at her mouth. "Want to move it next door with me?"

She shook her head at his unfamiliar, suggestive teasing. "I'm switching my bedroom with my studio because the light is better in that room now."

As an artist, she liked to take advantage of whatever natural light she could get. In summer, she used her smaller guest bedroom for sleeping so that the larger room could be filled with her canvases and paints and pottery wheel. But now with winter hard upon them, the light was different. More often than not, long shadows filled the room, so she was switching. If nothing else, it gave her a way to fill the time rather than think of Booker and Judith snuggled up in front of a warm fire, playing kissy-face and more.

Booker stepped around her and closed the door. "Maybe I can help. What else do you have to move?"

Now that was more like the Booker she knew and loved. "Just the bedroom furniture. I already moved the small stuff and my clothes." She turned to meander down the hallway and Booker followed. Closely. She could practically feel him breathing on her neck. Neil Diamond's Christmas album played softly in the background, barely drowning out the drumming of her heartbeat.

Today, even Neil hadn't been able to lift her spirits.

As they passed the kitchen, they walked beneath a sprig of mistletoe hung from a silver ribbon. Because she was a single woman without a steady date—without any date really— Frances had put it up as decoration, not for any practical use. She paid it little mind as she started under it, until Booker caught her by the upper arm.

Turning, she said, "What?"

Gently, he drew her all the way around to face him. He looked first into her eyes, letting her see the curious heat in his, then he looked at her mouth. His voice dropped. "This."

In the next instant, Frances found herself hauled up against his hard chest while his hands framed her face.

Startled, she thought, *He's going to kiss me.*

Just as quickly, she discounted that absurd notion. Booker was a friend, nothing more. He was involved with Judith. He didn't see her as a—

His mouth touched hers.

She went utterly still outside, but inside things were happening. Like her heart hitting her rib cage and her stomach fluttering and her blood taking off in a wild race through her system . . .

"Frances?" He whispered her name against her mouth.

Dazed, her eyes flickered open. "Hmm?"

Booker held her face tipped up, brushed her jaw with his thumbs, and kissed her again. It was a gentle, closed-mouth kiss, but there was nothing platonic about it. His mouth was warm, soft, moving carefully over hers. His tongue traced the seam of her lips with such enticing effect that her toes curled and her hands lifted to his hard shoulders. Booker groaned, tightened his hold—and Frances came back to her senses.

"*Booker.*" She shoved him away, suffused with indignation and hurt and an awful yearning. "What do you think you're doing?"

Because she was nearly as tall, her push had thrown him off-balance. He caught himself, grinned at her, and said, "Something I've been thinking about doing for a long time."

Frances touched her mouth, equally doubting and flustered. She could still taste him. "You have?"

"Yeah. I have." He closed the space between them again. Frances inhaled the clean scent of his aftershave and the headier scent of his body. She could practically feel the heat in his unwavering gaze. He touched her chin, tipped up her face, and asked, "Haven't you, Frances? Ever?"

Chapter Two

Frances swallowed hard. Think of him? Of course, she had. There were nights when she couldn't sleep at all, fantasizing about Booker, about kissing him and touching him, feeling his weight on top of her, naked flesh to naked flesh. But all she did was fantasize because he was already with someone else and she would never, ever be blamed for breaking up a couple.

She couldn't lie to him, but she wouldn't be a party to him cheating either. "Yes, I have."

His expression tightened, his voice went deep. "Tell me."

God, he was potent in seduce-mode. "No. Because I'm not going to do anything about it."

"Wanna bet?"

Oh, the wicked way he murmured that. "Booker Dean, have you forgotten that you're already involved? Have you forgotten about *Judith?*" Damn, she hadn't meant to sneer the woman's name. It wasn't Judith's fault that Booker had fallen in love with her long before Frances had even moved into his apartment complex. She scowled. "You know you don't really want to do this."

"Oh, I want to all right." He kept inching toward her, forcing her to back up. "You probably have no idea of all the things I want to do to you."

Her mouth fell open, then snapped shut. "Let me rephrase that. I won't let you do them."

He reached out and brushed her cheek with the back of his knuckles. His voice was soft, mesmerizing. "Even though Judith and I aren't together anymore?"

"You aren't . . ." Her eyes narrowed. "Since when?"

With a load of satisfaction, Booker said, "About twenty minutes ago."

Forget indignation. Frances was outraged. She stopped retreating and took a stand. Through stiffened lips, she said, "Judith breaks up with you twenty minutes ago and so you come tripping over here expecting . . . what? You want me to comfort you, Booker? Is that it? You want to use me to forget about her?"

Booker looked momentarily nonplussed, then annoyed. "No, damn it. That's just dumb. Besides, she didn't break up with me."

That surprised Frances. "You're the one who broke things off?"

He worked his jaw. "Well, not yet. Not officially. But see . . ."

Frances threw up her arms. "I don't believe this. Go home, Booker." She turned and stomped down the hall to her bedroom. *Not officially*, she mimicked in her mind. Damn. She hit a pillow, but it didn't help. She'd wanted Booker too long to play games like this.

Conflicting emotions wreaked havoc with her heart. She'd dreamed of Booker seeing her as more than a friend, but never would she allow him to use her to get over another woman.

She started to hit the pillow again, then Booker slipped his arms around her from behind. All along the length of her back, she felt him, hot, hard, most definitely male. Because he held a physical job, Booker's strength was evidenced in lean, hard muscles. When Frances started to jolt away, he carefully restrained her, gathering her close against his body, enfolding her in that delicious scent. "Just hold on and let me explain."

She'd melt if she stayed pressed to him like this. In a rasp, she whispered, "Let go."

"No."

His refusal gave her pause, then renewed her temper. She'd

never known Booker to be a dominating-type man. "What do you mean no? I said to let me go."

Instead, he immobilized her by kissing the side of her neck. Stunned, Frances registered the heat and firmness of his mouth, the soft touch of his damp tongue—and she registered his smile. "Honest to God, Frannie, you make me nuts. You've been making me nuts for a while now." His arms tightened in a bear hug and he rocked her side to side.

Holding herself stiff against the urge to relax in his embrace, Frances said, "Well it wasn't on purpose."

"I know," he soothed. "You can't help it."

"Booker—"

He interrupted her warning with another soft smooch, this one behind her ear. That small kiss, accompanied with the sigh of his breath, had her breathing accelerating and her temperature on the rise. She shivered.

"There, you see? You do it without even trying."

"Do . . . what?"

"Make me crazy." He pressed his nose into her hair. "With the way you smell—"

Smell? She tried for sarcasm to save her. "You mean like paint thinner and clay?"

"And woman and sex and *you,* Frannie Kennedy. I love how you smell." He took another deep breath, then growled to show his sincerity. "And the way you dress."

Now she rolled her eyes. "In paint-stained work clothes? C'mon Booker." Since they couldn't be more than friends, she'd made a point of *not* primping with him. In the last few weeks, he'd started coming over more often, staying longer when he did, and she'd come to appreciate how nice it was to be totally herself with someone. She could forget makeup and uncomfortably stylish clothes. She could laugh out loud without worrying if he found her inelegant. She could blow her nose when she had a cold or sniffle and cry at sad movies. She could cheer as loud as any guy when her favorite football team won, and she could even share a few dirty jokes with him without blushing.

Now he wanted to throw a kink in the works.

Booker's hands opened over her middle. He had large hands, rough from working in his lumberyard and doing custom millwork. With his fingers splayed, he was only a millimeter from her breasts with one hand, and closer than that to her left hipbone with the other.

Anticipation held her in thrall. Would he touch her? Would she let him?

His warm breath brushed her ear. "In soft loose smocks that tease because they hide your breasts, making my imagination go wild."

She didn't know Booker had ever noticed her breasts. They certainly weren't big enough to automatically draw attention.

". . . and snug leggings that make your ass look great."

Her *ass?* She tried to twist to see him, but he wouldn't let her.

". . . and thick socks that look so cute on your feet."

Being almost as tall as him meant her feet were proportionate—and not in the least cute. "Now you're just being ridiculous."

"Frannie, Frannie, Frannie. You'd be amazed at what appears sexual to the male mind, especially when it's been deprived. Like the funny way you always pin up your hair." He teased a twisted lock with his nose. "It's sort of sloppy and casual, but I can see your nape and those baby-fine curls there and it makes me horny as hell." To emphasize that, he took a gentle love bite at the side of her throat.

Frances swallowed down a gasp, both of shock and sexual spark. Against her behind, she felt the start of an impressive erection. She gave a small, nearly silent moan. It took all her willpower not to nestle up closer to that purely male reaction—*to her.*

But willpower was something she'd cultivated since moving next door to Booker Dean. When she'd first met him, she'd panicked because he was so appealing and she'd been a complete wreck, a typical state for her when she worked, and she worked almost all the time. But when she'd realized he was already taken and so off-limits, she'd given up and been herself and found a wonderful friendship that no matter how she tried wasn't quite enough.

It still wasn't enough, but she'd be damned before she got him on the rebound.

"So," she said, forcing the word out while closing her hands around his wrists to ensure he wouldn't move them up or down. "You're not officially over with Judith, but you expect me to just say, 'Hey, okay, let's go to bed'?"

He shuddered against her, asking roughly, "Would you?"

"No." She again started to lunge away but Booker held on and they stumbled into the wall.

"If you'll just settle down and listen, I'll explain." Cautiously, he turned her around so she faced him. Then, before she could protest, he looked at her mouth, appeared drawn there and he started kissing her again, light, teasing kisses. "I swear, Frannie, you have the sexiest mouth."

"In about two seconds, I'm going to unman you with my knee." He released her and stepped back so quickly, she almost smiled. "Now, if you insist, you can explain while you help me move my stuff." If he kept his hands busy moving her furniture, he couldn't have them busy feeling her up, and she wouldn't have to worry about resisting him.

He followed her to the bedroom, reacting to her antagonism with inexhaustible good humor. "Sure thing, Frannie." Muscles flexed and his shoulders strained when he hefted a nightstand high and started out the door with it. "Hey, do you realize your room will be right next to mine now?"

Frances froze in the process of lifting a plant. Good God, he was right. Only a thin apartment wall would separate them now. He came back into the room, saw her stunned expression, and clicked his tongue. "What are you thinking, Frances Kennedy? Can I trust you not to put your ear to the wall? Will you drill a hole and peek at me at night? I sleep naked you know."

Heat pulsed in her cheeks. "Booker . . ."

"In fact, if you actually want a peek, I'd be more than happy to—" He reached for the snap on his jeans.

Frances shoved the plant into his arms. "I was just wondering if I'd have to listen to you and Judith."

He chided her with a look. "Nope. I told you, that's over. Actually, it's been over for a month. I just wasn't sure how to finish it off."

She desperately wanted to believe that. "So what changed?"

With great relish, he confided, "She wants Axel."

"She *what?*"

Booker laughed. "Don't sound so shocked. I haven't met too many women who don't want Axel."

"Well, I certainly don't." Axel was a nice enough guy, and she could see why he'd be popular with the females. But it was this particular brother who pushed all her buttons. Not Axel. Not any other man.

"I'm really glad to hear that. He can have Judith, but I don't want him to even look at you funny."

Like a zombie, Frances moved to the end of her mattress and helped Booker lift it. Her thoughts were churning this way and that. "You don't seem upset that she might want your brother."

"No 'might' to it, and no, as I told Axel, I'm relieved." He winked at Frances. "Leaves me free and clear for other . . . pursuits."

Frances ignored that bit of nonsense for now. "Did Judith tell you she wanted Axel?"

"No." Booker wrestled his end of the mattress into the other room. "From my understanding, she just caught Axel alone and tried to molest him."

Frances snorted. "Yeah right. Like Axel ever needs to be coerced."

Booker paused to give her a long look around the side of the mattress. "He's my brother, honey. Whatever else he might be, he's loyal to family."

Somewhat chastened, Frances dropped her end of the mattress. "Meaning he wouldn't go behind your back with Judith?"

"That's right. She came on to him, he turned her down, but felt he had to let me know. Rightfully so because what man wants to tie himself to a woman who's after his brother?"

"Only an idiot."

"And I'm sure we'll both agree I'm not an idiot." He didn't wait for her agreement at all. "But as it turns out, I'm pleased to have the perfect opportunity to end things." He, too, let his end of the mattress rest on the floor. "I'd been working on that anyway."

Frances bit her lip and tried not to sound too hopeful. "You have?"

"Yeah, I have. Only I'm a nice guy and I didn't want to hurt her." His voice lowered. "We haven't been . . . close for a month anyway."

It had been about a month that he'd been coming around more often, staying longer, teasing her more. But did he mean he hadn't slept with Judith in a month? Her brows drew down in disbelief.

"Now Frannie, don't look at me like that. Have I ever lied to you?"

"No. But you've never acted interested either."

He sighed, lifted the mattress again and dragged it the rest of the way into the room. Frances thought he was going to let the subject drop until he said, "I've always been attracted to you, Frannie. From the first time I saw you, I knew I wanted you."

She swallowed hard, frowned, then turned away. Booker followed her back into the bedroom where they tackled the bedsprings next. Unable to keep it in, she finally grumbled, "You hid it well."

He grinned. "Really? Maybe I should have been an actor." They both strained to get the cumbersome bedsprings through the doorway. Once it was in place with the mattress, Booker dusted off his hands. "I must be more accomplished than I realized. I mean, I know I didn't come right out and tell you, but if all the attention didn't clue you in, then I thought for sure the occasional boner would be a giveaway."

Frances silently cursed herself for blushing again. She retreated back to her room to dismantle the bed frame.

Booker knelt beside her. "Frances?"

"I never noticed."

"Never noticed what?"

Keeping her attention on the task at hand, she blindly gestured toward his lap and gave a whopper of a lie. "Any . . . boners."

Booker clutched his heart theatrically and toppled back on his rear. "God, I'm wounded. You really know how to damage the old male vanity, hon."

Laughing, Frances lifted one half of the frame and stood. Truth was, she'd noticed a few erections here and there, but had always discounted them as some strange male phenomenon. Guys got hard for the most ridiculous reasons.

Booker came to his feet to face her. Losing his smile, he stared at her with beguiling seriousness and seductive charm. "How about now?"

"Now?"

Without looking away from her eyes, he took her wrist and carried her hand to his fly where a thick ridge had risen beneath his denims. The second her fingers touched him, he caught his breath and his voice went hoarse. "Can you notice this one?"

A rush of giddiness nearly took Frances's knees out from under her. He was long, thick and hard . . . how could she not notice? She thought of him naked, thought of him pressing inside her, filling her up, and her fingers curled tight around him. Booker's eyes closed and she heard the roughness of his breathing.

Filled with curiosity, she traced his length upward, then back down again, measuring him, teasing herself. Booker locked his jaw. "Keep that up and I'm going to lose it."

She barely heard his words. Lifting her other hand, she covered him completely, stroking, squeezing, reaching lower to feel the heavy weight of his testicles. His teeth clenched. "Frances, I've wanted you too long to have any patience. Add that to month-long celibacy, and I'm working on a hair trigger here."

So, it really had been a month? That meant something, didn't it?

He stood rigid before her, letting her do as she pleased. Or rather, as she dared. She wanted to push him to the floor and strip him naked, but everything had happened too quickly . . .

Releasing him, she stepped back. It took him a moment, but Booker finally got his eyes open. He looked in pain. He looked ready to jump her bones. Suggestively, he said, "Why don't we finish putting the bed together?"

"All right."

His eyes flared at her agreement.

Damn it, she hated her conscience sometimes. "But Booker, I can't . . . we can't, do anything until you've officially broken things off with Judith. You said you're a nice guy. Well, I'm a nice woman. And like your brother, I want no part of poaching."

Booker frowned. "Speaking with her is just a formality at this point."

"It's a formality I'll have to insist on." In the darkest part of her soul, Frances was afraid that Judith would beg him not to leave her, and he'd agree. She knew it was wrong to hope things would be over between them, especially if Judith would be hurt. But she wished it just the same.

Booker hesitated a long moment before agreeing. "All right. Let's get done here and I'll go call her. But it won't matter, Frannie, not to me."

Hoping that was true, Frances nodded. They spent the next hour setting up her bedroom. Booker even helped her remake the bed, then rearrange everything in her new studio so that the job was complete. The busy work afforded Frances a little time to think about the new turn of events.

When they'd finished and the last item was in place, Booker

caught both her hands and bent to kiss her. "If Judith is home, I could be back here in no time."

Booker Dean was more temptation than any woman should have to endure. Regretfully, Frances shook her head. "Booker, I need some time to adjust to this. You can't just expect me to take it all in stride."

"Do you want me, Frances?"

"Yes." She didn't mind admitting that much. "I have for a long time."

His triumphant smile was sexy and pure male.

"But I still need some time to think things through."

"How much time?"

"I don't know. At least until tomorrow."

Disappointment showed in the drawing of his brows, the darkening of his eyes. "Tomorrow, huh?"

Unable to continue meeting his gaze, Frances looked down at her feet. "You need time to think about this too, you know. You could still change your mind. You might be here on the rebound or because you want validation because Judith tried to cheat on you." Frances shrugged, feeling a little helpless, caught between wanting to say *yes* and having enough common sense to say *not yet*. "I want you, but I don't want to be used and I don't want regrets and even more than that, I don't want things to get weird between us if we do this, and then tomorrow or the next day or a month from now, you're back with Judith."

Booker said nothing to all that, and Frances had the feeling he waited for her to look at him. Finally she did and got trapped in the mesmerizing intensity of his dark gaze. She had the bed at her back, Booker in front of her, and a whole lot of desire crackling in the air between them.

One side of Booker's mouth tipped in a sensual smile, then he stepped up against her and toppled her onto the mattress. Before she could catch her breath, he came down over her. His solid chest crushed her breasts, his hard abdomen pressed into her stomach. Like a tidal wave, desire rolled through her.

Booker cupped her face, kissed her nose, her forehead, her chin. "I don't want Judith. I haven't wanted Judith since I got to know you. But I'll wait. I'll give you some time. And while you're thinking things over, Frances, think about this."

His earlier kisses had been teasing, tentative.

This one scorched her.

Using his thumbs, he nudged her chin down so her lips parted. He sank his tongue in, leisurely exploring while giving her that full-body contact she'd craved for so long.

Her hands gripped his shoulders, holding on. His hips moved in a carnal press and retreat, mimicking how he'd take her if only she'd say yes. Frances moaned, then moaned again when his fingers found her breast, gently cuddled her, traced her nipple—and then he was gone.

It wasn't easy, but she got her eyes open to see Booker standing between her legs at the side of the bed. He stared down at her, his face flushed, his chest heaving, his dark gaze fierce.

Frances pushed up on one elbow. "Booker?"

"If I don't go now, I won't go at all. But I want more than just a quick tumble, Frannie. You'll figure that out on your own, without me pushing you. So . . . good night." He took one step back from the bed. "Think about me tonight. And try trusting me just a little."

She watched him leave the room, then dropped back down to the mattress with a long groan. Good gracious, Booker on the make was even more exciting than she'd ever imagined. And if he was like this when she said no, how tantalizing would he be when she finally said yes?

Chapter Three

No way was she going to be able to sleep. It was midnight, but her body hummed and her mind was in turmoil. Had he called Judith yet? What had happened?

Frances punched the pillow, moaned in frustration, and rolled to her side. She'd asked for tonight to think. But all she could think about was whether he'd called Judith, what might have happened, if it was really over. Why didn't he call and tell her?

She moaned again. When she saw him tomorrow, she'd . . .

"Frances?"

She froze at the muffled call of her name. Eyes wide in the dark, she peered around but saw nothing. No one.

A knock sounded on the wall right behind her head. "C'mon Frannie. I hear you in there." The squeak of his bed resonated through the wall.

Frances jerked upright. "Booker?"

"Of course, it's Booker. I told you we'd be sleeping right next to each other." Silence, then: "Why did you moan?" And sounding a little wishful: "Thinking of me?"

"Yes."

Throbbing silence. "What *are* you doing over there, Frannie?"

The way he said that, she knew exactly what *he* thought she was doing. She punched the wall, heard him curse softly, and smiled. "Get your mind out of the gutter, you pervert. I was beating up my pillow."

"How come?"

Because you made me all hot and bothered and then walked away. "Because I can't sleep."

"And? You can't sleep because . . . ?"

Through her teeth, Frances snarled, "Because I'm wondering if you spoke with Judith and how it went, but you didn't bother to call and tell me."

"Oh."

A few seconds later, her phone pealed loudly, giving Frances a horrible start. She stared toward the nightstand in the dark, then groped across the bed until she found it. She lifted the receiver. "Hello?"

"I called her."

Her fingers curled tightly. "And?"

There was a definite shrug in Booker's tone. "Axel answered."

"*Axel* answered?" Frances collapsed back against the headboard. Man, Booker's brother hadn't wasted any time. Of course, where women were concerned, he seldom did.

But Booker didn't seem perturbed by his brother's rush into his ex's bed. "Yeah. He sounded winded, too, so I'm thinking I interrupted things."

Her eyes flared wide again. "You interrupted things?"

Laughing, Booker asked, "Are you going to repeat everything I say?"

"Maybe." She couldn't believe how cavalier he was about the whole thing.

"I want you."

Frances gripped the phone, swallowed hard.

"Not going to repeat that, huh?" He sighed, very put out. "Anyway, Axel put Judith on the line, she apologized, said she was drunk. Then I heard Axel grousing at her and pretty soon, she was giggling, then panting. I don't know what he did to her, but she liked it because she finally admitted that she'd been thinking about Axel for a long time, and because of that, she knew she wasn't ready to settle down."

"Um . . . wow." Frances cleared her throat. "I don't know what to say."

"I say all's well that ends well. At least with those two. Now to work on you." His voice dropped. "I need your trust, Frannie."

Knowing she'd never get to sleep now, Frances flipped on the lamp and got out of bed. A peek out the darkened window showed drifting snow and ice crystals covering every surface. It looked magical, perfectly picturesque for Christmastime, and perfect to help clear her mind.

With the phone caught between her shoulder and ear, she pulled on thickly lined nylon jogging pants. "It's not a matter of trust, Booker. You've just done a hundred and eighty turn, and we both need time to adjust."

"What are you doing?" He sounded suspicious.

"Nothing." She sat on the bed to pull on two pairs of socks and her all-weather running shoes.

"Frances Kennedy, are you getting dressed?"

A new alertness had entered his tone, so she hesitated before finally saying in a small voice, "Yes."

The phone clicked in her ear. Well. In a huff, Frances put the phone back in the cradle and stood. Over her T-shirt, she layered on a thermal shirt and finally a sweatshirt. After wrapping a muffler around her throat, pulling a wool hat low over her ears and grabbing up her mittens, she headed for the apartment door.

She opened it only to find Booker standing there in hastily donned jeans and nothing else. He pushed his way in, forcing her back inside.

"Oh no, you don't." He flattened himself against the closed door, arms spread, naked feet braced apart, blocking her from leaving. The sparse sprinkling of dark hair over his chest drew Frances's attention. She'd seen his bare chest before, but always with the awareness that she couldn't, shouldn't stare. Now she could. And she did.

His chest hair was crisp, spreading from nipple to nipple, and a line of silkier hair trailed happily from his chest down his abdomen. Fascinated, she visually traced it as it twirled around a tight navel, then dipped beneath his unsnapped jeans. Lord have mercy.

It wasn't easy, but Frances got her attention back on his face—and caught his indulgent look of satisfaction. "What are you doing here, Booker?" *Besides looking like sin personified.*

"Supplying some common sense, apparently." Vibrating tension brought him away from the door until he stood nose to nose with Frances. "It's too cold, too late and way too damn dark to be out running around by yourself."

"Wanna go with me?" She wouldn't mind the company.

"Hell no." He shivered for emphasis and began unwinding her muffler. "We'd both end up with pneumonia."

"I can't sleep. Running helps me relax."

Eyes twinkling, he opened his mouth and Frances, knowing good and well what his alternate suggestion would be, snapped, "No, don't say it, Booker. I told you I wanted time and damn it, I'll get time."

His grin sent a curl of heat through her stomach. He whipped off her hat, kissed her nose. "Okay. Then let's make cookies." Eyebrows bobbing, he added in a growl, "I *love* your cookies."

Well, that was nothing less than the truth. She'd already made him several batches of frosted Christmas cookies and they never lasted him long. She supposed baking would be as distracting as running. "All right. But you have to help."

Using both hands, he pushed his bed-rumpled hair away from his face. "My pleasure. Lead the way."

This time she dodged the mistletoe as she headed to the kitchen, making Booker laugh. She pulled out flour and sugar, eggs and other ingredients, and he got her big glass bowls off the top shelf.

"You know," Booker said thoughtfully, "while you're getting used to the idea, I could detail all the benefits of a more intimate relationship between us."

Frances bit back a moan. The intimate benefits were already more than apparent to her. She didn't need them detailed. Keeping her back to him and carefully measuring in vanilla, she said, "I have a good imagination, Booker. I don't need any help."

"But I want to tell you." He came up behind her, caught her hips in his hands and kissed her ear. "It occurred to me that there may be nuances involved that you haven't considered."

Her right hand held an egg suspended over a bowl. "Yeah? Like what?" She leaned into him, tilted her head to give him better advantage, and sighed when his kisses trailed to her throat. She'd dated plenty of times, even semiseriously once or twice, but she'd never known the side of her neck was that sensitive.

Then again, maybe it was just Booker. Everywhere he touched her made her senses riot.

She knew she should resist him, but it just wasn't possible.

"Like tonight," he whispered huskily. "When you're restless, I'll be right there to help." He smiled against her throat. "But if you insist on jogging at night, I can go with you. Or we can make more cookies."

"Sounds . . . interesting." Truth was, she couldn't clear her thoughts long enough to decide what made sense and what didn't. Not with Booker touching her.

"You wouldn't have to worry about finding a date."

"I never worry about that anyway."

The squeeze he gave her nearly took her breath. "I know. How come you never go out much?"

Because she loved him and he'd been with Judith. "I dated a lot before I moved here. But since then, I've had one job after another. Especially with the holidays." Recently, with her growing popularity, every small gallery around had wanted to put on a show with her work.

Booker stepped away from her, enabling her to draw a deep, fortifying breath. "That's another thing," he said. "When you're working nonstop the way you do sometimes, I can help with your dinner and chores."

Slowly, Frances turned to face him. What he suggested sounded a whole lot more involved than an affair. Because everything was so new, she didn't have the nerve to ask him to spell out his intentions. Instead, she said, "I can take care of myself."

His expression warmed with tenderness. "You're the strongest woman I know. I admire you a lot, Frannie."

He admired her.

"You're also smart and funny, and I love how I can be myself with you."

He'd said the *L* word, and it nearly stopped her heart. She watched him with wide eyes and growing tension.

"But Frannie, wouldn't it be nice to have someone to cuddle with at night? Wouldn't it be nice to go Christmas shopping together for gifts? To wake up Christmas morning and share all the magic and fun?"

It felt like her tongue had stuck to the roof of her mouth. He implied that he wanted to . . . move in?

"I'd like you to meet my folks. They're great. You can't judge them by Axel," he teased. "He's the black sheep of the family. Were you planning to go home on Christmas?"

He ran that all together too quickly, leaving her dazed. "Christmas Eve," she murmured, still trying to mentally catch up with him.

"Great. Then I could go there with you and we could hit my folk's place Christmas morning. Gramps and Gramma will be there. Hell, they're ninety now, but still have a wicked sense of humor. There'll be some aunts and uncles, too. Do you have big get-togethers? How many of your relatives will I get to meet?"

Her head spun. She almost dropped the stupid egg but caught herself in time. Turning back to the large bowl, she began adding ingredients. "There's, uh, about twenty of us. Lots of kids. My two sisters are already married."

"I bet they all tease you about being single."

Her chin lifted. "Actually, they consider me the strange artsy one in the bunch. They never know quite what to expect from me." For certain, they wouldn't expect Booker.

"Strange? Really?" He said it with amusement.

"And why not? Look how different I am from Judith."

"Yeah." She felt his gaze tracking over her body, pausing in prime places until she almost squirmed. "You're different all right."

Just what the hell did he mean by that? Flustered, she dumped in too much sugar. "Set the oven on three-fifty."

"Yes, ma'am." He took care of that before leaning beside her against the counter. Without a shirt and his jeans undone, he proved a mighty distraction. "Now, about these differences."

Frances stirred the batter with single-minded ferocity. "Judith is beautiful."

With a snort, Booker leaned around to see her face. "You're an artist, Frannie. You know you're easy on the eyes."

"I know I'm not a hag," she specified. "But I am too thin and probably too tall."

"You're damn near the same height as me."

"Exactly. And judging by Judith, you like women who are elegant. Judith always had her hair just right, her makeup perfect and her nails freshly painted."

Indulgently, Booker tucked her hair behind her ear. "And the only paint I see on you is often on your nose."

Rolling her eyes, Frances said, "Or under my nails, rather than on them." She hesitated a moment, unsure how many comparisons she wanted to make. "Judith has bigger boobs, too."

His grin came and went quickly. "She's got a nice rack on her, true. But Frannie?" When she glanced up at him, he said, "She's not you." He stroked the side of her throat. "You make me laugh, almost as much as you make me hot. I enjoy being with you, talking to you. I knew things were over with Judith when I decided I'd rather watch football with you than sleep with her."

Frances paused in her stirring. "Has it really been a month?"

"At least. It feels longer because I've wanted you more every damn day." When she stood there, just staring at him, he gently nudged her aside and began scooping the cookie dough into the press he'd taken from her cabinet. "I should have realized Judith felt the same when she didn't protest my lack of interest. But everyone kept talking about us being an item, hinting that we should get married. And it was the holidays, a bad time to dump someone. And so, like an idiot, I tried to figure out a way to end it without causing a big scene—so I could be with you."

He began turning the crank on the old press and a tree-shaped cookie appeared on the baking sheet. "You," he told her with a sideways glance of accusation, "kept treating me like some asexual buddy."

Frances gasped in affront. "That's how *you* treated *me*."

"Not by choice. I just wanted to make sure I didn't scare you off until I could tell you how I really felt."

The baking sheet now held two dozen small trees. Frances took it from him, opened the oven and bent at the waist to slide it in.

"Oh, sweetheart," he said from right behind her, "you don't know what you're advertising there."

Frances glanced around to see him staring at her behind. She jerked upright, her face flushed from his attention and the heat that wafted from the oven.

Booker reached out, caught her elbow and dragged her close. "You're too warm." So saying, he caught the hem of her sweatshirt and pulled it up and over her head. "Damn, how many layers are you wearing?"

"Enough to jog outside without freezing."

"Well, maybe you can be an early present and I'll just keep unwrapping you." He removed her thermal shirt too, leaving her in an oversized blue T-shirt and gray nylon jogging pants. He stared at her breasts and said, "I don't suppose you'd want to do a little making out? We could sort of ease into things with a lot of kissing, maybe a little petting. Then tomorrow when you've made up your mind—"

Frances threw her arms around his neck. "Yes."

Chapter Four

Surprised by her sudden acquiescence, Booker lifted her to the countertop and moved her knees apart to stand between them. Frances's eyes widened, but he didn't give her time to change her mind. He kissed her.

God, he'd never get used to her taste, her softness. The T-shirt hugged her small breasts, showing the strained outline of her puckered nipples. He slid his hands down her sides, enthralled by her narrow waist, the firmness of her supple muscles. As a runner, she stayed toned and trim. He couldn't wait to feel her legs around him, squeezing him tight.

But she wanted a day to think about it, so by God, he'd give her a day. Tonight he'd only tease, show her what they could have together in an effort to hedge his bets. It was a ruthless move, but then, he'd wanted her too damn long to play fair.

He took her mouth in a long drugging kiss, meant to distract her while he slipped his hands beneath her shirt. She felt warm and firm and soft and he knew he'd bust his jeans if he prolonged this too long. The silky skin of her back drew him first. She was so slight of build, so narrow that with his fingers spread, he could span her width. He rubbed back down her sides, then up to her breasts, just under them, not touching her yet despite the urge to weigh her in his palms, to learn her.

"Booker . . ." she groaned, and the way she said his name pushed him that much closer to the edge.

Using his thumbs, he stroked her nipples, felt them stiffen, and he couldn't take it. He leaned back, pulled the shirt up to bare her and inhaled sharply at the sight of her.

"Frannie." He could feel her hesitancy. Her breasts were small, perfectly shaped with dark pink nipples. He bent to take one puckered nipple into his mouth, drawing gently, flicking with his tongue.

Her reaction was electric. She stiffened, lacing her fingers tight into his hair, pulling him closer. Her legs opened wider around him and Booker used one arm to pull her to the very edge of the counter, in direct contact with his hips.

Her groan was long and gratifying.

Earlier, he'd been on the ragged edge, damn near ready to come in his pants. But now he had her where her wanted her. Almost. Naked would be better, but he'd make do.

"I'm going to make you come, Frannie."

Her eyes snapped open and she stiffened, but Booker didn't let her gather her wits enough to retreat. Carefully, he laid her back on the counter, kissing her deeply again until she sighed and clung to him. Stroking her, he smoothed his hand over her shoulder, down her side, and to her hip. The elastic waistband of her jogging pants proved accommodating.

Her stomach sucked in and she gasped.

"Shhh . . ." he told her, then groaned when he found her panties damp. "God, I've dreamed of touching you like this."

He heard her fast shallow breaths and lifted his head. Eyes wide, she stared at the ceiling. Her face was warm, her breasts rising and falling as she panted, her nipples achingly tight.

Booker gently pushed one finger inside her, gritting his teeth against the instant clasp of her body. Her lips parted on a deep inhalation. "How's that feel?" he asked her, slipping his finger in and out, his voice so low and hoarse he barely recognized himself.

Rather than answer, her neck arched and her eyes closed. With his heart slamming hard enough to shake his body,

Booker went back to her breasts—at the same time working in a second finger. She was tight, but so wet and hot he knew she would enjoy the slight stretch of ultra-sensitive flesh.

Her legs opened wider.

Nipping gently with his lips, he teased her nipple. He circled with his tongue, held her with his teeth and tugged until she cried out, rolling her hips against his hand, bathing his fingers in slick moisture. He found her clitoris with his thumb, pressed, and then let her set her pace.

"Booker," she whispered, then again, a little louder, a little more shrill, *"Booker."*

God, yes, he thought, thrilled with her response. He held her closer to still her movements. While thrusting his fingers harder, faster, he sucked strongly at her nipple. In a sudden rush of sensation, she climaxed, her body bowing on the countertop, her cries loud and sweet. Booker had to fight back his own orgasm so he didn't embarrass himself by coming in his pants.

Slowly, Frannie subsided, her body going limp by small degrees. She'd managed to knock the clip out of her hair and it tumbled around her face, a little tangled, a little sweaty. Booker leaned over her, smiling, feeling pretty damn good except for a straining, painful erection.

He touched her lax mouth, brushed a pale blond lock away from her forehead. "I love you, Frannie."

Her eyes snapped open—and the oven dinged.

Good timing, Booker decided. He knew he could take her now and all her protestations wouldn't mean a thing. She was soft, limp, open to him in body and emotions. Her gently parted lips told him so. The flush of her skin told him so. Her heavy, unfocused eyes told him so.

But he'd promised her and because he loved her, because he wanted her for the rest of his life, not just tonight, he slid his arms under her shoulders and lifted her off the counter. She was unsteady on her feet, weaving until he steadied her.

Her T-shirt fell into place. He helped readjust her displaced jogging pants. After a teasing flick on her nose, he said, "The cookies will burn," and went to fetch a potholder to remove the tray from the oven. The air filled with the humid scents of sugary cookies, and the more subtle scent of aroused woman.

When he turned to face Frances again, she hadn't moved. She was still staring at him, mute, but also drowsy with satisfaction.

Booker sighed. "I'm going to go now. If I don't, you won't get that time you need to think about things."

That brought her around, her eyes blinking and her shoulders straightening. "You need time to think too, to make sure—"

"No." He reached out and brushed one fingertip over her left breast, making her shudder anew. "I know what I want."

"You mean right now?" She swallowed. "Or tomorrow?"

Smiling, Booker told her, "I already got what I wanted right now. Thank you."

She blinked rapidly again. "You're welcome."

"Tomorrow I'd love to have you naked, so I can really love you proper. So I can come with you. Inside you."

She rolled her lips in on a soft moan.

"After that," he said, looking at her directly, makng sure she understood, "I want *everything*. Every day, every night, the rest of our lives."

She drew a shuddering breath, opened her mouth to speak, and Booker put a finger to her lips. "No, honey. Just do your thinking, okay? We'll talk in the morning."

"But—"

"Can you sleep now? I don't have to worry about you slipping outside?"

"I can sleep."

She already looked halfway there, amusing him and blunting the lust with tenderness. He cupped her jaw. "I love you, Frannie," he stated again, then he went to her door and walked out.

Frances woke slowly, a smile on her mouth. He loved her. Her Christmas wishes had come true. Feeling energized despite the fact she'd only had a few hours sleep, she threw off the covers and went to the window. More snow had fallen, blanketing the world in a dazzling display of silver and white. It was so awe-inspiring it took her breath away.

A tap sounded on her bedroom wall. "G'morning, beautiful."

Almost dancing in her happiness, Frances dashed back to the bed and laid her hand on the wall. "Good morning, Booker."

"I miss you."

She hugged herself in giddy pleasure. "It hasn't been that long. Why are you up?"

"Because a sexy broad turned me inside out last night, then sent me to my lonely bed. Oh wait. Do you mean why am I out of bed?"

She chuckled. "Booker Dean, you know exactly what I meant." He *had* gone home alone, all because he was so considerate and wonderful . . . and he said he loved her. She wanted to stand up and sing.

"Well, as to that, I was hoping that same sexy broad would have something special to say to me today. I've been laying here just waiting."

Frances fell back on the mattress, arms wide, heart full. Oh, she had things to say to him. Lots and lots of things. What he'd done to her last night, how he'd made her feel . . .

She sat back up and spoke close to the wall. "She just might." Booker said today he wanted her naked, then he wanted her for the rest of their lives. She badly wanted to give him whatever he wanted. Struck with sudden, very daring inspiration, Frances glanced at the clock. She bit her lip, hesitated, then forced herself to say, "I'll need an hour, okay?"

"Right. One hour. But keep in mind I'll be holding my breath." He tapped on the wall, and Frances knew he'd left the room. She jumped up and dashed into the shower. This was going to be the most magical Christmas ever—one that would start her on a new life with the man she loved.

* * *

Booker got out of the shower at the sound of knocking on his door. Frances? Damn, he hoped so. He pulled a towel around his hips and went to greet her.

Unfortunately, it was Axel and Cary, not Frances. They sported a box of doughnuts, beard-shadowed cheeks, and red-rimmed eyes.

"Morning, Booker," Axel said as he walked in, then nudged the door shut behind him. "Did you lock me out on purpose?"

Booker headed to his bedroom to dress. "It's only seven in the morning. I always lock my door at night when I sleep."

Cary said, "See? It wasn't personal." Then to Booker, "I'm going to put on coffee."

Booker emerged wearing jeans and carrying a shirt and sneakers. "No. Your coffee sucks. I'll get it." Feeling a touch of déjà vu, Booker pulled his shirt over his head, pushed his feet into his sneakers, and began coffee preparations. "All right. Why the early-morning visit?"

Cary grinned. "You are so damn suspicious, Booker. Hell, we're just heading home after pulling an all-nighter."

"Together?"

"No." Axel fished out a fat jelly doughnut and took a large bite. "We hooked up for breakfast, then decided you might want doughnuts too."

"You were with Judith all night?"

Axel paused in the middle of chewing. "Is that okay?"

"I keep telling you that it is. Just don't ever try it with Frannie. I don't even want you looking at her. Got it?"

"I'll wear blinders when the girl is around."

"See that you do." He finished the coffee. "I'm kind of amazed at your speed with Judith, though."

Grinning, Axel said, "Yeah, well, she's been converted."

"Axel-fied?" Cary asked.

"Exactly. And who can think of marriage when having so much fun being single?"

Booker's front door opened again and Frances called softly, "Booker?"

Knowing he grinned like a sap and not caring in the least,

Booker saluted his brother and Cary. "I'll be right back." He would allow his brother one cup of coffee, and then he'd oust him for some alone-time with Frannie.

She stood uncertainly inside his door, her bare feet shifting on his carpet, her hands playing with the belt to her robe. She hadn't dressed yet? Excellent.

For once, she had her hair loose too, freshly brushed and hanging past her shoulders. She chewed on her bottom lip. Her continued shyness charmed him.

Booker looked her over, realized she appeared naked beneath the robe, and all kinds of delightful possibilities rolled through him. "Good morning," he murmured, already thinking ahead to how quickly he could get rid of his brother and get Frannie into bed.

Her smile trembled. "Do you remember what you said yesterday, Booker?" Her hands continued to fidget with her belt.

He walked closer. "I said a lot of things."

"You said you wanted me naked."

Heat raced up his spine. "Yeah, I—"

She jerked the belt loose and dropped her robe. It pooled around her slim ankles leaving her gloriously, beautifully nude.

Booker froze, his eyes going wide, his cock leaping to attention. Lord, she devastated his senses. He couldn't blink, couldn't move.

And then from behind him, Axel said, "I don't suppose I should be witnessing this?"

Frannie's screech was shrill enough to shatter glass. The damn robe was on the floor and she dropped down to grab it, twisting at the same time so that her rump faced them instead of her front. And good Lord, the view . . .

Cary coughed. Axel choked.

Belatedly, Booker reeled on his brother. He blasted him with a look and gave him a hard shove that sent him stumbling back into Cary, toppling them both into the kitchen. Neither Axel nor Cary seemed to mind the attack. They were both too busy laughing.

Booker slugged his brother hard in the arm.

"*Ow.*"

"Damn it, Axel, I told you I didn't want you looking at her."

In his defense, Axel said, "I didn't know I'd get to see her in the buff, now did I?" and he rubbed at his shoulder where Booker had hit him. "It's a reflex. Naked woman equals staring. Any man still breathing would look at that, and you damn well know it."

"I would," Cary said, and Booker slugged him too. But Cary just continued to snicker and grin.

Booker's front door slammed shut.

Damn it! He rounded on his brother again. "Now see what you two have done?"

"Us? We're innocent bystanders. In fact, I think I may have wounded myself when she dropped that robe. My eyeballs hit the floor."

Cary nodded. "Coffee came straight out my nose. Hurt like hell."

Booker pointed a finger at them both. "*Leave.*" Then he went into his bedroom and sat on the bed nearest to the wall. He could hear funny noises in Frances's room. Probably her thumping her fists on the bed.

"Frannie?"

The noise stopped, then in an agonized whisper, "I'm going to kill your brother, Booker."

"Not if I kill him first." He smiled. At least she was still talking to him. "Mind if I come over?"

"Yes!"

He rose from the bed, turned—and ran into Axel. After they'd both regained their balance, Booker scowled. "I told you to leave."

"I thought I'd apologize."

Frannie yelled, "Go to hell, Axel!"

Axel grinned. "She's got a temper, doesn't she?"

Booker pushed past him. "Go home, okay?" He went through his apartment and next door to Frannie's. Her door wasn't locked, so he walked on in, but made a point of locking it behind him.

He found Frances on her bed, facedown, a pillow over her head. She'd pulled the robe back on, but when she'd flung herself on the bed, it had fluttered up to her knees. Her smooth calves and bare feet drew him.

God, he had it bad. "Frances?"

She went utterly still, then gripped the pillow over her head more firmly.

"Are you trying to smother yourself, honey?"

"Maybe," came her muffled reply.

Booker sat on the bed beside her. "I'm sorry you got embarrassed." He was so damn horny, he could barely speak. He wanted to soothe her, to make her feel better, but more than that he wanted to disperse with the robe, turn her to her back and look at her some more. That flash peek at her naked body had only whet an already ravenous appetite.

"Embarrassed?" she repeated with incredulity. "I'm *mortified*. I'll never be able to face your brother again."

Through the wall, Axel said, "That's okay. The rear view was pretty spectacular, too."

Frannie lifted the pillow and stared at the wall with the meanest look Booker had ever seen. Before she could say anything rash, he touched her shoulder. "Ignore Axel. He's an idiot."

"I am," Axel agreed. And then, more sincerely, "I'm sorry I embarrassed you, hon. Booker will beat the hell out of me later, I'm sure, because I bumbled into his fantasy. And I've no doubt you *are* his fantasy. You only have to look at his face when he talks about you."

Frannie twisted about, her narrowed gaze colliding with Booker's heated expression. "Really?"

"Cross my heart."

Axel sighed. "There. All's well that ends well?"

Booker growled. "Will you *go away*, Axel?"

Cary said, "I'll drag him off, Booker. You two just go about your business."

Frannie's expression said, Yeah, right. They both knew Cary and Axel probably had their ears pressed to the wall with no intention of budging.

She was still red-faced, Booker noted, but at least she appeared less murderous. Tired of waiting, Booker scooped her up into his arms and carried her into her living room, away from prying ears. He settled onto the sofa with Frances on his lap. She hadn't turned any lights on yet, so the Christmas tree provided the only real glow in the room. The lights blinked behind her, forming a soft halo against her fair hair.

"I love you, Frances."

She curled into him, hiding her face in his neck. "Even though I just made a gigantic fool of myself?"

"You didn't. You pleased the hell out of me." He smoothed her waist, enjoying the feel of her beneath the terrycloth, the dips and hollows and swells of her body—soon to be his for the taking. Maybe even his forever.

"Axel's right, you know. You are my fantasy, and knowing what you likely intended when you came over to my place has me fully loaded and ready to go." He nibbled on her ear, kissed her temple.

"Yeah?" She wiggled against his erection, letting him know she understood his meaning.

"Damn right. Now if I could just get you to let loose of this robe . . ."

Wearing a beautiful smile, she did, and Booker spread it open so he could look at her to his heart's content. Curled on his lap, every part of her was within reach. Her breasts, her soft belly, her smooth thighs. Those dark blond curls over her mound.

Booker drew a shuddering breath. Physically, he didn't know where to start, where to touch or taste her first.

Emotionally, he knew exactly what he wanted. Gaze glued to her breasts, voice gruff with tenderness, he said, "As long as you're being agreeable, do you suppose you could tell me that you love me too?"

"I do." He glanced up to find her face rosy with pleasure, anticipation and . . . love. "I have for such a long time."

He hadn't realized he was so tense until her quick agreement sank in. He let out a long breath. "Do you suppose you could agree to marry me?"

"Yes."

She squeaked from his sudden tight embrace, but Booker couldn't seem to loosen his hold. She pressed her palms against him until she could turn on his lap, facing him. She shrugged off the robe, opened his shirt and pressed herself to him chest to chest—heart to heart.

Booker's hands roamed freely down her back to her bottom, along the sides of her thighs. Again, he scooped her up, keeping her tight to his chest until he laid her gently on the floor beneath the tree.

As he shrugged off his clothes, his hands already shaking with anticipation, he smiled. "Christmas dinner is going to be interesting." He pulled a condom from his wallet and tossed it to the floor beside her.

"If your brother says one word to me, if he even looks at me funny, I'll clout him."

Booker came down over her. She hadn't refused dinner, and that was all he cared about. He wanted his family to meet her. They'd love her as much as he did. "As I said, interesting."

For several minutes, he simply enjoyed kissing her, touching her. There was no music in the background this time, but Frannie's soft moans and small whimpers were better than any holiday tune.

When he slipped his fingers between her thighs, she arched up. Wet, hot. He stroked two fingers deep, working them in and out of her at a leisurely pace, feeling the grasp and release of her body. Her eyelids sank down, her lips parted.

"Come for me, Frannie." He brought his thumb into play, using her own wetness to glide over her clitoris, softly, easily, repeatedly.

"*Booker.*"

"That's it." He kissed her mouth hard, swallowing her cries, drowning in satisfaction. When she quieted, he rolled the condom on in record time, held her knees high and wide, and pushed into her.

They both groaned.

To Booker's delight, he felt Frances begin tightening all over again. Her short nails stung his shoulders, her runner's thighs held him tight to her. He pumped into her fast, deep—and as she arched high, her mouth open on a raw cry, he came.

Though it was frosty and cold outside, they were both now warm and sweaty. Frances's heart continued to gallop under his cheek. He remained deep inside her, and he never wanted to move.

She was quiet so long, he finally forced himself up to his elbows. Looking at her, at her sated, sleepy contentment, filled his heart to overflowing. "What are you thinking about?"

Lazily she smiled, her eyes opening the tiniest bit. "I got what I wanted for Christmas."

"Me, too."

"But Christmas morning isn't for several more days. I'd like to know just how you plan to top this, Booker Dean. Because I can tell you, it isn't going to be easy."

The grin tugged at his mouth, then won. He laughed out loud. "Oh, I dunno. I think I can come up with something."

"Yeah?"

"Yeah." He lowered himself to kiss her throat, her flushed breasts, each and every rib. Little by little, he scooted down her body. When he reached his destination, he whispered, "Now this is a gift I won't mind getting every morning for the rest of my life."

With a small moan, Frannie agreed.

All She Wants for Christmas

Janelle Denison

Chapter One

"Ho, ho, ho! Merry Christmas everyone!"

Even though Faith Roberts had been anticipating his arrival, she shivered as the husky greeting slipped down her spine and an all-too-familiar heat gathered deep in her belly. There was only one man lately who'd been able to elicit such a thrilling response, and his visit at today's festive, holiday celebration was no exception.

"It's Santa!" one child exclaimed in joyful excitement, and that's all it took for the activity room in the children's ward to break out in squeals of delight. The kids erupted into a mad rush toward the jolly man in the red suit and gathered around him, all sixteen of them vying for his attention, all at once.

Faith laughed, not that she could blame the little imps, or the young nurses who'd left their stations to watch Matthew Carlton, pediatric surgeon, in action. Even dressed in a bright red Santa suit, complete with a padded tummy, fluffy white beard, and wire-rimmed glasses, the man still managed to exude mass quantities of sex appeal, and no one of the female gender seemed immune to his easygoing charm and affable personality.

Especially her. And if all went as planned, by the end of this holiday party Santa would be granting Faith her fondest wish.

All she wanted for Christmas this year was one hot, unforgettable night of passion with playboy Matthew Carlton before she moved on to the next phase of her life and started dating seriously again. No more wondering what it would feel like to have Matthew's mouth on hers and his hands sliding across her curves. No more tossing and turning in her bed all alone as she fantasized about having that solid body of his moving over hers, sliding deep inside where she was soft and warm and wet. She craved the real thing, and if his interest in her was any indication, she didn't think he'd refuse her seductive request.

She'd spent the last six months skirting his flirtatious advances and turning down dinner invitations because of his love 'em and leave 'em reputation around the hospital, but after a year of remaining single and cautious due to a past relationship gone bad, she was ready to give in to the attraction and restless desire she'd been fighting for too long. Ready to give in to temptation and enjoy every sensual delight he had to offer. And this time she'd do so with her eyes wide open, and keep her heart out of the equation.

As Santa made his way to the red velvet throne next to the gaily decorated Christmas tree, with his entourage of youngsters in tow, his twinkling blue eyes swept the area and stopped on her for a moment. Faith saw his beard twitch with a smile, and he winked at her before he settled himself in his chair and returned his attention to the ecstatic kids.

Another rush of heat tingled along her skin and scattered across her breasts, pebbling her nipples into tight aching points. Doing her best to subdue her body's reaction to Dr. Sexy, as he'd been appropriately dubbed by the female hospital staff, she immersed herself in the carefree, festive mood that had been created for the sick and recovering children who'd be staying in the hospital through Christmas.

While everyone had shuffled forward to greet Santa, and her good friend, Chayse Douglas, snapped pictures to document the occasion, Faith remained behind with five-year-old April, who sat on her lap clutching her soft worn blanket. She watched the commotion from afar with big round eyes, fascinated but unsure whether she wanted to join in the melee.

Faith didn't push the little girl, certain she'd come around once she saw Santa pull gifts from the big velvet bag he'd brought with him and discovered he'd given the kids precisely what they'd asked for. Last week, as a volunteer in the children's ward, Faith had helped each child write a letter to Santa; then afterward she'd gone shopping with Chayse to make sure that all the kids received at least one item that they'd asked for.

As the procession around Santa continued, Chayse came over to Faith, sat in the vacant seat beside her, and loaded a new roll of film into her camera. "Do you think Santa would be up to being a hunk in the Outdoor Men calendar project I'm doing for charity next year?"

Faith chuckled at the frustration threading through her friend's voice, knowing the source of her discontent. "I take it you haven't been able to recruit Adrian Wilde to pose as your last subject yet, hmm?"

"No, but not for a lack of trying," Chayse grumbled beneath her breath. "The man is absolutely aggravating, and so darn gorgeous and sexy that I refuse to give up on him."

"So, are you interested in him for more than just charitable reasons?" Faith asked curiously, and loosened her arms around April when the girl shifted restlessly on her lap, seemingly trying to gather the courage to approach Santa.

Chayse dug into her camera bag for a different lens. "No more or less than you want Dr. Sexy for more than his pediatric skills, I suppose."

"Touché, though I'm also very attracted to that soft spot he has for kids," she said in her own defense, and let her gaze drift back to Matthew, who had a bright-eyed boy perched on his knee and was listening avidly to what he had to say.

As a third-grade schoolteacher having always loved children, Faith appreciated how gentle and focused Matthew was with the kids in the hospital. Being attentive was all part of his job, of course, but Matthew's caring was genuine. She could see it in his striking blue eyes as he strolled through the children's ward a few times a week, making sure to stop and visit each child, no matter how sick, and the way he handled them with an abundance of gentleness and compassion. He even entertained them with sleight-of-hand magic tricks that brought a bit of joy and amusement into their sometimes lonely, confined days.

But as great as he was with the younger generation, he was a reputed ladies' man who enjoyed playing the field. He had one broken engagement under his belt, and he'd dated a few of the nurses in the hospital who hadn't been shy about admitting that he was "the best they'd ever had."

Faith knew and accepted that Matthew wasn't a forever kind of guy, and that was fine with her, since what she wanted from him was just one night of erotic, breath-stealing pleasure, to finally get him out of her mind, dreams, and nightly fantasies.

Stroking a hand over April's soft hair, Faith glanced back at her friend, who was busy fiddling with her camera settings, and decided to let Chayse in on her plan. "I'm going to ask Santa over there for a very intimate Christmas present this year, one only *he* can deliver personally."

Chayse's grin widened, and her violet-hued eyes glimmered with amusement. "Well, it's about time you treated yourself to such a decadent and yummy gift, especially after the way things ended with Martin."

Martin, a successful lawyer, who'd strung her along with false promises until someone better, and more exciting and sophisticated, had piqued his interest and libido, shattering both her heart and her trust. But she was no longer that guileless woman who believed in fairy tale endings, especially not with a man who was known for his prowess with the female gender.

Matthew might agree to an affair with her, but she wasn't so naive that she'd ever believe she was the type of woman he'd eventually marry. And she knew that particular score upfront, and she wasn't looking for anything long term, either.

"It's the *right* time," Faith countered with a shrug. "With my sister living in Houston with her husband and new family, and my parents off on vacation in Paris, it's the perfect Christmas gift to myself." She hated to admit it, but she'd been dreading spending the holidays alone, without her parents or sister, for the first time ever. If Matthew agreed to her wish, he'd provide her with a nice sensual kind of distraction, and plenty of fond Christmas memories to look back on.

"I'm certain Santa is just the man to give you exactly what you want and need," Chayse said.

He was definitely that. But for all she knew, he might already have plans for the evening. It was Saturday, and two days away from Christmas, a time when many people were booked up with parties, celebrations, or family affairs.

Everyone except her, of course.

Chasye stood and slipped the camera strap around her neck, her gaze suddenly serious, as if she had direct insight into the thoughts tumbling through Faith's mind. "By the way, you know you can always spend the holidays with me if things don't work out with Dr. Sexy."

"Thank you." Faith smiled gratefully. "I might just take you up on that offer."

"Good luck with Santa." With a quick, sassy wink, Chayse went back to taking pictures.

For the next half hour, Faith watched the festivities along with April, waiting patiently for the little girl to come out of her shell and join the fun. Finally, all the children had their turn with Santa and were busy playing with the toys he'd given them, but there was still one present left.

Holding a gaily wrapped gift in his hand, Santa looked over the rim of his wire-rimmed glasses, searching the room for the recipient. "Is April here today?" he asked.

The little girl stiffened in surprise, and not sure whether April would speak up, Faith gently coaxed her to approach Santa for her gift. "Come on, sweetie, I'll go with you."

With April clasping Faith's hand tightly, they made their way to Santa. The young girl didn't want to sit on his lap, but standing so close to him, she stared up at him in awe as he handed her the last present. She opened the gift tentatively, and her entire face transformed with gleeful excitement once the box was unwrapped.

"I got the doll I wanted," she squealed in excitement. "Thank you, Santa!" She rushed off to share her gift with the friends she'd made during her stay in the hospital.

Feeling warm and fuzzy inside, Faith smiled from April, to Matthew. "Very well done, Santa."

"Thank you," he murmured in that low, velvet-lined voice that sent shivers down her spine. Before she realized his intent, his gloved fingers wrapped around her wrist and he pulled her onto his lap.

Suddenly self-conscious with the nurses and kids looking on in avid interest, and very aware of his hard muscular thighs beneath her bottom and legs, she tried to make light of the situation. "Don't you think I'm a bit too big to be sitting on your lap?"

"Not at all. You fit just right." His eyes sparkled playfully, and the tilt of his moustache hinted at the sexy-as-sin smile hidden beneath. "So, what about you, Faith? Have you been naughty or nice this year?"

He'd placed his gloved hand on her knee, and the heat of his touch seeped through her slacks and spread upward, wreaking havoc with her sexually deprived body. She inhaled a deep steady breath, and the warm male scent of him invaded her senses, increasing the wanting unfurling in the pit of her belly.

"Oh, I've been very nice." Too nice and good, but all that was about to change. And he'd just presented her with the perfect opportunity to act on her intentions, to be the kind of bold assertive woman she'd always admired from afar but had never been.

"So, what would you like for Christmas?" he asked quite innocently, but there was no mistaking the sexy dare in his gaze.

Caught up in the sensual awareness thrumming between them, Faith seized the moment and made it hers. Cupping her hand over his ear so that no one could hear her very private wish, she whispered, "I want to be naughty, Santa. Very naughty. With you." She gently nipped his lobe to prove how brazen she was willing to be, and heard him suck in a startled breath. "I want one night of unforgettable, anything-goes sex with you, any way I please, and any way you want."

She pulled back, not certain what to expect, but the arousing heat and desire in Matthew's eyes reassured her that she'd definitely piqued his interest, and his libido, with her shameless request. And his next words confirmed her hunch.

"Well now, since you've been so good this year, I think your request can be arranged," he drawled, and followed that up with a hearty, jovial "Ho, ho, ho!" that had everyone wondering what, exactly, she'd asked for.

Chapter Two

Finished with his St. Nick duties, Matthew headed into the nurses' lounge to change out of his Santa suit and wait for Faith to join him. After initially stunning him with her unabashed and very naughty proposition, he'd told her to meet him in the private lounge so they could discuss the details of her Christmas wish, which he was more than willing to fulfill, in every way.

Taking off the fluffy white wig and beard he'd donned for the children, he set them in the rental box, along with the wire-rimmed glasses, then combed his fingers through his hair to restore some order to the thick strands. For the past six months, he'd been waiting patiently for a moment like the one Faith had presented this afternoon. He'd bided his time, subtly flirting and pursuing her despite her rejecting his invitations to lunch or dinner, hoping she'd eventually come around and take a chance on him.

A slow grin lifted the corner of his lips as he unbuckled the wide black leather belt around his padded waist. Never in his wildest dreams would he have thought that Faith would turn the tables on him and make such a brazen advance, or issue such a seductive overture. Not that he was complaining. She'd just given him the opportunity he'd been angling for, and he had no qualms using her request to his advantage.

There was no denying the chemistry between them, and

while she might just want a one-night affair to sate her desires, he craved something far more long-term with her. Over the ensuing months he'd come to realize that she was the kind of woman he'd been searching years to find—genuinely sweet and caring, inherently sensual, and one of the few women who didn't have one eye on being the wife of a pediatric surgeon, and the other eye on his bank account and all that his money might be able to buy them.

Since he'd had so much time to get to know Faith on a casual, amicable level, he'd learned that what you saw was what you got. And because she'd never tried to pretend otherwise like so many other women he'd dated, he was already half in love with her. Now, if all he had was twenty-four hours to convince her that what was between them was more than a sizzling attraction, then he was going to make the most of every minute with her—physically and emotionally.

But first, they'd start with their basic mutual attraction because that was the reason she'd finally come to him. From there he was certain that trust and intimacy, the foundation of any solid relationship, would develop naturally.

Just as he unzipped the fancy, fur-trimmed coat, Faith entered the room and leaned against the closed door. She tipped her head, causing her auburn hair to frame her classical features in soft layers, beckoning him to run his fingers through those silky strands like so many times before.

An irresistible smile curved her glossy lips and her green eyes glowed bright with anticipation as they met his gaze from across the room. "Hi there," she said, the husky tone of her voice flowing through him, warm and smooth, like fine aged whiskey.

He took in her black sweater top, embroidered with candy canes for the holiday, and admired the way the knit fabric outlined her full breasts, tapered into a trim waist, and followed the curve of her hips to a pair of black slacks. "Hi, yourself. I was beginning to think you'd changed your mind," he teased.

She licked her bottom lip. "Not a chance."

"Me either." He shrugged out of the heavy coat and removed the padding around his waist, which left him wearing a plain white cotton undershirt and baggy pants held up by nothing more than a pair of black suspenders. "Would you lock the door so I can finish changing?"

"Oh." Her eyes widened as realization dawned. "I can come back in a few minutes when you're dressed."

"No, I want you to stay," he said, before she could slip right back out of the lounge. "Lock the door, Faith."

Cheeks flushed pink, she obeyed his order, but he could tell she did so tentatively. For as daring and impudent as she'd been with him in the children's ward less than an hour ago, now that she was completely alone with him she appeared much too reserved for a woman supposedly intent on seducing him.

That was about to change.

"Faith, you're the one who asked for this, and in order for me to fulfill your Christmas wish, every bit of inhibition stops here and now," he said with purpose. "You wanted a night of unforgettable, anything-goes sex with me, any way you please and any way I desire. I plan to take you up on that offer, and that means no modesty allowed between us, in any way. Agreed?"

"Agreed." She exhaled a breath and nodded, seemingly in need of that pep talk that gave her permission to embrace the wanton he knew was tucked inside that conservative facade of hers.

"Good." Satisfied with her acquiescence that left the door wide open to all kinds of erotic possibilities, and needing her within touching distance, he crooked his finger at her. "How about you come on over here and help me take off these snug boots?" It was as good an ice-breaker as any, a way to dispel any last bit of tension with a more playful overture.

He sat down in a nearby chair and watched her approach, enjoying the subtle sway of her hips and the sexy self-assurance that lit her eyes as she neared. Now that he'd established that he wouldn't accept anything less than an equal partnership in their affair, she wasn't holding back, and all that feminine confidence thrilled and aroused him.

When she reached him, he motioned for her to turn around. "To get the best grip and leverage, I need to slip my foot between your legs from behind so you can grab the heel and give it a good firm tug," he explained.

She lifted a brow skeptically but did as he suggested and faced away from him. When he had his leg positioned between hers, she leaned forward from the waist and grabbed the heel of the black vinyl boot. A surge of heat spiraled straight to his groin, making his cock swell thickly as he imagined her in this exact same position but completely naked—legs spread, bottom tilted in invitation, and the pink wet folds of her sex tempting him to take her in such a provocative position.

"Tell me when to pull," she said, unaware of what an opportunist he truly was. But she was about to find out.

"In a minute. I'm admiring the fantastic view and indulging in a very carnal fantasy." He reached out and gently caressed and squeezed her buttocks. "You have a great ass, you know that?"

She glanced around at him, all that glorious hair of hers tumbling over her shoulder and framing her face in a wild disarray. "Are you trying to shock me?"

"Not at all," he drawled, and grinned like the devious rogue he planned to be with her tonight. "I'm just speaking what's been on my mind for months now. And since we'll be spending the night together, hopefully most of it naked, I figure that gives me permission to speak what's on my mind."

She laughed and relaxed. "I suppose it does."

He let his thumbs drift along the crevice of her bottom and lightly stroked and teased between her legs. "Then I guess I can tell you that I'd love to fuck you in this position, with me taking you from behind, hard and fast and deep."

Her breath caught and her eyes darkened at his frank sexual dialogue and very intimate touch. "Matthew . . ."

He liked the way his name sounded on her lips, a soft,

sweet plea that let him know she was his for the taking. When the time came. "But first, we'll take it slow and easy and work our way up to that particular fantasy," he said, and let his hands settle on the feminine curve of her waist. "Pull off my boot, sweetheart."

Regaining her composure, she tugged hard on the heel, and the tight-fitting shoe slowly eased right off his foot. She grinned at him, looking amazed at her efforts. "Hey, that really did work well!"

He chuckled. "Of course it did. The view was just an added bonus for me."

She helped him remove his other boot and put both of them in the rental box. Then he stood, slipped the suspenders down his arms and let the bulky, red velvet trousers drop to the floor. Her gaze flickered down the length of him, taking in his snug boxer briefs that outlined every detail of his solid erection.

He reached for his jeans and stepped into them. "If you don't quit staring at me like that, there's no way I'll be able to zip up my pants and walk out of here without being accused of indecent exposure."

A light shade of pink swept across her cheeks. "Sorry," she said, not sounding apologetic at all for checking him out.

Shaking his head in amusement, and despite his own discomfort, he did his best to fasten the front of his jeans. "There's something I want to ask you," he said, switching the mood from sexy and frisky to something more serious. He needed to know what was going through her head as far as he was concerned, which would give him a better idea of what he was ultimately up against with her. "You've been turning me down for the past six months. What made you change your mind about me?"

Faith mulled over his question for a quick moment, thinking about how to best answer it. "I've been turning you down, yes, but that doesn't mean I don't want you."

"Which makes your request all the more intriguing," he murmured, and covered his broad muscled chest with a beige cable-knit sweater.

She shrugged her shoulders and strove for a nonchalant attitude. "Maybe it's a simple matter of wanting each other—"

"And getting it out of our systems?" he finished for her.

Hearing her thoughts coming from his lips, she had to admit that her plan had a shallow ring to it. Then again, she was being honest with him, and their agreement thus far was all about mutual pleasure, nothing more. "Sure. Why not?"

He stared at her, his gaze direct and intense. "And you think one night together is going to accomplish that?"

There was a wealth of doubts in his statement that surprised her, yet she had to remain firm. One night would have to be enough, because anything more would mean involving her heart and emotions, and she wasn't willing to risk that part of herself with him, knowing they had no real future together.

Beyond their attraction, he was way out of her league socially, and she'd already traveled down that road with Martin. She was a simple schoolteacher who lived modestly, and from what she knew of Matthew Carlton, he'd grown up in a very wealthy, privileged household. And apparently, judging by his broken engagement and the slew of women he'd dated, he wasn't looking for anything long term or permanent.

Well, neither was she, she reminded herself determinedly. "That's all I'm asking for, Matthew. I wouldn't think my request would be a problem for you."

A slight frown etched his brows. "And why is that?" he asked, obviously interested in hearing her explanation.

She leaned against the wooden table behind her that employees used for their meal breaks and braced her hands on either side of her hips. "You do have a certain reputation around the hospital for being quite the ladies' man."

"Trust me, that reputation is highly overrated," he muttered, seemingly very bothered by her perception of him.

She regarded him speculatively. "Are you denying that you've dated some of the nurses in this hospital and all of them on a short-term basis?"

"No. I've gone out with a few of them, all on casual,

friendly dates." He shrugged, as if the time he'd spent with those women was insignificant. "Nothing serious at all, but that's by choice, and the women knew that up-front."

"Exactly." Those same women had shared intimate details of those dates, fueling the gossip around the hospital about Matthew's notorious reputation. "And I'm letting you know that I respect your rules, because I'm not looking for anything serious, either."

He ran a hand through his hair, the gesture reflecting the sudden frustration she saw flitting across his expression, though she had no idea what had him so bothered when she was willing to make their affair as uncomplicated as possible between them.

"One night is all I want," she told him again, her tone adamant.

That brief moment of discontent faded, and his mouth quirked into a slow, sexy smile that tightened her nipples and made her melt inside, despite her convictions. "Okay, I'll agree to that," he said. "For now."

A contradictory statement if she ever heard one. His gaze glimmered with ulterior motives as he slowly stepped toward her, and her heart beat wildly in her chest as he grasped her waist and pushed her back against the table, giving her no choice but to sit on the hard wooden surface.

"Umm, what are you doing?" she asked curiously, though she wasn't at all opposed to whatever he had in mind. Not when her body was already humming in keen anticipation.

"Something I've been wanting to do for months now." Splaying his palms against her knees, he pushed her legs wide apart so her thighs bracketed his lean hips.

A slow, insidious ache spread through her limbs, a need so strong it nearly overwhelmed her. A need as hot as the wanting that blazed like blue fire in Matthew's eyes. "And what's that?" she asked breathlessly.

The grin that eased up the corner of his sensual mouth was pure unadulterated male. "I want to see how well we fit together."

Chapter Three

Matthew had no doubt that their bodies would be a perfect match, that physically they'd complement each other flawlessly. But this moment was all about giving Faith a preview of what was to come. A bit of foreplay to increase the hunger already smoldering between them, and show her just how amazing making love was going to be . . . his reputed reputation be damned.

Cupping her bottom in his palms, he pulled her forward and pressed the hard ridge beneath the fly of his jeans against her sex. A moan slipped from her throat, and if it wasn't for their clothing, he would have been inside her by now. Deep inside her. Mindlessly lost in the softness and heat of her body.

Pushing that erotic image from his mind, he framed her jaw in his hands, lowered his head, and nibbled delicately on her plump lower lip. "I want to see how compatible our mouths are, and I want to taste you deep inside," he whispered in between soft nips of his teeth and the lazy coaxing stroke of his tongue. "I want to feel your breasts against my chest, your belly against mine, and your legs wrapped tight around my waist."

"Yes," she breathed and parted her lips for him, offering him everything he asked for. Everything he craved. Her passion. Her desire. Her heat.

With a raw primal groan, he slid his hand into the silky mass of her hair, tilted her head, and angled her mouth beneath his for a deeper, more satisfying possession. His tongue delved into the honeyed warmth as he kissed her hotly, greedily, thoroughly. His other hand slipped beneath the hem of her sweater, and he groaned once again when his fingertips encountered soft baby-smooth skin. Skimming higher, he traced the undersides of her full breasts, then enclosed a taut mound in his hand and kneaded the generous flesh. The fabric of her bra was thin and insubstantial, all satin and sheer lace, enabling him to roll and pluck her taut nipple between his fingers.

Her breathing deepened, and she slid her arms around his neck, pulling him closer, a little wild and a whole lot needy. She arched into his touch, causing her breasts to crush against his chest and their bellies to brush and align. When she hooked her long slender legs around his hips and rocked against his stiff cock, it was all he could do not to come right then and there in his too-tight jeans.

Knowing things were spiraling way out of control, and quickly, he pulled his mouth from hers, reluctantly released her lush breast, and buried his face against her throat. She smelled so good, so sweet and deliciously feminine, and he couldn't stop from taking a soft bite from her neck.

She gasped, and he soothed the sting with the damp stroke of his tongue, then nuzzled the soft underside of her jaw. "God, that kiss was so worth waiting for." *She* was worth waiting for, and his goal was to prove that to her over the course of the next twenty-four hours.

"Umm, yes, that was very, very nice," she agreed, her voice a sultry purr of sound as her palms slid lazily over his shoulders and down to his chest.

He was tempted to strip off his cable-knit sweater and T-shirt, just so he could feel her hands stroking his bare flesh. But here in the nurses' lounge wasn't the place, and they'd already lingered longer than he'd intended.

"There's a whole lot more where that kiss came from," he promised, and lifted his head.

He met her gaze, saw the unquenched desire in her eyes, and a reciprocating heat washed over him in waves. "I want this evening to be special and memorable for you. A night you'll never forget." A night that would, he hoped, change her opinion of him and open her eyes to what was truly between them.

Her lips, damp and puffy from their shared kisses, lifted into a slumberous smile. "I want that, too."

"In order for me to give you that night to remember, I need some time to get a few things taken care of." He tenderly brushed back a wayward strand of hair from her cheek and grazed his thumb along her jaw. "Do you mind waiting for me in the children's ward for, say, about an hour?"

"An hour and no more," she said sassily, then leaned forward and took his mouth in a kiss that staked a sensual, mind-blowing claim on him.

Less than an hour later, Faith found herself sitting in Matthew's Lexus Coupe as he maneuvered the sporty vehicle into the circular drive in front of Chicago's St. Claire Hotel, an elegant, five-star establishment that was known for its opulence and extravagant amenities. Matthew came to a stop at the curb, and a valet was immediately there, opening the passenger door and offering his hand to help her from the car.

She stepped out onto the sidewalk, pulled her winter coat closer around her body to ward off the chill in the December air, and stared in awe at the beautiful architecture of the old building. The exterior of the hotel was gilded in gold accents and adorned with lavish Christmas decorations and an abundance of twinkling lights, and as she glanced around and took in the rich look of the hotel's guests, she couldn't help but feel a little intimidated by the excessive wealth surrounding her.

Matthew came around the front of the car and met up with

her on the sidewalk carrying a small leather duffle bag, and an easygoing smile in place. "Have you ever been to the St. Claire before?"

She shook her head, though he was obviously very comfortable in such a luxurious environment. "No. A place like this isn't exactly within my vacation budget," she said wryly. "What are *we* doing here?"

With a hand pressed against her lower back, he guided her toward the double doors leading to the lobby, which a doorman promptly opened for them. "This is where we're spending the night."

Stunned, her jaw nearly hit the floor as two things registered at once. First, that he was actually going to pay the astronomical price they charged for a room. And second, he was giving her the entire night together, until the next morning, sleeping in the same bed, when she'd only expected a handful of pleasurable hours with him.

Oh, wow.

She glanced up at his face, struck anew by just how good-looking he was, how astonishingly sexy and confident. And for the moment, for the night, this incredible man was all hers, and she decided that she was going to enjoy him and everything else about their short time together. Including their stay at the St. Claire. "You sure do know how to dazzle and spoil a woman, don't you?"

He winked at her. "You haven't seen anything yet, sweetheart. Before the night is over, you'll feel completely and totally pampered."

Silently admitting she liked the sound of that, she looped her arm through his and whispered in his ear, "And seduced, I hope."

"Oh, yeah, seduced *and* sated," he said, his tone positively sinful.

Faith stood by his side as he checked in at the registration desk and mentioned the reservations he'd made an hour ago. It was then that she realized what those "things" were that

Matthew had mentioned to her in the lounge that he needed to take care of. At the time, she'd briefly wondered if he had another date he needed to cancel to spend the evening with her, and was relieved to find out that he was merely a man who liked to plan things and be prepared.

Staying in a hotel was the ideal arrangement for their tryst, as well. It eliminated the intimacy of having him in her apartment, or her in his domain. In the morning they'd part ways, no muss, no fuss, and no evidence of their night together to deal with once they checked out.

Yes, it was the perfect plan, except she realized she didn't have an overnight bag with her, and he did. As soon as they'd secured their room key and were walking across the lavishly decorated lobby, she said, "Matthew, I don't have a change of clothes, or toiletries—"

"Trust me, you're not going to need much," he said before she could finish, the intimate insinuation threading through the tone of his voice quickening her pulse. "And what necessities you do need, I've got covered."

Before she could argue, he steered her into the hotel's boutique, a specialty shop that offered guests everything from men and women's casual and formal wear, to jewelry, to accessories and even high-priced gifts and collectibles. She immediately felt out of her element and overwhelmed by the high-priced items.

Matthew smiled at her, oblivious to her sudden discomfort. "I hope you don't mind, but before you and I head up to our room, I have a few last-minute Christmas gifts I need to buy, and I was hoping you could help me pick out a few things for my sister, Tracy."

"Me?" she exclaimed incredulously. "I don't even *know* your sister."

That didn't seem to be an issue for him as he led her over to the women's section of the boutique. "Let's see. She's twenty-two, the baby of the family, and a senior at Yale who's home for the Christmas holiday. She's about your size, maybe an

inch or two shorter, her taste runs to more modern than traditional, and she loves the color purple."

Faith rolled her eyes at him. "I still don't know her well
enough to judge what she'd like." And no way did she want to
be responsible for any kind of gift he bought at these outrageous, overinflated prices.

"Okay, then how about your opinion, from a woman's
point of view?" he suggested, and selected a designer purse
from a nearby shelf and showed it to her. "What do you think
of this?"

The four-hundred-dollar price tag flashed in front of Faith's
eyes, and her heart nearly stopped in her chest. She was certain
Matthew didn't want to know what she thought of a purse
that cost more than her monthly car payment. Luckily the approach of a woman—a saleslady, Faith assumed—saved her
from responding.

"Hey, Dr. Carlton," the beautiful, sophisticated blonde said
in a friendly, bemused greeting. "How have you been?"

Matthew put the purse back on the display and smiled
fondly at the other woman. "I've been great, Ash." He kissed
the woman's cheek affectionately, then made introductions.
"Ashley, this is Faith Roberts. Faith, Ashley St. Claire. The St.
Claires are long-time friends of the family."

Oh, yes, she was most definitely *way* out of her league,
Faith thought. "It's nice to meet you." She shook Ashley's
hand, and instantly felt enveloped in a gracious and friendly
warmth that dispelled a bit of her insecurities.

"It's a pleasure to meet you, too." Ashley smiled from Faith
back to Matthew, her eyes sparkling inquisitively. "I haven't
seen you in a while. What brings you by?"

"Last-minute Christmas gifts," he said, waving a hand over
the display of women's accessories and keeping his explanation for their presence as discreet as possible, which Faith appreciated. "I didn't want to fight the crowds down on Michigan
Ave., and I remembered how much my mother and Tracy love
the stuff here."

Matthew glanced back at Faith and gently squeezed her

hand. "Would you excuse us for a moment?" he asked her. "I have some business I need to discuss with Ashley."

"Sure. Go ahead. I'll be right over here looking at the collectibles." And keeping her hands to herself, because she wasn't about to test the "you break, you buy" policy.

With her fingers clasped behind her back, Faith pretended interest in a collection of crystals and prisms while watching Matthew and Ashley out of the corner of her eye. His dark head was bent close to hers, their voices too low for her to decipher. Ashley looked her way a few times, nodded at something he said, and made some kind of reply of her own. When Matthew gestured toward the women's section of the boutique, Faith decided to let them have their conversation . . . privately, without her trying to figure out what they were talking about.

As she continued to gaze at the crystals, she found herself drawn to a three-dimensional prism. The multitude of cuts were striking, enabling the overhead lights to catch on the many facets, which sent shards of rich brilliant colors against the wall and ceiling.

Mesmerized, and despite her vow to keep her hands to herself, she reached out and touched the prism, her breath catching as those same colors spun around her in a dizzying display of vibrant reds, purples, greens and blues.

"It's beautiful, isn't it?"

She jumped at the sound of Matthew's low, seductive voice right behind her. She'd been so enthralled with the crystals, she hadn't heard him approach. "Yes, it's absolutely exquisite."

She turned around, glad to have him back and all to herself again. "Ready to finish finding something for your sister?"

He nodded. "I certainly am."

"How about a scarf?" she said, opting for a more practical gift. She picked up a lavender-hued wrap, the cashmere weave infinitely soft against her fingertips. "She'll get a few months' wear out of it when she goes back to school for the winter season."

"See, you *are* good at this." Grinning, he reached for the

other coordinating accessories. "I'll get her the hat and gloves and matching socks, too."

She couldn't fault him for being so generous with his sister, a quality she found endearing and such a natural part of his giving personality. Something stirred within her at those admiring thoughts, a startling warmth that threatened to breach the barriers she'd erected around her heart nearly a year ago.

Doing her best to dismiss the emotional tug demanding her attention, she continued their easy conversation. "Is Tracy your only sibling?"

"No." He moved on to a case displaying fine jewelry, peered at the selection, then gestured Ashley back over to them. "I have an older brother, James, who is married to an incredible woman. They have three great kids, all boys, and a fourth one on the way, due this spring, which they're hoping is a girl."

The love for his family was tangible, and made her miss her own parents and sister even more. "Do you all get together for Christmas?"

"Absolutely. Christmas Eve my parents have a huge party for close friends, and then Christmas morning is a private gathering for just our family. We open presents and have brunch and hang out for the day." An indulgent grin curved his lips. "I usually end up on the floor with my nephews playing with them and whatever new toys Santa has brought them."

"That sounds nice," she said, unable to keep the wistful note from her voice. A part of her actually envied his big family, the nephews he obviously adored, and their traditional Christmas ritual. And just how involved he was in it all.

When Ashley arrived at the display case, Matthew pointed out a piece of jewelry for her to show him. She withdrew the dainty, pearl drop choker with a trio of diamonds offsetting smaller pearls along the delicate silver chain and placed it in his big hand.

"Let me see how this looks on you," Matthew said, and

Faith held up her hair and let him clasp the choker around her neck, thinking his sister or mother were very lucky, indeed. The necklace was beautiful, and as she looked into the small hand mirror Ashley offered, for a moment she felt like a princess wearing such an exquisite piece of jewelry.

Matthew fumbled with the clasp as he removed the choker, his fingers brushing erotically against the nape of her neck, causing her to shiver. "I'll take the necklace, and the matching earrings, too," he said to Ashley.

Grasping Faith's hand in his, he continued checking out other items in the jewelry case, but nothing else seemed to catch his eye. "So, how are you spending your Christmas?" he asked. "With family?"

"No," she said quietly. "They're all out of town." She explained where her sister now lived, and how her parents had decided to take a vacation for the holidays.

He looked taken aback. "You're all alone for Christmas?"

The concern in his eyes tugged on her heart and emotions, more than was wise, and she forced a casual shrug. "I won't be *all* alone. I'll be spending the day with Charlie."

"Charlie?" His brows pulled into an adorable, possessive frown that almost made her laugh. "Who's Charlie?"

Was that jealousy she heard in his deep voice? she wondered, more than a little surprised that he'd feel that way with her, considering his own untamable reputation. "Charlie is my cat."

"Oh." He visibly relaxed. "Good thing I like cats."

They spent another half hour in the boutique, with Matthew doing what looked to be more Christmas shopping while Faith gathered a few essentials to get her through the night: hairbrush, toothbrush and paste and a small compact of makeup. Matthew insisted on paying for her items, and instead of issuing a protest in front of Ashley, she let him use his American Express card to purchase everything.

He asked that the items be delivered to his suite, and once they were out of Ashley's range of hearing, Matthew dipped his head toward Faith's and murmured huskily in her ear, "Are you ready to head up to the room so I can have my wicked way with you?"

She thought he'd never ask, and excitement stirred through her. "Lead the way."

Chapter Four

Matthew teased her in the elevator on the ride up to the twenty-second floor, despite the fact that guests came and went along the way. Standing in the back of the small cubicle, he slipped his hand inside her coat and caressed her bottom and ran his fingers down between her thighs. He nuzzled her neck and whispered in her ear all the wonderful decadent things he wanted to do to her, with her, making Faith hot and anxious and impatient to be alone with him

As soon as they were in their suite with the double doors shut and locked behind them, Matthew pinned her against the nearest wall and kissed her senseless. A long deep kiss that made her breasts swell at the sensation of his hot silky tongue sliding oh-so-erotically into her mouth.

He pushed her coat off her shoulders, and shrugged out of his own, letting both fall to the marble floor. Then he was back, his hands tangling in her hair and his muscled body pressing insistently against hers. She felt the hard length of his erection right at the crux of her thighs, the heat of him burning into her. With a small moan she pushed closer, seeking more pressure, more friction, and felt herself grow wet with wanting, with the desperate need to have all that hot male flesh filling her completely. His large palms slid down her back and roughly grasped her bottom, separating her legs wider, lifting her into his pelvis, and moving rhythmically against her.

The encounter was deliciously aggressive, unmistakably carnal in its intent, and unlike anything she'd ever experienced before. It had been so long since she'd been with a man sexually, too long since she'd been the sole focus of a man's lust, and the force of Matthew's desire thrilled her. She wanted to rip off their clothes and let him take her right there, up against the wall, but he seemed to have his own agenda.

His mouth continued its hungry assault, and his fingers dipped between her legs, caressing and rubbing her aching, swollen sex through the fabric of her slacks. Her heart raced, her mind spun, and her lower body tingled and pulsed. Her thighs clenched his hand tightly as the tension built, and then there was no stopping the climax that rippled through her or the deep, raw moan that escaped her throat. The pleasure that shook her was amazingly wild and intense—especially for a fully clothed orgasm, which had never, ever happened to her before.

Matthew ended the kiss and looked at her, his features reflecting the same shock she felt.

"Oh, Lord . . ." She ducked her head against his chest and laughed, both amazed and embarrassed at her uncontrollable response. "Ummm, it's been a long time."

Tucking his fingers beneath her chin, he lifted her gaze back to his. His smile was crooked, his expression searching. "How long?"

Her face felt warm, flushed. Like her entire body. "A little over a year." And even at that, foreplay with Martin had never been so exciting, so combustible.

"Was it a serious relationship?"

She hadn't expected him to be so interested in her past, but his direct gaze demanded an answer, and also awakened too many insecurities she didn't want intruding on their time together. "Nine months worth of serious." And she didn't want to discuss the hows and whys of her hurtful breakup with Martin with a man who didn't seem to know the meaning of the phrase *permanent commitment*.

Which brought her around to the reason they were there, in

a very plush and extravagant suite for the night. She slid a hand between their bodies and curled her fingers around his solid erection, barely able to hold all of him in her palm. Lifting on her toes, she nipped gently on his bottom lip. "How about I return the favor?"

He groaned as she stroked and squeezed him. "As great as that sounds and feels, I want to wait until we're both naked."

"Unlike me," she said humorously.

"I loved the way you let go and came apart like that. It was so damn sexy." The hot look simmering in his eyes backed up his words. "Your lack of inhibition is a good thing, especially tonight, with me." He ran a finger down the slope of her nose, then grabbed her hand. "Come on, I've got a surprise waiting for you, and I want you to enjoy it before it gets cold."

Infinitely curious about what he'd planned, she followed him through the spacious living room, past the kitchenette that dispelled her guess that he'd ordered up a warm meal for them, to the outrageously huge master bedroom with a four-poster, king-size bed. He opened a set of double doors that connected to an enormous bathroom with a huge sunken tub dominating the room, filled with fragrant, steaming water, a froth of bubbles, and gardenia petals floating on top. Sitting on the rim was an ice bucket with chilled champagne and two glasses.

Pampered, indeed. Inhaling the rich floral scent filling the air, she glanced at Matthew in astonishment. "How in the world did you arrange to have this done when we got here?"

"I have my ways." He gave her a slow, sweet kiss that curled her toes, then let her go. "Why don't you take a bath and relax before I order up dinner?"

Before she could suggest otherwise, he stepped out of the bathroom and closed the doors behind him to give her the privacy she didn't want. She was disappointed that he hadn't stayed with her so they could enjoy the bath together, but she wasn't about to pass up the chance to indulge in such a decadent treat on her own.

She stripped off her clothes and secured her hair into a

twist so it didn't get wet. Stepping into the silken, heated water, she sat down and sank all the way up to her shoulders, enveloping her senses in the heady scent of gardenias. With a content sigh, she did as he'd ordered. She let her lashes drift shut and relaxed both her mind and her body.

Matthew opened the door to the bellman, who'd arrived to deliver his numerous purchases from the hotel's boutique, along with a plastic garment bag. He had the hotel employee set the packages on the floor in the living room, then tipped him generously for his time, service, and just because it was the giving season. The man thanked him profusely, then was gone.

Most of what he'd bought were Christmas gifts for his sister and mother, but there had been a few things that he'd deemed as necessities for Faith. Other than the clothes she had on when they'd arrived, she didn't have anything else to wear, and while she'd been shopping for her toiletries he'd picked out a dress and undergarments for her to wear tonight.

Judging by how conscious she'd been of the price tags on the items in the boutique, he knew she wasn't going to be happy that he'd spent so much money on her, but figured it was his prerogative to do so. And what a refreshing change it was to have a woman not want to relieve him of his money. Which made him want to spend it all the more on Faith.

He carried the garment bag and a few of the smaller packages into the bedroom, thinking back to their discussion in the boutique, about her spending the holidays alone. He couldn't imagine being without his family on Christmas, and hoped if all went well, Faith would spend the day with him and his parents, siblings, and nephews.

And then there was their brief but revealing conversation about her past relationship, one that had been serious for her and had lasted nearly a year. One that had obviously made her wary of him and his intentions. But before he could ask what had happened, she'd quickly changed the subject. Though he wouldn't let her avoid the topic for long, because he had a feeling whatever happened in that last relationship was a big part of the reason she'd been so resistant from the beginning.

And why had she finally changed her mind, he wondered as he laid out the dress he'd bought for her on the bed, along with sexy undergarments he hadn't been able to resist. Sure, she'd told him that it was a simple matter of giving in to their attraction and indulging in one night of hot, unforgettable sex. But Matthew didn't buy her convenient excuse and had to believe that there was something deeper behind her motivations. Something more emotional he'd be able to use to his advantage before their time together was over.

There was so much he wanted to know about Faith, so much he wanted to learn. So many different facets to her personality, much like that prism she'd been admiring earlier. And every brilliant layer that she revealed about herself only made him want her that much more . . . insecurities, vulnerabilities, and all. And when he finally had her beneath him, making love to her face-to-face, he'd make damn sure she knew that one night wouldn't be nearly enough to slake his need or desire for her. That what he felt for her went beyond sex and involved his heart and emotions.

But first, she was expecting to be seduced, and that tub was more than big enough for two.

He stripped out of his clothes, and wrapped a towel around his hips that he'd taken from the spare bathroom. He was still hard with wanting her, and he grinned wryly as his erection made itself known.

He knocked lightly on the bathroom door as a warning, then entered. Faith was immersed in the water and bubbles, and her lashes drifted open when she heard him come in. Her gaze lazily took in his bare chest, slow and appraising, and an appreciative smile curved her lips.

"Mind if I join you?" he asked, unable to keep the rasp of arousal from his voice. Unable to deny how beautiful she was, inside and out, and how much he ached to have her in his life.

"I was hoping you would," she murmured, and shifted beneath the water, causing tiny waves and gardenia petals to lap over the upper swells of her breasts, teasing him with thoughts of her naked body beneath the bubbles. "I could use some help scrubbing my back."

He waggled his brows playfully at her. "I'll scrub yours if you scrub mine."

"Deal," she said eagerly, making room for him.

He dropped the towel from around his waist and watched her eyes widen as she took in his size and length. She licked her lips, wetting them, fueling fantasies of her sweet mouth on him, taking him deep. Sucking softly. Using her tongue to lap and swirl over the head of his cock.

He shuddered at the provocative thought and climbed into the tub with her.

"You don't mind smelling like a flower?" she asked, her eyes dancing with a teasing light.

"Not if it means being in here with you."

"Ahh, such a sacrifice." She reached for the washcloth and added a large dollop of liquid soap. "You first," she said, and made him turn around so she was kneeling behind him and had access to his back.

He relaxed as she washed his shoulders, enjoying the rough texture of the cloth against his skin, down his spine, and along his thighs . . . until at some point it was only her hands and fingers skimming along his flesh below the water, touching and caressing and exploring.

She moved closer from behind, her knees widening on either side of his hips. The position caused her breasts to flatten against his back, and his jaw clenched as her palms glided around to his chest and her thumbs rasped across his rigid nipples. Then those slender fingers of hers were traveling downward, feathering along his taut stomach and lower still.

She nipped at his neck and nibbled her way to his ear, her breath hot and damp against his skin. "You have such an incredible body," she whispered, then took his throbbing penis in her hand and stroked him in her tight grasp.

He reacted with a jerk of his hips and a rough sound of pleasure he was helpless to hold back. His release simmered right below the surface, and not wanting it to be over so soon for him, he pulled her hand away and turned around, pinning her against the side of the tub and maneuvering her sleek wet body beneath his.

He stared into her eyes, brimming with a lighthearted tenderness and passion he felt, as well. "Now it's my turn to get even," he growled, and proceeded to tease her just as mercilessly as she'd aroused him.

Forgoing the cloth, he used his hands to wash her, to trace her voluptuous curves, her breasts, her belly. He kissed her, too, as she squirmed and slipped against him. Her skin was like satin and her legs tangled with his as he continued to familiarize himself with every secret spot on her body.

He found a ticklish area just below her ribs, and she laughed and writhed, nearly dunking herself in her mirth. He loved the playful, unfettered sound that drew a reciprocating chuckle from him, as well. Loved how comfortable she was with him, so trusting, without any inhibitions to get in the way of their pleasure and enjoyment of each other's bodies, and he hoped the fun, sexy moment would pave the way to a deeper, more intimate trust later.

He slid his hand between her thighs and brushed his fingers along the slippery folds of her sex, so infinitely soft and warm. He pressed deeper, and she gasped and wriggled and arched into his touch, but he deliberately kept her climax just out of her reach.

When he knew he'd tormented them both enough, he reached for the removable shower head attached to the tub's spigot. "Now for the rinse cycle," he said, and set the handheld unit to a steady, pulsating spray. "Sit up on the edge of the tub, right over there in the corner, so I can wash off the bubbles."

She hesitated for only a brief moment before doing as he asked, but sat with her knees clamped together, more prim than he would have liked. He gazed at her naked upper body, lush and curvaceous and perfectly built with high full breasts crowned with tight nipples and the gentle flare of her hips.

"You are so beautiful, so sexy," he rasped, wanting her with a hunger he could barely contain. He aimed the warm water at her chest, watching as it flowed down her gorgeous body like liquid silk.

With a soft, surrendering sigh, she closed her eyes and let her head fall back against the marbled wall. "Oh, God . . . that feels incredible."

He felt the pulse of his blood in his groin, a mounting ache in his balls. "Touch your breasts, Faith," he urged huskily. "Help me wash away the soap."

His request was completely unnecessary, but there was something incredibly erotic about a woman caressing herself so sensually, and Faith was no exception. Her hands cupped her breasts and her fingers plucked at her nipples as the water continued its gentle cascade down her body.

He wanted to lap every bit of moisture off her, wanted to taste every inch of her on his tongue, and it was then that he noticed she hadn't touched the champagne, and he was suddenly feeling very thirsty. Letting the showerhead drop into the tub, he reached for the chilled bottle, popped the cork, and poured the icy, bubbly drink over her chest.

She sucked in a startled breath, her eyes flaring wide with disbelief, but before she could object to being doused in the cold champagne, he was warming her with his mouth. She shuddered at the insistent tugging of his lips as he suckled her breast and rasped his tongue over her beaded nipple. With her hands twisting restlessly in his hair, and her breathing as ragged as his, he treated her other breast to the same sensual torture.

He lapped his way down her ribs, swept his tongue across her quivering belly, needing to sample her elsewhere. Everywhere. But her thighs were still pressed together, keeping him from his ultimate goal.

He drew back, looked up into her eyes that were hazy with desire, and traced the seam of her thighs with his finger, coaxing them to part. "I'm still very thirsty. Spread your legs for me, sweetheart."

She bit her bottom lip and let her thighs fall open, enabling him to see all of her, vulnerable and open to him in the most intimate way. Closing his thumb over the opening of the bottle, he shook the contents, hard, then released the pressure building beneath his finger. The frothing champagne sprayed between her thighs, bathing her in the sparkling, carbonated liquid.

She inhaled a quick, shallow gasp, and he could only imagine what she was feeling—the cold champagne in heated places, the shimmer of effervescent fizz on her sensitive flesh, tingling along her sex like a dozen tiny tongues pleasuring her all at once.

Her hands moved to touch herself, and he caught her wrists and held them at her sides. "Let me . . ." he said, and bent his head, taking her in his mouth, his tongue hot and rough and determined. He found her clit and sucked gently, greedily, the flavor of champagne and hot, honeyed woman a heady combination that went straight to his already straining penis.

He tongued her deeper, and she gave a stifled scream and climaxed, shaking with the force of her release.

Once he coaxed every last sensation from her quaking body, he pulled her back into the water so that she was straddling his waist and his shaft was nestled between her smooth trembling thighs. He looked up at her face, into her dazed eyes, needing her more than his next breath.

He didn't have a condom handy, but he was more than willing to improvise, especially when he knew it wouldn't take much to make him climax. He brought her hand to his erection and circled her fingers tight around his cock.

"Make me come," he growled, and crushed his mouth to hers.

His tongue delved deep, matching the long heated stroke of her palm. Wild lust and savage longing mingled, and he couldn't hold back any longer. Didn't want to.

He let go and came in a fierce searing rush, surrendering completely to the insane pleasure of it all.

Chapter Five

Faith reached for the plush robe hanging from the back of the bathroom door and slipped inside the soft terry material, while the best lover she'd ever had finished with his own shower after their very illicit tryst in the tub. Her body still thrummed from her recent champagne-induced orgasm, and her heart . . . oh, Lord, her heart was in the process of taking a very dangerous free fall for Dr. Matthew Carlton.

The thought sent a startling jolt of reality through her. It was just sex, she told herself as she tightened the sash on the robe and valiantly ignored the tempting outline of Matthew's body against the fogged shower doors. Nothing but a few amazing, unforgettable orgasms so far—undoubtedly the best she'd ever had—just as she'd asked him for. And the rest of the night promised to be equally outstanding and memorable.

She just never expected that being with Matthew would feel so perfectly right, beyond physical attraction and in ways she'd never imagined. She was drawn to him as a man who loved his family and made time for them, a big brother with a generous spirit who enjoyed spoiling his sister, and that sensitive, compassionate side she'd glimpsed many times as a pediatric surgeon. And mostly, a man who'd gone out of his way to treat this as more than a one-night stand.

He was a man who possessed so many outstanding qualities, yet she couldn't stop the doubts tightening her chest—the fear of believing in the impossible with a man out of her league personally and professionally, and ultimately getting hurt when he decided the newness and excitement of their affair had finally worn off. That particular lesson with Martin was still too fresh in her mind to forget.

Vowing to keep her distance emotionally, and praying that she had the willpower to do so for the next twelve hours or so, she headed into the adjoining master bedroom and came to a sudden stop when she caught sight of the garments laid out on the bed. Certain that Matthew wasn't planning on wearing a dress and provocative undergarments this evening, she could only assume that the items were for her.

She stepped closer, brushed the tips of her fingers along the sexy black dress she recognized from the boutique downstairs, and experienced a blend of mixed feelings over wanting to look desirable for Matthew, and refusing to accept anything more from him tonight than sex. Gifts certainly weren't part of their deal . . . but then again, neither had been staying the night in one of Chicago's most luxurious hotels.

Hearing him exit the bathroom behind her, she turned around, not sure what to say, or what to do.

He must have sensed her uncertainty, because he approached slowly, cautiously, securing the sash on his own robe around his waist. "Will you wear that for me tonight?"

He'd *asked*, a polite request not a demand, making the choice solely hers, and that simple gesture made a lump rise to her throat. Then there was that sincerity she saw in his dark eyes, along with a deeper longing that made her ache to do and be anything he wanted.

Damn her traitorous emotions, anyway!

She smiled, just for him. "I'd love to wear the dress and other things for you."

He looked immensely pleased with her decision. "Then I'll leave you to get dressed while I change in the spare bedroom." He kissed her on the cheek, his lips warm and smooth and much too fleeting. "I'll meet you in the dining room when you're done."

Then he was gone.

It took Faith a good half hour to get ready, to clip her hair up in a stylish knot, reapply her makeup, and put on the lingerie and outfit Matthew had bought specifically for her. Standing in front of the dresser mirror, she took in the elegant long-sleeved, off-the-shoulder dress and the strappy shoes that were about a half size too big but would more than do for an hour or so. Her stockings were black, too, matching the garter belt, panties, and strapless bra ensemble he'd bought for her.

All traces of the conservative schoolteacher had vanished, replaced by a sensual, sophisticated woman with seduction on her mind. The new look thrilled her, but also made her more than a little nervous, because for as much as she enjoyed the temporary transformation, it didn't change her modest lifestyle or who and what she was. And she hoped with all her heart that wasn't his intent.

She headed out to the dining room, the delicious smell of dinner awaiting her, along with Matthew, dressed in a white dress shirt he'd left unbuttoned at the throat and brown slacks he must have purchased at the boutique, as well.

His gaze surveyed her appreciatively, from the low-cut bodice down to the knee-length hem of the dress. "You look gorgeous."

She felt her cheeks flush, but had to admit she liked feeling so beautiful. So pampered and spoiled by him. "Thank you."

He pretended a frown and tapped a finger against his lips. "Something's missing."

She glanced down at herself, unable to imagine what she'd forgotten. "And what's that?"

"Accessories." He produced a flat velvet box, opened it, and showed her what he had in mind.

She gasped, her heart stuttering in her chest as she caught sight of the pearl-and-diamond choker and earrings she'd tried on at the boutique. "Matthew." She shook her head, in disbelief and denial. "I can't accept those!"

"Sure you can." A confident man, he merely smiled, undaunted by her refusal. "How about you consider it a memento of our special night together?"

"That's one hell of an expensive memento, as was the dress!" She laughed, the sound strained, certain she'd never have another reason to wear such a lavish gift. "I'd be just as happy with a key chain souvenir from the gift shop downstairs."

He chuckled and stepped behind her, securing the choker around her neck before she could object. "But that wouldn't go nearly as well with your outfit."

He coaxed her to put on the earrings, too, and she did so while telling herself that she couldn't, wouldn't, keep the jewelry. She'd wear it for now, for the night because it was all part of the fantasy, but she'd leave in the morning with only the items she'd come here with . . . and her heart intact.

Seemingly satisfied with himself, Matthew bowed gallantly and swept his hand toward the formal dining room. "Dinner awaits us," he announced, and escorted her to her table.

Sitting beside him, Faith positively glowed. Matthew loved the way she looked in that sexy black dress, and the way the necklace she'd been so reluctant to accept from him sparkled in the candlelight. As they dined on beef tenderloin, he enjoyed the way her eyes shone and her expression turned animated as she talked about her third-grade class of eight-year-olds as if they were her own.

He understood her dedication to her job and the kids she taught, because he felt the same way with his young patients. Those sick children all became a part of his life in some way, even if only for a brief time, leaving a lasting impression that never completely faded.

Just as Faith was leaving a lasting impression on his heart and emotions. On his soul. It was as though he'd found his other half, a woman who accepted him for who he was on the inside, not what he presented on the outside. She was meant for him, of this he had no doubts.

Now it was a matter of making her realize that, too.

They fed each other dessert, a rich, delicious chocolate soufflé they washed down with sips of fine champagne while he regaled her with amusing stories about his childhood and siblings, hoping she'd see just what an ordinary guy he was, despite his medical degree and the old family money he'd been born into. He also made sure Faith knew he took nothing for granted, that his parents had taught him to work hard and earn his way in life, and he was doing that quite well.

But for as much as they'd shared during dinner, there was still one important issue they needed to discuss tonight, before they went any further. And he had a feeling if he wasn't careful in his approach, their night together might end before it truly had a chance to begin.

He scooted out his chair, stood, and held his hand toward Faith. "Care to dance?"

"Ahh, dancing," she said on a soft wistful sigh as she placed her fingers in his palm and allowed him to help her up. "Now there's something I haven't done in a long while."

He guided her to the middle of the spacious dining room, wrapped an arm around her waist, and pulled her close. The area was dimly lit, the music drifting from the stereo speakers light and instrumental. "It's not something I do often either . . . usually just at the occasional social function, but tonight it gives me the perfect excuse to hold you in my arms."

She slid her arms around his neck, her fingers playing through his hair, her breasts warm and firm against his chest. "Ulterior motives, hmm?"

He caressed her spine, aligning their lower bodies, their thighs. "Guilty as charged."

She smiled up at him as they swayed together, her earlier caution with him completely gone. Her damp lips parted, and he knew she wanted him to kiss her, that she was more than willing to let things progress from there. He wanted that too. Soon.

He took the hand he was holding and pressed her palm over his beating heart, needing that intimate connection between them before he shattered the tranquility of the moment.

"Faith . . . what happened between you and the last guy you were dating?"

She stiffened, and that quickly he could feel her erecting those protective walls around her again. "Why does it matter?"

"Because I don't want to make the same stupid mistake he did and end up losing you." While his tone was teasing to put her at ease, he was totally serious.

She drew a deep breath, which did nothing to dispel the internal pain he saw flash across her features. "Matthew, we agreed on this one night, no more—"

He pressed two fingers against her soft lips to quiet her. "Just humor me and answer my question, okay? And if there's anything you want to ask me in return about my past relationships, I'm an open book."

She arched a brow, a hint of disdain glimmering in the depths of her eyes. "Including your broken engagement?"

He wasn't surprised she knew about that—the gossip among the single women in the hospital was ruthless, and most of the time, inaccurate or overinflated. It was that severed engagement and the dating that followed that had instigated his current reputation as a player, and he'd felt no need to defend himself . . . until now, when it ultimately mattered.

"I have absolutely nothing to hide from you," he said gently. "I'd like to hope that you feel the same way."

She glanced away for a long, quiet moment, then her gaze returned to his, her reserve firmly back in place. "I met Martin at a mutual friend's party, and he pursued me, until I finally gave in and went out to dinner with him. Once we started dating, things between us seemed to turn serious very quickly."

Matthew remained silent, listening, holding her close in his embrace and offering his caring and support the only way he could.

"Martin was a very successful lawyer, and I was always aware of the differences in our social standing when we were with his friends or colleagues. And when I tried to talk to him about my concerns, he'd dismiss them as inconsequential, promising me that those things didn't matter to him."

Her fingers absently traced the seam at the collar of his shirt, her gaze focused on something over his shoulder. "After nine months of seeing each other, he told me he wanted to get married and have kids. And just when I let my guard down and allowed myself to believe that maybe, just maybe, I could fit into his life and be what he wanted, I discovered that he didn't want those things with me after all. Something better came along for him."

"I can't imagine what that would be," he said in disbelief.

She inhaled a deep breath and looked back at him. "He met a sophisticated, well-bred woman who came from a wealthy family and had political connections that suited his career. And suddenly, he decided that an elementary-school teacher didn't fit his image as a lawyer, and that was the end of that."

Matthew swore, low and succinct, furious at the other man's callous treatment. "Martin was a fool to let you go," he said gruffly. But that jerk's loss was definitely Matthew's gain. *If* he was able to get around the insecurities Faith's ex-boyfriend had instilled in her.

Her lips pursed tightly. "No, I was the fool, for letting him sucker me in with all the right words and for allowing him to use me the way he did."

He hated how disillusioned she'd been, but understood it well and used it to his advantage. "You and I seem to have something in common with our past relationships."

She frowned at him, her disbelief plain. "I can't imagine how, unless your fiancée was fooled by you, as well?"

That judgmental remark should have stung, but didn't, because Matthew now understood Faith's pain and felt it as his own. "No, I was the one who was almost fooled by Alison."

She stared at him in the flickering candlelight, her expression perplexed by his statement, and he explained while he had the chance.

"I don't deny that I was the one who broke things off with Alison. I overheard her talking to a friend on the phone about how she was finally going to become a surgeon's wife, and just how she planned on spending my money. She's not the first woman who's looked at me and seen dollar signs or the prestige of being a doctor's wife, but Alison hid it better than most. So, just like you, since then, I've been cautious."

She digested that information, seemingly shocked by the revelation. "And what about your reputation for 'playing around,' for being a playboy?" she asked curiously.

"I won't deny that the gossip about me around the hospital has run rampant the past year, but it's pure exaggeration and rumors." It was time to set the record straight, to lay the truth bare, because with Faith it mattered what she thought of him. "I told you, my reputation is highly overrated. Yes, I took a few of the nurses out for a casual date, but none of them got more than a peck on the cheek at the end of the evening."

He drew small soothing circles with his thumb against the base of her spine, and felt some of the tension in her body drain away. "With the women at the hospital, it's worse than a men's locker room when it comes to gossiping about the opposite sex. And after my broken engagement, I guess I became fair game. After I took one of the women out for a cup of coffee, the next day I heard through the grapevine that the two of us made out in her car before I took her home. Then I went out with another nurse, just to a movie, and the next thing you know gossip was circulating that she'd spent the night at my place." He shook his head, still unable to believe how the stories about him had snowballed. "It was as though everyone was trying to one up each other, and no one wanted to look like they'd been rejected by me when every woman had already reported how good I was sexually." He rolled his eyes at that.

She laughed, clearly humored by it all, and he was glad that she was able to find levity in the situation. "That must have done wonders for your ego."

He shrugged, knowing that his ego was firmly intact. "I'll admit, it became a huge source of amusement, but it never occurred to me that the rumors and gossip would hurt my chances with a woman who truly meant something to me." He tenderly stroked his knuckles down her cheek. "You're that woman, Faith."

Her eyes widened, but despite all that he'd revealed, her uncertainties were still a tangible thing, lingering in those guarded eyes of hers. "Matthew—"

Again, he pressed his fingers to her lips, silencing her. "I don't want to talk anymore, Faith." He'd given her enough to think about, and now he wanted to show her that what was between them was different than what they'd each experienced in their past relationships. That he was different than the man who'd used her, then destroyed her trust.

Grasping his wrist, she pulled his hand away, the insecurities in her gaze giving way to the same desire and hunger racing through him. "Then what do you want to do?"

"I want to make love to you . . . all night long." He dropped a kiss on her bare shoulder and trailed his lips up to her ear. "What do you say we take this up to the bedroom where I can love you properly on a big soft bed?"

Chapter Six

Faith's stomach tumbled as Matthew's choice of words flitted through her mind and her heart, adding to the conflicting feelings swirling within her—especially the need to trust him and all he'd told her, but his warm damp mouth and the slow slide of his hands along her back to her bottom were wreaking havoc with her thought process. At the moment, the only thing she knew for absolute certainty was that she ached to make love with him, too. And, in the morning, she hoped she'd be better able to sort through her emotions and put everything back into perspective before they went their separate ways.

With that decision made, she took his big hand in her smaller one and led the way into the bedroom. He turned on the lamp next to the bed, casting a soft glow in the room, and she caught sight of the condoms he'd left on the nightstand. When he stood in front of her again, his eyes adoring and filled with breath-taking emotion, she felt yet another chink in her armor fall away. This time, though, she didn't have the will to fight her surrender to this man who made her feel new and exciting things.

He lowered his head, and she met him halfway, her lips parting eagerly for his. The kiss they shared was slow and sensual, his mouth soft yet firm, his tongue lazily seducing her mind and senses.

Moaning, she arched closer to his hard muscular body. She twined her arms around his neck and felt his hands lift to her hair. He pulled out the clip holding up the heavy strands, and then the silky mass was tumbling around her shoulders and he was sifting the tresses through his fingers, tugging on them gently, adding to all the other deliciously arousing sensations rippling through her.

Kicking off her shoes, she dragged her flattened palms across his shoulders and down his chest. She found the buttons on his shirt and started unfastening them, wanting him naked. Wanting to feel his strong powerful body beneath her fingertips, against her lips—just as his lips were skimming down her neck, his tongue tasting, his mouth open, his breath damp and hot. She pulled the hem of his shirt from his trousers and shoved it off his broad shoulders at the same time he lowered the zipper on her dress and gently pushed the outfit in the same direction. She felt the fabric slither down her body, along with her strapless bra, leaving her dressed in a very scanty lingerie ensemble.

She shivered as the cool air hit her bared skin, and her nipples puckered tightly. She laughed, sounding more nervous than she intended. "It's chilly in here."

He glanced down the length of her, taking in her full breasts and the garter, panties, and stockings that encased her long legs. The grin that curved his mouth was pure sin. "Don't worry, sweetheart. I've got enough body heat for the two of us and I promise I'll warm you up."

She believed him, because beneath the hands she'd flattened on his chest, his flesh was hot, feverish. "You can warm me in a minute," she said, and splaying her fingers, she glided her palms down his torso to his belly, which clenched beneath her touch. "I want to have my way with you first."

He groaned as she leaned forward and laved his nipples with her tongue while her fingers unbuckled his belt, undid his slacks, and let them drop to the floor. She slid her hands into the waistband of his briefs, cupped his taut buttocks in her palms, and dragged his underwear down his thighs as her mouth traversed a path lower, tasting his skin and inhaling his scent.

Then she was kneeling before him, his pants and briefs kicked aside and his long thick erection curving upward, nearly reaching his navel. She licked her lips, fascinated by the size of him. Reaching out, she wrapped her fingers around his shaft, squeezing him gently. A drop of precome gathered on the tip, and she used her thumb to spread the silky drop of moisture over the head of his cock.

His fingers slid into her hair and curved against the back of her head, urging her forward. "Take me in your mouth," he rasped.

She did as he asked, enveloping him in the wet heat of her mouth, her tongue swirling and lapping down the rigid length of him. Then she took him as deep as she could and suckled slowly, rhythmically, greedily.

His entire body shuddered, and he exhaled sharply, dragging her mouth back up to his. He kissed her with an intensity that left her reeling and maneuvered her backward, until the back of her knees hit the edge of the mattress and he was pressing her down onto the middle of the bed. She went willingly, gasping as he caressed her breasts and plucked at the stiff peaks with his lips and teeth, then soothed her nipples with his soft tongue. His mouth continued down her ribs, scattering hot damp kisses across her belly, until he was kneeling between her spread legs.

He sat up, reaching for a condom and in seconds sheathed himself. She was still wearing her panties, and she desperately wanted them off, but Matthew had other ideas in mind. His hot hands skimmed up her thighs, widening them even more, and then his fingers were fanning out over her mound and his thumbs were easing beneath the crotch of her underwear, sliding slowly, unerringly along her swollen folds, her aching cleft, teasing her with the promise of an explosive orgasm.

She moaned fretfully, grabbed handfuls of the comforter,

and arched into his illicit touch, the word *please* escaping her throat. She was hot and slippery wet, trembling, her climax building momentum only to ebb when he deliberately changed the rhythm of his caresses.

He lifted his head, staring up at her from between her legs. His dark lashes cast shadows on his cheekbones, and his silky hair fell over his forehead, his eyes hungry, primal. "Come for me while I watch," he murmured.

He stroked again, one thumb gliding purposefully across her clit and the other pushing into her, then slowly withdrawing, again and again, until she was panting, then screaming and climaxing as the dual sensations washed over her.

As she lay there, trying to regain her strength to move, she felt him remove her garter belt and slide her panties down her legs, along with her stockings. She expected him to finally mount her, but she was learning quickly that Matthew wasn't a man who conformed to anyone's expectations but his own.

He settled himself between her thighs again, draping her legs over his broad shoulders. He looked his fill of her, stroked his fingers along her slick folds, increasing the heat where he touched her. On a soft, needy groan, he lowered his head, his breath hot against her overly sensitive flesh.

She grabbed a handful of his hair, certain she couldn't take another orgasm so soon after the first. "Nooo . . ."

"Oh, yes . . ."

His tongue touched her first, stealing her breath and stripping her of every last bit of inhibition. His skillful mouth pleasured her, slowly, leisurely, and everything he did to her, every soft, deep, erotic kiss, every lick, every suctioning swirl, felt exquisite. He worshiped her selflessly, leading her to the brink once again, until she was tumbling, tumbling, tumbling over the edge and shamelessly begging him to take her.

He reared up over her, and she felt the head of his erection slide along her sex, unerringly finding the entrance to her body. She closed her eyes, arching into him and wrapping her calves along the back of his thighs as he flexed his hips and drove into her, high and hard and deep . . . possessing her completely. Not just her body, but her heart and soul as well. And she was helpless to stop the invasion. Realized she didn't want to.

A sob rose up into her throat, and she gripped his straining biceps, waiting for him to move. Other than his choppy breathing, he remained still, but she could feel him throbbing within her, his entire body taut from holding back.

His warm fingers touched her face and gently smoothed strands of her hair off her cheek. "Open your eyes and look at me, Faith."

She swallowed hard, instinctively knowing this moment was more than just about hot, unforgettable sex. He was going to make love to her, and he wanted her to be sure she knew it, too.

Pushing aside the fears and insecurities she'd been carrying with her for too long, she opened herself up to Matthew and met his gaze, taking that first tentative step in trusting him with her heart and emotions.

He smiled, seemingly relieved that she hadn't shut him out, and it amazed her that this strong, confident man had a few vulnerabilities of his own and wasn't afraid to display them with her.

He stared deeply into her eyes, his own so dark and beautiful, like twin windows into his soul. "I want you to know that I'm falling in love with you."

His declaration was more than she'd anticipated, and she shook her head in denial. "Matthew . . . no."

"Yes," he refuted softly. "What I feel for you is real, Faith. I want you for more than just one night. I want you forever. All you have to do is trust me and believe in yourself and what you feel, too."

That said, he framed her face in his hands, kissed her, and made her feel. He rocked against her, into her, and every muscle clenched, pulled, and tightened around his shaft. He growled against her mouth and thrust into her, deeply, then deeper still, pumping in a hard, steady rhythm that had her hips lifting off the bed, straining, seeking yet another end to the thrum of desire coiling tighter and tighter within her belly. Her climax rolled through her, lifting her body against his, stretching her nerves to the breaking point one last time.

She whimpered as she came, stunned at this man's sexual and emotional power over her, and he was right there with her . . . her name a sweet promise on his lips as he lost himself in the same immense pleasure consuming her.

Flat on her stomach, replete and sated after a night of the most erotic lovemaking Faith had ever known, she eased awake by slow degrees. She was disappointed to find herself alone, but judging by the scent of coffee teasing her nose, she guessed that Matthew was in the other room, waiting for her to join him.

Smiling at the provocative, unforgettable memories dancing in her head, she buried her face in her pillow, inhaling the intoxicating scent of Matthew and of sex and all that they'd shared in this big bed. Seemingly unable to get enough of each other, they'd made love numerous times during the night. Hot and hurried. Slow and languorous. Intense and demanding. In ways that had thrilled Faith and allowed Matthew to fulfill a few fantasies he'd whispered in her ear.

She'd surrendered to him in every way. A scary prospect, that. Scarier still was the knowledge that Matthew was falling in love with her. And if she was honest with herself, she'd been fighting her feelings for him for months, too. He'd just been able to verbalize his emotions, while she'd clung tight to her insecurities for fear of being hurt again.

She'd asked Matthew for one night of unforgettable sex, and he'd given her that and a whole lot more. He could have reaped the benefits of a one-night stand and enjoyed their time together and been on his way in the morning. That's what she'd expected him to do since she'd fallen victim to the gossip about him around the hospital. But now she'd learned a lot about Matthew, and one of the most important traits he possessed was that he was a man of integrity—when it came to his work, his family, and his relationships. When it came to *her*.

Last night he'd told her that all she had to do was trust him and believe in herself and what she felt inside. A part of her was still scared and cautious, but listening to her heart, she knew she couldn't just walk away after last night. She wanted more with him, and that meant taking chances and opening her heart to the possibility of love.

Because ultimately, Matthew Carlton was a risk she was willing to take.

Matthew glanced up from the morning paper he was perusing when he heard the bedroom door open, not certain what to expect from Faith the morning after. Especially after he'd bared himself to her, physically and emotionally.

She was wrapped in one of the hotel robes, the hair he'd tousled during the night brushed so that it fell around her shoulders in soft layers. She strolled across the expanse of space separating them, and unable to gauge her mood or read her expression, he offered up a smile, despite the anxious feeling settling in the pit of his belly.

"Good morning," he greeted.

"Morning," she murmured, her voice husky with remnants of sleep.

"Would you like some coffee or fruit?" he asked, motioning to the continental breakfast he'd had room service deliver for the two of them. *If* she stayed long enough to eat. Then there was the one present he still had left to give her, a Christmas gift he wanted her to take with her, no matter how this morning ended.

"Maybe in a little bit," she said, and slid onto his jean-clad lap, surprising him with the playful move, until she spoke her next words. "Thank you for the most unforgettable night of my life. Never would I have imagined that sex could be so incredible; you more than fulfilled my Christmas wish."

So, she was still thinking in terms of sex and an affair. His hopes plummeted, but he managed, just barely, to keep calm instead of making demands. "It was my pleasure." He reached for the gift on the table, wrapped in bright Christmas paper. "I have something I want to give to you, and I won't take no for an answer."

"Another memento?" she murmured as she took the present from him and lightly touched the gold bow on top.

"Yeah, something like that," he replied gruffly.

She shifted on his thighs as she ripped off the paper, and the lapels of her robe gaped open, offering him a view of the creamy slope of her breast. He hardened in a rush, aching to take that soft mound of flesh in his hand, his mouth . . .

She opened the box, peeled back layers of tissue, and gasped when she revealed the beautiful prism she'd admired down in the boutique yesterday. "Oh, Matthew." She pressed a hand to her heart, her eyes filling with moisture. "How did you know I secretly wanted this?"

"Because I was watching you with that prism and how fascinated you were." He went on to explain to her what he saw in that crystal, the different facets that reminded him so much of her, and each brilliant layer that represented such an intriguing part of who she was.

"Thank you." She stroked her fingers over the glossy surface before putting it back in its box and setting it back on the table. "I'll treasure it always."

Still, he couldn't read her tone, and all he could think was the worst . . . that he hadn't been able to sway her last night to believe in him. Frustration welled inside of him, and unable to be passive about the situation any longer, he let his thoughts be known. "Dammit, Faith, I'm not letting you walk out of here today, leaving me behind and acting as though we never spent the night together. A night that was way more than sex."

She blinked at him, seemingly taken aback by his sudden outburst. "I could never do that—"

"Forget falling in love, I'm in love with you," he said, forging on determinedly and stating his case before she could stop him. "And I know you felt things last night, an intimate connection that superceded a mere affair. I know everything between us has happened quickly, and I know it scares you, but I'd never deliberately hurt you like that jerk you were dating did. I don't care that you're a schoolteacher and I'm a surgeon. Those differences don't matter to me, and they won't make a bit of difference to my family, either." He knew he was rambling, but couldn't help himself because he didn't want to give her the opportunity to say no to him. "I swear we'll take things slow and easy, one day at a time until you realize how serious I am, but in order to do that you have to give us a chance."

"I know," she said softly, affectionately.

His mouth opened, and then he snapped it shut again and frowned, certain he'd misheard her. "Excuse me?"

She pressed her cool palms against his cheeks and in her eyes he saw enough emotion to make him believe in true love, soul mates, happily-ever-afters and them. "I wasn't going to walk out of here today. Not without you by my side. I woke up this morning, and after everything that happened between us yesterday, everything we shared about our pasts and relationships, I knew that you'd be the one person I could trust with my heart." A small teasing smile tipped the corner of her mouth. "And I figured if there was going to be any gossip about the two of us at the hospital, it ought to be fact, not fiction."

He laughed, and reassured that this wonderful woman was his, he lifted her up so she was sitting on the table, then stood, pushing her knees apart and slowly sliding his hands beneath the hem of her robe and up her soft, smooth thighs. "It's Christmas Eve, and I want you to spend tonight and tomorrow with me and my family."

"I'd love to," she said happily, and sucked in a breath when his fingers encountered her soft, wet heat.

He grinned rakishly as other more pressing matters made themselves known. "God, I'm suddenly ravenous."

"Me, too." Knowing exactly what he was starving for, he

watched as she untied the sash around her waist, and with a shrug of her shoulders the robe slipped down her arms and off.

Faith sat there, gloriously naked, trust and love shimmering in her eyes, along with a wealth of passion for him. Cupping the back of his head, she brought his mouth to her breast and murmured, "Breakfast is served."

Turning Up the Heat

Susan Donovan

Chapter One

The longer Valerie sat, the colder she got.

She perched on a hard dining room chair, teeth chattering, the silk shawl pulled tight across her shoulders. Her eyes darted from the front door to the leg of lamb—now congealing in the candlelight—in the center of the table.

She silently analyzed the situation again and had to admit it was pitiful. She was all alone—on Christmas Eve, no less—and everything she'd done to keep loneliness at bay had backfired.

Yes, she'd prepared a festive meal, but it was for a party of one. Yes, she was wearing a beautiful new dress and had taken an hour to do her hair and makeup—but the glamorous result was for her eyes only.

And now, to add insult to injury, the heater had stopped working. So there she sat, waiting for the doorbell to ring. Waiting for some greasy, wrench-wielding furnace repairman guy to come in and fix it.

With a pensive smile, Valerie gripped the shawl even tighter across her chest and wondered if she'd ever be warm again. She wondered if any woman this cold and lonely could ever again feel the heat.

"Merry Christmas to me," she whispered, standing up.

Valerie grabbed the silver platter of lamb in one hand and the cut-glass salad bowl in the other and headed to the kitchen, knowing that if she let herself get all pessimistic about this, she'd have to admit that repairmen were like all men—they just got to be more direct about it. They showed up whenever they felt like it. They made you wait. Like their time was more important than yours. Like it didn't matter that you were freezing your buns off.

Then they left you with a bill.

Valerie went back to the table and blew out the candles. A jagged swirl of white smoke made a beeline right into her nostrils and made her cough, made her nose run and her eyes tear. She grabbed the sweet potato soufflé, the rolls, the green beans with almonds and tossed all the leftovers into Tupperware and into the fridge. She didn't even burp the lids—that's how miserable she felt.

She leaned up against the cabinets and looked down at her feet. The black suede sling-backs cost a hundred and fifty big ones. The sheer black thigh-highs were twenty. And she didn't even want to *think* about what she'd paid for the red velvet cocktail dress. Or the leg of lamb. Or the wine.

Her eyes were watering quite a bit now, and she didn't think she could blame it on the smoke. It was just plain sad that a woman would go to all this trouble to keep her spirits up, only to fail miserably. It was sad that she would pretend to be some red-hot holiday sex kitten only to have no one notice.

Valerie ripped off a jagged section of paper towel dotted with little red snowmen, and blew her nose.

Who was she kidding? There was nothing left to do but put on her baggy, green plaid, flannel pajamas, crawl under the down comforter, and watch *When Harry Met Sally* for the nine-millionth time.

Valerie pushed herself away from the cabinets and was heading down the hallway when the doorbell rang. Great. She couldn't wait to meet her "date" for the evening—the guy from Ferguson Heating and Cooling.

As her hand hit the doorknob, Valerie decided the guy would have to be the cream of the crop—the one repairman who wasn't married or in a relationship. The one poor loser who didn't mind working for holiday overtime on the most special night of the year. A guy who'd be bald, with a beer gut and droopy repairman drawers. A guy with a name like Lloyd or Cletus or Earl.

A guy who was as big a loser as she was.

"Ms. Matthews?"

The blood roared through her head. Her body went ice-hot. And her hands began to shake. But in general, if this was what it felt like to have a hallucination, Valerie decided it was pretty manageable.

She stared at the man in the blue zippered jacket who stood on her stoop. His name was machine-stitched across what looked like an exceptionally well developed chest.

Earl. At least she'd been right about one thing.

"Ms. Matthews?" He lowered his head to catch her eye. "I'm with Ferguson Heating and Cooling. I understand you're having some problems with your unit."

Her unit. Yes, indeed. Her unit had definitely started to act up.

Valerie scanned the specimen who stood before her. The snow swirled behind him and the porch light glittered off the individual flakes, creating a moving halo of tiny gold and white stars around his handsome head.

He looked like an angel. An angel with rich brown curls and mesmerizing blue eyes. An angel with a straight, strong nose. An angel carrying a clipboard and a rounded metal tool-box that looked like it weighed a ton.

A studly snow angel named Earl.

"Can I come in, Ms. Matthews? It's a bit nippy out here. And you—" Earl stopped. Valerie watched—and felt—his eyes slide up and down her clingy red velvet dress, to her stockings, to her shoes, and back up again. Real slow. His gaze fastened on the tops of her breasts, suddenly revealed as the shawl slid down her shoulders.

He cleared his throat. "Looks like you might be chilly."

Valerie managed to get her feet to work, and she took a few choppy steps backward, pulling the door wider as she went.

Earl stepped inside, bringing with him a churn of snow, a gust of cold air, the smell of winter.

And a smile hotter than August in Hades.

"How about we warm you up, Ms. Matthews?" Earl stood over her, his mouth still forming that sizzler of a smile, his eyes shining. Valerie watched, fascinated, as a single snowflake dangled from a spiky lower eyelash, fell to the rise of his smooth cheek, and melted on contact.

Just like she was doing.

"Do you think Mr. Matthews could show me where the furnace is?"

The silence hung heavy between them. Eventually, she said, "Who's he?"

Those were the first words Valerie had managed to utter and they came out scratchy and low, like she was catching a cold.

Earl's smile mellowed, and then turned sly. "I see," was all he said.

And without a word—without her permission—Earl took a few long strides on long legs and was suddenly standing in the middle of her living room, like he owned the place.

She watched his head swivel on a sturdy male neck, surveying the scene. His gaze stopped on the dining room table, and Valerie saw what he saw—puddles of cold candle wax on the white linen tablecloth, indentations where the serving dishes had been. The remnants of a table for one.

His eyes met hers for an instant, and she saw a flash of kindness in them—concern even—before he began a slow examination of the living room. She watched him scan over the comfortable Art Deco couch in muted green that she loved so much, the Christmas tree twinkling with tiny white lights, and the fireplace, hung with cheerful stockings.

He whipped his head around. "How about I start a fire for you, Ms. Matthews? Keep you toasty warm while I work?"

Toasty was good, she thought.

Then he set the toolbox and clipboard on the floor near an armchair, and walked across the room. The man took up a lot of space, Valerie noticed. He was nearly as tall as the tree, with wide shoulders and . . . *oh, my.*

This Earl person unzipped his repairman jacket and tossed it on the floor near the hearth. She watched as he squatted in front of the fireplace, his navy blue Dickies stretched taut across his butt and thighs. He attempted to open the metal fireplace screen but, as usual, the chain stuck.

He glanced over his shoulder, one stray curl cupping a perfect earlobe. "A little lubrication should fix her right up."

Valerie felt the sudden need to sit down. She groped around with both hands for the arm of the couch and collapsed onto the cushions, studying him. She watched as Earl built the cutest little teepee in the fireplace grate, crumpled newspaper at the bottom, sticks of kindling balanced over that, big logs at the top.

She watched his arms—well-formed and solid. His hands were broad but surprisingly smooth and clean for a workman. His pale blue denim shirt was pressed and tucked in at a trim waist. He moved with grace. Like an athlete. He was a joy to observe.

She sighed, leaned her elbows on her knees, and propped her chin on a fist. She didn't realize that she'd started humming "Joy to the World," until Earl swiveled his head around again and flashed her that smile.

"How did you know that's my favorite Christmas carol?"

Valerie jumped from the couch.

He stood up as well.

And as Valerie and Earl looked into each other's eyes, something fierce and electric passed between them in the silence of the cold living room.

Then Earl said, "Got a match?"

Chapter Two

Earl knew this woman—this hot, raven-haired, creamy-skinned woman poured into a red velvet dress. He'd first seen her at a company cocktail party a few years back. She'd been the caterer. He'd never forgotten her.

And here she was—all alone on Christmas Eve—looking up at him with huge green peepers. There were some things in the universe so outrageous that they defied explanation. There were some things that made him just want to pump his fist in the air and shout, *"Hell, yes!"*

Being alone with Valerie Matthews was definitely one of them.

She stood not five inches away from the front of his work shirt, licking her full lips in nervousness.

This was just too damn good to be true.

"A match?" She blinked. He could see her luscious breasts move up and down in that low-cut dress as she took shallow, rapid breaths. He could see her blood pound just beneath the silken skin of her throat.

"To start the fire, Ms. Matthews."

"Sure. Of course."

He watched her spin away on a pair of pretty shoes. He listened to the *click-click* of her high heels as she walked away across hardwood floors into the kitchen, the wispy fringe of shawl skimming a delectably round red-velvet ass.

She was all gift wrapped. And for some inexplicable reason, there was no man here to do the unwrapping.

He smiled to himself. Fortunately, he was used to taking charge in situations like this. He was the type of guy you could count on to handle the pressure. He was accustomed to stepping up to the mound in the ninth, three men on base, with no choice but to make the clutch play.

And as Ms. Matthews walked back to him, tentatively holding out a little square box of kitchen matches, he thought of several things he'd like to clutch—those hips, that waist, that face. He knew instinctively what her pleasing flesh would feel like in his hands. She would be round, soft, and all woman. She would feel as if she were made for him, body and soul.

"This is all I have," she said.

Her words cut through him. She looked so vulnerable standing there, so sweet, so alone. She looked like the kind of woman who needed a man to keep her warm . . . all night long.

He let his fingers brush over her delicate little hand as he took the box of matches. She jumped at the contact. "What you have is perfect, Ms. Matthews."

"Please call me Valerie."

Oh, that made him smile. He planned on calling her Valerie. When they'd gotten to know each other a little better. When the time was right. And he wanted to hear her call him Earl.

All in good time.

With a private smile, Earl returned to the fireplace and struck the match. It gave him great pleasure to see the spark catch at a crisp corner of newsprint. He watched it evolve into a single red flame that spread, went orange and yellow as it grew, licking along the surface of split hardwood.

Valerie was suddenly at his side, staring down at the blaze. "Thank you," she whispered.

The sound of her voice was like the slide of skin on skin.

"It's kind of silly, I know, but I didn't even think of making a fire." She looked up at him sheepishly. "I'm usually a very resourceful woman. I think I was preoccupied."

He watched her rub her upper arms, the silk shawl brushing over her flesh. She shook her head slowly, then stared into the flames. "I really can't remember the last Christmas Eve I spent alone."

Earl nodded slowly, looked into the growing fire, then moved his gaze to her face once more. This woman clearly needed some cheering up. And though technically he was just there to fix her furnace, he'd never minded a challenge.

"I've had a few of those myself," Earl said. "I remember one year, I got stuck in a snowstorm at Logan Airport. Spent Christmas Eve sitting on the floor by my gate."

Her eyes went wide.

"Good hot dogs, though. I must have had seven of 'em."

She smiled at him.

Such a beautiful smile. Such a sexy red mouth. Such lovely, long legs and bright eyes. And those dark curls just skimming those pale shoulders . . .

Without thinking, Earl reached for her, pulling her shawl up over her collarbones. Then he spun her around to face him and tugged the silk tight across her breasts.

She gasped, bringing her hands to cover his.

"You might want to keep this on for a little longer." He removed his hands from under her soft palms. "Until it warms up."

Ms. Matthews gripped the shawl so tightly that her knuckles turned white. She stared at him. Blinking.

"How about you take me where I need to go?"

"Of course," she said, shaking her head. "Follow me."

Earl extended his hand and she walked in front of him. He picked up his jacket, toolbox and clipboard on the way, never taking his eyes off that moving red velvet package, following like the dawg on a leash he was, through the kitchen, down the hall, down the basement stairs, into the doorway that led to the furnace room.

She flicked the switch, and the room went bright with fluorescent light. Her hair gleamed. Her skin looked soft and translucent. Her eyes sea-green.

"Over here, Earl," she said.

It was a newer oil burner under service contract with Ferguson's for three years. Nothing but regular maintenance and cleaning, according to the computer printout on his clipboard.

Valerie dragged a tall work stool from against the wall. "Would you like to use this?"

He smiled at her. This sweet little holiday babe looked so out of place surrounded by stacked paint cans, power tools and pegboard. "I prefer to do it standing up," he said.

He noticed the flicker in her eyes. She was interested, all right, but too much of a lady to let him know it right away. It made him smile. "But feel free to have a seat and keep me company."

"You don't mind?" Her voice was squeaky.

"Not at all. I'd be honored." He turned his back to her, grinning to himself. Man, this was wild. She was already half gone for him—he could tell.

As he opened the toolbox, he thought about all the possible scenarios that might have led to Ms. Matthews being alone on Christmas Eve. Had she just dumped a boyfriend? Had she expected someone to join her, only to be stood up at the last minute? Had she been hurt so badly that she preferred being with no one over being with the wrong one?

He glanced quickly back at the woman in question before he opened the service panel. She lowered her eyes, bit her bottom lip, then raised her lashes and flashed him a look of longing.

Oh, Mama! Earl pretended he didn't understand the message relayed in that green gaze, but it was now clear to him that Ms. Matthews had been lonely too long.

And he had what she needed . . . exactly what she needed.

He chuckled softly to himself and shook his head. He was many things, but he wasn't a jerk. And as appealing as this woman was, he wasn't sure he could live with himself if he thought he'd taken advantage of a vulnerable female.

Once the panel was removed, it took him two seconds to figure out why the furnace wasn't working. He suppressed his laugh. There could be a couple explanations for this, but they all boiled down to the fact that the furnace wasn't producing heat because somebody had cut the power. The main power switch was set to OFF.

Not that he was going to come right out and tell his customer that.

He feigned a grave expression and looked over his shoulder. "Could be a while, Ms. Matthews," he said.

"Valerie, remember?"

Then she shot him a wide smile that said: *Let's be real close friends*. She crossed those shapely legs, and from his bent position he could see that she wore thigh-high stockings with stretchy black lace trim, held in place as if by magic.

In that instant, Earl sensed a sudden and forceful shift in the balance of power, and had to wonder just who the vulnerable party was here.

Because, as any man knew, a woman in thigh-highs meant business. A woman in thigh-highs had plans. And Earl decided he'd give his left nut to make sure her plans included him.

He licked his suddenly parched lips and stood up straight.

"Can I get you something to drink, Earl? You probably can't have wine on duty, but I have a great bottle of Australian Shiraz that's going to waste. Can I tempt you?"

Now *that* was a loaded question. And the answer was *Please do*.

"This is my last call for the night, Ms. Matthews." He wiped his hands on a rag, studying the way she leaned back on an outstretched palm, perched just on the edge of the stool. Her sheer black legs were crossed seductively. Her high-heeled foot was swinging.

He swallowed hard. "And I'd love that glass of wine."

Chapter Three

Valerie's hands shook as she penetrated the cork with the sharp edge of the corkscrew and turned, turned, seeing the shiny metal bury itself into the yielding, red-stained pulp.

This was ridiculous. She needed to get a grip on herself. She could hardly remember the last time she'd been this turned on, and the idea that she would even *consider* falling for an anonymous furnace repairman would have made her laugh if she wasn't so aroused.

It was moments like this that made her wonder about herself, wonder just where her sexual limits might be. What exactly it would take for her to pull back and declare, "Stop right there. This is the end of the road."

All she knew was that she was thirty-three, and though she'd had her share of lovers, she'd never arrived at that place.

Valerie pulled out the cork with a satisfying *pop!* and sighed. She knew full well that having a hardworking man come to her rescue had always been the meat and potatoes of her sexual fantasy life, and apparently, the fantasy extended all the way to appliance repairmen.

At least one particular repairman.

She poured two goblets. Yes, she should have let the wine breathe, but she didn't want to wait. She wanted to go back downstairs with Earl. She wanted to watch him use his tools and look back at her over his nicely sculpted shoulder and talk about lubrication.

She was on her way to the basement door when she stopped. What if—no she *couldn't!* Oh, yes she *could!* She was going to take off her underwear! She was going to be a bad, bad girl . . .

Valerie placed the wineglasses on the chopping block and giggled. Just knowing that she wasn't wearing anything beneath her dress would make things hotter and wilder and more adventurous, wouldn't it? And if she got the courage, maybe she'd find a way to share her secret with Earl.

She laughed outright and pulled her dress up to her waist. She had to admit she was stunned by her level of daring tonight. She'd never really considered herself a complete wild woman. She'd always tried to make smart decisions about men. She'd almost always kept her head.

Valerie hooked her fingers into the stretchy, smooth fabric of the red thong and shimmied it down her hips, feeling the luxurious satin tickle the whole way down her legs.

But tonight? Tonight was apparently different. Maybe it was Earl. He was new and exciting. And handsome—God, yes he was handsome. But he seemed approachable. Familiar even. Like maybe she'd seen him somewhere before.

Or maybe it was just that it was Christmas Eve, a night set aside for gift-giving. And maybe—just maybe—she wanted to give her gifts to Earl.

Was that so bad?

Valerie stared at the panties dangling in her hand, wondering what to do with them, when she heard the clank of a tool hit the concrete basement floor and Earl's voice hiss out a muffled curse.

In her hurry, and at a loss for a better idea, she tossed the thong in the refrigerator and yanked her dress back down. Then she grabbed the wine and headed downstairs. She was almost afraid to poke her head in the furnace room.

"Everything okay in there?"

Earl spun around, and she had to admit he looked exceptionally pleased to see her. He also looked exceptionally attractive. She wondered if he could tell she'd ditched her underpants.

"Fine." She watched him wipe his brow, then toss a wrench into the toolbox. He sighed heavily.

"All fixed?" Valerie walked toward him, holding out the crystal wineglass. She saw his eyes go wider with each step she took.

His fingers cupped hers as he took the goblet. They lingered there a second longer than necessary.

"I'm afraid your unit needs a part," he said, and she could have sworn he raised one eyebrow at her in a kind of silent challenge.

"Oh, *really?*" Valerie returned to the stool, crossing her legs again, reclining back on one hand, shaking out her hair. "Is it a big part? Something important?"

"Very" was all Earl said. Then he leaned up against the steel support beam that ran from floor to ceiling, crossing his ankles, raising the glass to his lips.

"This is delicious." She watched one corner of his mouth crook up. "But I have to warn you—wine on an empty stomach makes me a little tipsy."

She couldn't help but laugh, and he joined her. She loved the sound of his laugh—deep and lusty and reverberating off the roughed-in walls. She let the sound cover her like a protective blanket, warm and secure.

"So, Earl. Is that a backhanded way of telling me you'd like a little something to eat before you head out?"

His grin spread and he lowered his head in embarrassment, a rich brown lock of hair spilling onto his brow. She'd always been a sucker for a man with a little bit of hair—enough to twirl in her fingers when they kissed, enough to grab onto during sex.

"Guess so," he said, raising those deep blue eyes. "That is, if you wouldn't mind. Something sure smelled good when I came in here."

Valerie sighed. "All right. I guess I can heat up something for you. A man shouldn't go walking around hungry."

"No, ma'am," Earl said, straightening up. "Not a good way to go through life."

"Well, come on up, then." Valerie popped off the stool and felt him right behind her as she flicked off the light and headed up the steps. She heard his breath and the tap of his footsteps. She felt his heat. She knew damn well that his eyes were plastered right on her butt.

As they progressed step by step, Valerie told herself this was her chance. She could cross the line into bad-girl territory with one simple movement. She could do it. She *could.*

With a deep breath, Valerie stopped suddenly as if to adjust her high heel, knowing that the bending motion had given Earl a view he may not have anticipated.

Still bent over, she looked back over her shoulder and smiled. The poor man looked stunned. He'd gone pale. He'd obviously just discovered her secret.

"Sorry," she whispered, fiddling with the shoe strap. "Something felt like it was poking into me."

Valerie watched Earl's Adam's apple take an up-and-down slide. Then he cleared his throat. "Oh, my God," he said.

Back in the kitchen, Earl seemed to regroup rather quickly, and offered to help her. *Such a gentleman,* she thought. *Even when hungry.* But she knew his motivation. She'd certainly seen the drill enough times to know how it was for men— food, *then* sex.

"There are some leftovers in the fridge," she said. "I'm not sure how microwaved leg of lamb tastes, but I think we're going to find out."

Earl laughed and put his hands on his hips. "Lamb? You made a leg of lamb just for yourself?"

Valerie shrugged.

"Hey, I'm sorry. I didn't mean . . . it's just—" Earl ran a hand through his hair. "It's so special. So fancy. And leg of lamb is my all-time favorite. You must be a great cook."

She smiled at him. This man in her kitchen was cute, sweet and handy with mechanical things. She could get used to a man like that.

"I am, Earl," she said.

He smiled back, then opened the refrigerator, pulling out three Tupperware containers, the last of which was draped with a red satin thong.

He stared at it, a quizzical frown creasing his brow.

"Hmm," he said, picking it up between a thumb and forefinger, studying the scant strips of satin leading to a small red triangle. "Quite festive, Ms. Matthews."

Valerie felt her face burn with what she knew was a combination of delight and embarrassment—and the delight was winning out. She'd been quite the brazen hussy this evening. She was kind of proud of herself.

Then Earl placed the thong on his head, pulling the stringy side panels down under his chin. "Did one of Santa's elves lose his hat?"

She burst out laughing. He looked utterly goofy.

"No, wait," he said, looping the underwear around his upper arm and holding it tight to his side. "An evening bag."

Earl began to sashay across the kitchen, one wrist limp.

She shook her head, still laughing. She absolutely loved this guy's sense of humor—how lucky could she get? What were the chances?

Then Earl stopped. He moved the thong down to the crotch of his Dickie's and stretched it wide across his hips, shaking his head with disappointment.

"Nope. Wouldn't fit. I'm an extra-large." He raised his gaze to hers and grinned.

"Really?" Valerie leaned against the counter and folded her arms across her chest, suddenly noticing that she wasn't quite as cold as she'd been a few moments ago. The house was starting to feel comfy.

"Okay, maybe I lied," Earl said, balling up the thong. He

shoved it in his pants pocket and gave it a pat. "My size is actually extra, *extra*-large."

A still-grinning Earl opened the Tupperware lids and leaned down to scan the contents. She saw his face light up. "This looks delicious, Valerie. Really." He shot her a sideways glance. "Got any mint chutney to go with?"

Chapter Four

As succulent as the lamb was—and it was mighty succulent—
Earl couldn't focus on eating. All he could think about was the
woman across the table from him, and the sweet little slice of
heaven he'd glimpsed under the hem of her dress.

How tender she'd looked. How mysterious all the swirls
and shadows seemed. How he'd longed to run a finger up the
inside of her thigh and press into that wet valley of flesh.

In his opinion, there was nothing as erotic as a newly found
woman. Unexplored territory. Fresh female.

Earl took a gulp of wine and studied the stroke of luck sitting just arm's length away. Valerie Matthews sat calmly,
bathed in candlelight, like she hadn't tossed her panties in the
fridge and given him a peek at paradise on the basement steps.
Women could be so cruel.

But damn, they could be fun.

And he liked this one. Oh, he liked this one just fine.

"So, Earl, how long have you been a furnace repairman?"
Valerie dabbed at the corner of her luscious lips with a white
linen napkin and leaned back in her chair, her smile reflected
in those evergreen eyes.

"Not long," he said. "And it's HVAC technician, actually.
Heating, ventilation, *and* air-conditioning. I do it all."

"You don't say."

As Valerie absently toyed with her glass, it dawned on Earl

that she'd eaten a hearty portion of everything, though she'd obviously had dinner an hour or so earlier. Not that there was anything wrong with a woman with a healthy appetite.

He also noted she'd barely touched her wine. Maybe she was afraid a little alcohol would make her lose control. It wouldn't be the first time a woman in his presence met that fate.

Earl sighed. She'd draped her shawl on the back of the chair a moment ago, and the view of her sculpted collarbones, smooth shoulders and slim arms was now unobstructed. Valerie Matthews was all green eyes, red dress, and porcelain skin. She was a Christmas ornament made of flesh and bone.

Earl placed his napkin on the table and smiled at her.

"I want to thank you for this, Ms. Matthews. It was real nice of you."

She returned his smile, tilting her head just a bit. The curls brushed her shoulder. "It's my pleasure." She lowered her gaze, staring at her hands—smooth, narrow hands, he noted.

"You're actually pretty good company." Valerie raised her head again. "Things were looking pretty grim earlier tonight."

Her expression held so much yearning that Earl forgot to breathe.

They stared at each other a long, hot moment before he could get his lungs to work again. And as he fiddled with the tablecloth, he hoped desperately that she couldn't tell how much he wanted her, how she'd gotten to him.

"I know this sounds strange, but have we met before?"

Earl's head snapped up at the question, only to be met by a mysterious grin that teased him. Challenged him. Earl felt himself being drawn in by that grin—and the challenge.

And right then he had to stop himself from laughing out loud, because it was obvious where this evening was headed. He really was going to get this Valerie Matthews naked, her beautiful, long legs spread open, waiting for him, on the floor in front of the fire. There was absolutely no doubt in his mind.

A small voice that he immediately identified as his conscience began to whisper in his brain. It asked him what kind of man walked into a woman's house on Christmas Eve with an ulterior motive like that? What kind of man wormed his way into a hot meal and a hot babe on what was supposed to be a service call?

"I think maybe," he said, knowing full well they had. "At a private party given by some people I know. You catered it. Quite a few years ago, I think."

She nodded. "Ah-ha! Thought so. I never forget a face, Earl."

"I sure never forgot yours, Ms. Matthews."

Or the rest of her, for that matter.

She raised one eyebrow and ran a fingertip around the rim of her wineglass. "Hmm." She cocked her head. "I was wondering—"

"Yes?" Earl felt his pulse race. How bold would she be? How blunt would she get?

"Do you want me—"

"Yes."

"—to serve dessert?"

Boy, did he feel stupid. "That would be nice," was the only thing he could think to say.

She offered him a flirty little smile and cleared her throat. "Um, in case you were wondering, I'm . . . uh . . . not dating anyone special."

Valerie then used her eyes instead of words to ask the next logical question, and Earl had to laugh. It never ceased to amaze him how women could carry on a conversation without using actual words.

"Nope," he said. "Me either."

Her emerald eyes twinkled. "How about that dessert, Earl? I made a lemon custard tart."

His mouth fell open, then slammed shut. "Hot damn," he whispered.

Everything she'd prepared had been outstanding, even reheated. This woman was batting a thousand in Earl's book—she could cook *and* she was beautiful, sexy and sweet. Plus, she liked to run around without underwear—a definite bonus.

He watched her rise up from her chair and *click-click* her way across the kitchen to retrieve the dessert. She brought it into the dining room on a silver pedestal plate that she held directly in front of her luscious cleavage.

He knew she did that on purpose, but his mouth began to water anyway.

"I've always been partial to tarts," Earl said.

She tipped her head back and roared with laughter, and the sound of it rained down on him like a shower of stars. He was tempted to close his eyes, turn his face up toward the heavens, and let it cover him in sparkles.

Valerie wiped the tears from her eyes as she stopped laughing. "Why don't you make yourself useful and get the silver cake server out of the drawer? Second down, left of the sink."

He was up in a flash. By the time she got around to asking him to get two plates and two forks, he already stood behind her—holding two plates and two forks—feeling quite proud of himself.

His reward was her sweet smile and the touch of her hand on his right bicep—landing as soft as a snowflake. And though both her smile and her touch were warm, they sent chills through him. Earl knew they were chills of anticipation.

As they ate dessert, he felt proud that he had her laughing hard just by telling stories about his work, his nosy neighbor Mr. Hurley, and his family—four wild brothers. He enjoyed listening to her talk about her catering business and the bigshot clients she had. Seems it was a fancy enterprise. Just like her.

Valerie sighed and leaned back in her chair with a contented smile. She looked like a queen, he decided, all serene beauty and grace. She looked like a woman who should be spoiled and treasured.

Earl couldn't help himself. In one fluid motion, he was up out of his chair and standing behind her. He reached down, down, feeling the heat pulse from her body as he grew closer. The scent of cinnamon and cloves and warm female slammed into his brain. And then—just like that—she was sheltered inside his arms.

He grabbed her dessert plate.

"I'll clean up," he said, turning with the dirty dishes and walking into the kitchen. "Do you think you could find some music that might motivate me?"

He was careful to hide his smile, appreciating the silent woman behind him. He imagined that her breath was starting to get a little choppy. Her pulse quick and light. He imagined that the sight of a man doing the dishes was having the desired effect.

He paid her no attention as he returned for the remaining dishes, but a moment later he heard the slide of velvet on stockings as she stood from the chair and crossed the room. He took a quick peek at her retreating form. She had a softly swaying gait. She was graceful in heels. She was sleek and red and round in all the right places.

Without warning, she looked over her shoulder and said, "How about a little bit of everything, Earl?"

Damn, she'd caught him ogling. He needed to be more aloof. Cooler. But he had to admit that a little bit of everything was what he had in mind as well. Maybe a lot of it.

"Sounds like a plan," he said, returning his attention to the sink.

As strains of Marvin Gaye spilled into the room, Earl sensed her standing behind him. He could smell her. He could feel her. She opened a kitchen drawer just to the right of his hip.

"Here, Earl. I think you might need this."

When her fingers brushed against the front of his Dickie's, he nearly dropped a plate.

Chapter Five

Oh, she was naughty to the core! She was torturing Earl, but she couldn't stop herself. Teasing—the hors d' oeuvres of sex—had always made her famished for the main course.

Besides, Earl didn't seem to mind. As she reached around his waist with the apron strings, she brushed her fingers across the fly of his trousers, and she heard him gasp.

She felt him swell.

It was all very rewarding.

"I wouldn't want you to get the front of your pants all wet," she breathed in his ear.

She felt his big body shudder.

Then he turned slightly, bringing his handsome face inches from hers. "Do you get wet when you do the dishes, Ms. Matthews?"

She giggled, pressing her body against his nicely formed backside as she tied the strings in a bow. "It happens sometimes, yes," she said.

When she was done, Valerie gave that butt of his a friendly little pat. She'd wanted to do that since the moment he walked in her house.

"Thanks, Earl."

His response came out in a croak she thought might have been the words: "No problem."

As Valerie moved into the living room, she could feel the

heat of Earl's stare again. He'd been staring at her all night. This time, she could feel his eyes make their way from her shoes, up the back of her legs, lingering on her butt, up the long line of her back, to the shoulders, arms, neck and hair.

She knew with certainty that Earl was thinking about her walking around without underwear. She knew he was trying to stay cool, and failing miserably.

She put a little extra *oomph* in the swing of her hips and shook out her curls.

They were adults. Clearly they both wanted the same thing. The only question was who would be the first to cross the line?

Valerie stood staring down into the fire, listening to the crackle of wood, the mellow rhythm of Motown, and the comforting clatter Earl was making in her kitchen. Outside the picture window, she could see the snow coming down in large icy flakes, and her thoughts moved to people who were alone tonight. It humbled her to think that if it weren't for pure chance, she might be one of them.

She looked around her home and sighed with pleasure. She felt languid, relaxed, and suddenly hot.

Valerie brought a hand to her throat and felt a thin sheen of perspiration. She stroked up the side of her flushed face, to her hairline, where tiny curls stuck to her damp forehead.

"It's hotter than hell in here," she mumbled to herself, stepping back from the fire just a bit.

"Did you say something?"

She jumped. He'd snuck up on her, and she nearly backed into him. In fact, Earl was so close that she could feel his breath on the nape of her neck.

"No," she said, suddenly aware of how nervous she felt. Her belly was fluttering. Her pulse was hammering. Her mouth was dry. The two of them were playing a game, but apparently, it was a game her body took quite seriously.

Earl came around to her side and handed her the wineglasses. Then he slowly, so slowly, lowered himself down to a squat at her feet and looked up at her with those true blue eyes.

"Maybe I should heat things up a bit more," Earl said, offering her a wicked smile. He pulled the chain on the fireplace screen, and the sharp screeching sound made them both flinch.

He sighed. "I really should fix that."

"Lubrication, right?" she whispered.

He tossed a few logs on the grate and rose up again. "Lubrication is key." He accepted the wine she handed him. "Shall we make a toast?"

Valerie faced him. He was a truly gorgeous man, with that strong and straight nose, firm jaw, smooth tawny skin—all of it seeming to serve only one purpose, and that was to be the backdrop for those sexy eyes.

They shone down on her with humor and intelligence and a flash of desire that heated her blood. And at that moment, she would have given anything to know what the man was thinking. Just how sure of himself was he? Just what were his plans for her? For this night? Just what kind of woman did he assume she was?

She clinked her glass against his. "To Christmas Eves and heroes. You're mine tonight. Thanks for coming out."

"My pleasure," he said simply.

And as she leaned her head back and took a tiny sip, she heard the CD player shuffle and send more husky-voiced soul classics gliding through the room. The music, the man, the mood—she was ready to say yes to nearly anything.

Then she felt him come closer. The tips of her breasts barely brushed his solar plexus. And she felt his body begin to move, to sway just a bit, and she let herself be drawn into him.

"Nice song," Earl said.

The front of her thighs brushed against his rough cotton work pants. Her knees grazed just below his. She heard the soft *whoosh* of his breath, felt his heat. She smelled him; he smelled like clean winter air.

The words came out before she could stop them. "Do you believe in everlasting love, Earl?"

He laughed a little and shrugged. "Sure I do, Ms. Matthews,

just look at parents and their kids. That usually lasts for the duration."

She smiled at his answer. "But what about romantic love?"

"Ah, now that's a different story."

It was then that she felt his hand touch her hip. It landed with an easy sense of ownership that made her tremble.

"Are we talking about passion?"

Valerie blinked. She swallowed. She answered him in a meek voice. "Yes. That kind of love."

"I see." Earl spread his fingers wide and caressed her hip, his touch beginning to wander onto some very sensitive territory.

His gaze locked on hers. "I believe that if you want something to last, you gotta keep things interesting. I think passionate love between a man and a woman can last, but it's rare."

His hand moved up to the small of her back, and she felt him pull her closer. The dainty toe of her sling backs bumped up against a pair of steel-toed work boots.

"And you, Ms. Matthews? Do you think love can last?"

It was difficult to carry on a conversation with his hands on her. The press of his palm held just the right amount of pressure. The feel of his body against hers was making her ears ring and her head spin.

And all she could think was that there had been a time in her life when she would have answered his question with a quick no. But tonight—oh, my.

Tonight, on this Christmas Eve, Valerie was brimming with optimism.

Chapter Six

As he gazed down into Valerie Matthew's lovely face, Earl recalled the way she'd looked just moments ago, standing alone before the fireplace. She'd turned off the lamp, and the room's only light had come from the fire and the white twinkle of the Christmas tree. The whole picture had seemed magical to him—as if she were standing in a dream world, waiting for him to come to her. As if she were his fantasy made flesh.

She'd stood with one hip jutted out, the opposite toe tapping to the beat. She began to move, smooth and sultry, her hips making a half circle that seemed at once an honest appreciation of the music and an overt attempt at seduction.

It had worked.

And now, with his hands on her body and his eyes locked with hers, he knew it was his turn to seduce her.

He set his wineglass on the mantel. And with his left hand, he touched that sweet spot he loved so much—just where the dip of a woman's waist swelled out to form her hip. So unlike a man's body. So unlike any other spot on Earth.

Earl allowed his palm to sink down in the red velvet hollow, where he hoped the subtle pressure would convince, suggest, and encourage.

He loved the way she responded.

And that's when it hit him: Valerie Matthews was the kind of woman a man could get lost in. The kind who could take a man, love him right, and send him back into the world better for knowing her.

She was the kind of woman Earl had always wished for.

She inched even closer. She wiggled a bit. And he pressed his palm in a little tighter, letting his body sway. And he wondered if this woman would follow his lead, and how far she'd go.

Then Valerie reached up with a graceful sweep of her arm and ditched her wineglass, too. Both her arms curled around his neck and he felt her there—sweet and light and holding on to him, asking him to dance with her.

In those eyes, he saw what she was really asking for. And he felt his heart do a back flip.

He cleared his throat. "Uh . . . do you like to dance, Ms. Matthews?"

She smiled seductively. "Depends on the dance partner, Earl."

He moved his other hand to the small of her back, letting his palm rest in the second sweetest spot on Earth. He spread his fingers wide, touching the swell of her ass, the muscles of her back.

He studied her mouth, the lips parted slightly, so pretty and feminine. So fucking hot.

He felt his knees tremble. He took a steadying breath. He decided it was time to take little Valerie Matthews on a test-drive.

"Do you like to kiss, Ms. Matthews?"

"Depends on who's doing the kissing, Earl."

He scooped her into the front of his body with one smooth movement of his forearm. The other hand found the nape of her neck, the warm silk of her lustrous dark hair, and he cupped the back of her head in his big palm.

He watched her eyes flash. Her lips open. A pink flush raced over her cheeks, her throat, her chest. Earl recognized the flush of her sexual arousal.

They swayed together. Earl felt the slide of expensive red velvet along the plain cotton of his uniform, and the contrast was strangely exciting to him. She was elegance. He was ordinary. He reminded himself that this woman was a stranger, and his cock nearly burst through the zipper of his pants.

He saw the instant she became aware of his erection, and felt her push instinctively against his hard flesh. He watched her eyelids grow heavy with the knowledge of him.

Then he began to nudge against her in time with the music. And she accepted his rhythm with the give of her belly, the arch of her back. Her eyes never left his.

"So you like it when big handsome men come to your rescue, Ms. Matthews?"

She gasped.

"Tell me how you reward them, aside from pulling off your panties and flashing them."

He watched her mouth fall open in what he thought might be outrage. It made him smile.

"Do you have any idea what that did to me?"

"No," she whispered. "I mean . . . yes."

He chuckled, then grabbed her hair and tilted her head back so that her eyes looked right into his.

"Do you want me, Ms. Matthews?"

She moaned. Her lips fell open enough for him to see inside her mouth to that wet pink tongue he was going to own in just a matter of seconds.

"Do you want me, Valerie?"

A little cry escaped her throat and she licked her lips.

"Does it excite you that this stranger who walked in here tonight—this basic workman, nothing like the fancy big shots you probably usually date—is going to give it to you good?"

Valerie stared. She managed a little nod of her head, despite the fact that his fist was now gripping her hair tight.

"You weren't just leading me on, were you, baby?" Earl chose right then to slide his hand lower and caress her ass—all of it in one hand—right in the center. He pulled her tight against him.

"You just loved teasing me like that, didn't you? Bending over so I'd get a peek at those sweet little pussy lips."

She blinked.

"Did you think I wouldn't do anything about it? Did you think I could live without having you after that? Did you think I could just walk out of here without getting my cock inside you?"

She shook her head, her eyes wide with what he thought was a combination of amusement and surprise. This was too good, so good that he was in imminent danger of shooting inside his Dickie's.

He grabbed the velvet hem of that little dress.

"You know that dresses like this were meant to be taken off nice and slow, Ms. Matthews."

She gulped as he slid it over her hips to her waist. This was going so well, he decided to up the ante.

Earl slid his fingers over the silky curve of bare hip, over the top of her thigh, along the outer edge of her pussy.

"And naughty women who take off their underwear should get exactly what they want. So why don't you tell me what you want, Ms. Matthews."

He gently pushed one thick finger in between the lips of her sex, sliding it inside her. She was slick and soft and hotter than any furnace he'd ever had the pleasure to repair.

"Why don't you tell Mr. Earl what you want for Christmas?"

She whispered something. It was faint—and she'd swallowed the words in a frantic gulp of air when his finger penetrated her—so he couldn't understand her.

He lowered his lips to hers. He covered her open mouth while pushing a second finger into her, meeting her moan with his own. She was nice and tight. And oh, he loved it that she couldn't even gasp properly because her mouth was full of his tongue.

Earl ended the kiss. He smiled down at her. Valerie's eyes were closed and he felt her body tensing in his arms. Her pussy was gripping hard. Her breath was shallow and fast.

"Tell me." He heard his voice come out rougher than he intended, but he was so aroused that he couldn't stop himself. He pulled his fingers all the way out of her, then played gently with her hard little clit. She began to break apart in his arms.

Her eyes flashed open, her gaze sharp on his yet miles away. He knew exactly what that meant.

"Tell me what you want!" Earl's fingers pumped and stroked and flicked.

"I want you!" she screamed. "All of you!"

"What's my name?" His fingers were flying.

"Earl! Earl! Oh God, Earl!"

Boy, did he love hearing that.

Chapter Seven

As her body and her soul hung on the edge, suspended in the timelessness just before orgasm, it dawned on Valerie that this man was a stranger—that the blue eyes boring into hers were those of a *complete stranger.*

And she blew.

The climax had a pulse and a drum rougher and harder than anything she could recall. There was simply not enough oxygen in the room, or in the universe. The walls were caving in. The sweat sliding down her spine brought pinpricks of agonizing pleasure.

And the tide just kept going, even as she felt his repairman fingers pull out of her body. Even as she felt his hands grip the low drape of velvet at the neckline of her dress. Even as she heard the *rrrip!* of fabric and sensed the warm air hit her damp skin.

She was in a state of awe, reverberating with aftershocks of delight, as she stood before this sexy stranger in nothing but her sheer black thigh-highs, heels, and tattered velvet. Astonished, she looked down at her belly, and watched a single teardrop of sweat take the long slow crawl to her navel, where it pooled.

Her legs began to shake when Earl dropped to his knees before her to flick the very tip of his tongue into her belly button, to drink from her, to slurp her little indentation dry.

"Oh, *Gawd!*"

Aparently, Earl wasn't satisfied with just a single drop of her liquid, because he'd moved his lips and tongue lower, and was now feeding at the top of her mound, his hands simultaneously ripping open his work shirt, throwing it off his torso, unbuckling his belt, unzipping his pants.

The scene was surreal. She felt strangely disconnected, yet intensely excited. She looked straight down into his angel eyes, watching his mouth spread into a smile as his tongue sought out the match head of her being, and her thighs began to tremble. Valerie had to hold on to his head to stay standing.

She grabbed that gorgeous head of hair as if it were a lifeline.

"Oh, Earl!"

He kept smiling, kept flicking at her with that wicked tongue, and the sight of his wet mouth covering her dark curls was too much for her. Too much.

She started to fall.

And Earl caught her.

He collapsed with her onto the soft green sofa and struggled out of his pants and shoes with her sprawled across his lap.

Then she felt his muscular arms around her back, his hands moving across her skin as if memorizing every inch of her, taking inventory of the unknown woman now blissfully lolling on top of him.

From behind her disheveled hair, Valerie could just make out his expression. He seemed as if he was in a trance. Mouth loose. Eyes unfocused. She suddenly felt his hand grip her wrist.

"Feel this, Ms. Matthews," Earl said.

He guided her hand down to his cock. She gasped. He was long and startlingly thick. She noted with curiosity that he didn't feel perfectly cylindrical in her grip—how unusual. How stimulating. She looked down to where he pressed her hand.

The head of his penis was broad and plump and leaking a

stream of clear fluid. She rubbed the pad of her thumb in a slow circle around it, smearing the slick liquid all over him, as his fingers stroked the inside of her wrist.

"Extra, extra-large," she whispered.

"Furnace repairmen don't lie," he said.

"HVAC technicians, you mean."

"Whatever the hell I am."

She started to giggle, but abruptly stopped when she felt his other hand press down on the back of her head. She knew exactly what that meant, and a flash of anticipation raced through her bloodstream.

"Earl?"

"Hold still. Do not move."

He leaned forward, and she heard him grabbing his work pants. What could he possibly be doing?

Then she saw a flash of bright red, and felt him take her hand from his penis. He pulled it around to her back, and brought her other arm around to meet it. In just seconds, he'd tied her wrists together with what was obviously her thong.

"Put your mouth on me, Ms. Matthews."

"But—"

"Please put your mouth on me. You know you want to."

The words were dark and powerful. They excited her. How helpless she felt, especially when his hands returned to her head and began to push her down again.

He was right. There was no point in denying it; she wanted to do exactly that. Her tongue was on fire with the need to taste him. Her lips felt swollen with the promise of sucking him.

But Earl shouldn't get his way so soon! Where was the fun in that?

"No," she said, pushing back against him, struggling to get away from his grasp.

Earl's laugh was loud and wicked. Then he pushed harder.

"Did you just say no to me?"

"Yes."

"See? You've already changed your mind."

Why bother trying to fight him? He was so strong, so much bigger than her. Not that this was a bad thing . . .

And as her mouth descended, a shiver ran through her entire being. Once again, she reminded herself that she didn't know Earl from Adam. Yes, she liked him. Yes, she felt comfortable with him. But he was just the furnace repairman, a stranger.

And then he was inside her mouth.

Oh, she was so bad, but she couldn't help it! All she wanted was to get one hand free so she could touch herself between her legs in the way she so desperately needed. She began to wiggle her butt around in the air.

"Hell yes, Ms. Matthews." Earl's hands eased up on the pressure. He began to stroke her hair, and she felt his fingers massage her scalp, slow and easy. Valerie found herself moving her hips at the same pace.

Earl tasted smooth. The shape of him felt exotic and new cradled on her tongue. And as she pushed down, allowing more and more of him into her throat, her nose made contact with the springy hairs at the base of his sex. And he smelled clean and male and aroused.

"You're so good at this, baby. Has anyone ever told you how good you are?" One of his hands took long strokes through her hair, combing through it to the ends. She mimicked those long, slow movements with the bob of her mouth. Then she felt his other hand tug at the thong around her wrists.

"I've always remembered you, Ms. Matthews. I always wondered how wild you were."

His words were hoarse and soft and they surprised her so much she stopped, raising her eyes to his.

"From the night I first saw you—at that party." He licked his lips. "I watched you all night. How you moved. How you smiled. I couldn't take my eyes off you."

She wanted to say something but his hands guided her mouth back to him.

"I wanted you to be mine. From that night on."

Valerie felt his fingers spread over her bottom, reach around, and enter her from behind. At that instant, she knew she would do anything Earl asked.

"You like this, don't you, sweetheart?"

It was hard to talk with her mouth full, so she just let loose with a moan of appreciation. She looked up to see Earl's mischievous smile. His blue eyes glittered.

"Are you all mine, Valerie?"

Earl removed his hand from her pussy and brought it to her face. He slid his fingers down her cheek to her mouth, using an index finger to trace the outline of her swollen lips several times before he pushed it between her teeth.

As if she had no will of her own, Valerie began to lick and suck at his finger, tasting herself.

He abruptly removed it, and laid his hand gently at her throat.

"Answer me."

She swallowed hard, feeling his hand move as her throat constricted. He had control of her. He owned her. She knew this as deeply and perfectly as she'd ever known anything in her life.

"All yours." The words came out very faint.

"And what do you want for Christmas?"

"Your cock."

Earl grinned. "Now?"

"Now!"

And as she felt herself being untied, picked up under the arms, and carried through space until she was deposited on her back before the hearth, the only image that raced through her mind was how this situation would look to a third party— her naked white skin against the red Aubusson carpet, Earl's golden-brown body lowering itself upon her—and what a wanton woman she would appear to be.

She was giving herself to a stranger—a stranger who apparently liked to tie her up! A stranger who talked dirty to her! Did she have no shame?

And as Earl lifted her legs, pulled her knees apart and pushed into her, the procession of fantasy lovers who had been there before raced through her mind. Each one of them so special to her. Each one of them a kind rescuer and a wonderful lover—the lifeguard, the cop, the fireman, the doctor, the Navy SEAL, the bodyguard.

Valerie came like a crazy woman.

She came all over her latest real-life fantasy—all over Earl the furnace repairman.

Chapter Eight

If there was anything better in this life, Earl had never experienced it. It was Christmas Eve, his birthday, and the Fourth-of-Fucking-July all wrapped up in this hot woman beneath him, moaning his name.

"Earl . . . oh, Earl! Oh, God. *Yesss!*"

She was spread wide open under him, the silky and firm surface of her thighs cradling each thrust of his hips. Her eyes were shut tight now, sealed with thick black lashes, her brow creased from the force of the pleasure.

She was his, all right. *All his.*

And he was going to take his time with her. He was in no hurry to finish. It was going to be a long night—a long night of making Valerie Matthews forget that she was ever lonely. A night of sex so hot that it would burn away everything that had ever come before it, every man who had come before Earl, the furnace guy.

Her nails were raking across his shoulders. He lifted her butt off the rug and pulled her even tighter to his pelvis, getting a good view of how they struggled to consume each other, how perfectly they fit together.

"Give it up, Valerie. I want you to come for me again, you hot little thing."

She began to howl, and the sound penetrated Earl's soul. God, how he loved to make a woman howl. How he loved that instant that things got too intense, too fiery to contain, that second when she gripped him in waves of erotic contractions, when he felt her body milk him, when he melted into her, became her, felt so much love for her that he couldn't hold it inside another second . . .

"God, I love you so much, Val!" He heard the words rush from his mouth as his semen exploded from his body, and it didn't matter anymore.

The game had been fun, but the reality was so much better. Better than anything he'd ever hoped for.

"Oh, baby! I love you, too!" She sobbed underneath him, taking his seed, gripping him with arms, legs, body.

He collapsed into her, immediately rolling to his side and taking her with him, bringing her on top of his body. Then they lay still, holding on, sticking together with sweat, breathing hard. She continued to cry softly.

He stroked her back. "You okay, Val?"

She nodded her head up and down, snuggling into his chest. Then he heard her say, "What did you do, Earl? Set the thermostat to a hundred degrees or something?"

He chuckled. Maybe he had turned the furnace up a little too high after he restored the power, but the house had been a freaking meat locker!

"Just wanted to warm you up, babe."

She laughed a little into his shoulder.

Earl caressed her hair, and let the knowledge settle into him bone-deep—the woman in his arms was his whole life, the reason he was put on Earth. He would do anything to protect her and keep her safe and make her happy. Anything. And a sharp pang of guilt sliced through him.

"Did I go too far this year?" He crushed her to him as he whispered in her ear. "The tying-up thing? Forcing your head down? The words I used? Was it too much?"

She shook her head, sniffling. "I loved it, honey. It was fun."

He sighed in relief, and loosened his grip on her. Sometimes these Christmas Eves got a little out of hand, like with the Navy SEAL thing back in 2001. She nearly drowned!

It seemed that each year they raised the bar a notch, and Valerie still managed to surprise him.

She was definitely more creative, so he was happy to let her come up with the role-playing scenario each year and just give him his assignment. And it always seemed that once it started, the scene took on a life of its own, and she made him crazy—every damn time. But he never wanted to hurt her, or scare her.

He loved his wife more than anything.

"You were so hot this year, Val."

She rose up on his chest and smiled down on him. "And you were the sexiest furnace repair man in the world, though you didn't do such a convincing job with the tools. I thought you were going to hurt yourself down there."

"Yeah, but the clipboard was a nice touch, don't you think? Did you see I even went to Ferguson's to get a printout of our service records?"

"I noticed, honey. Very nice. And the name embroidered on the uniform—now *that* was impressive."

"Yeah—it was free with the three-piece set. And your dress. God, Val. I'm sorry I ripped it apart like that."

She giggled. "Seems to happen every year." She kissed his nose. "I don't mind at all. Hey! Did you like the new lamb recipe? Did you taste the coriander?"

"Oh babe, it was great. And the tart was fabulous."

"Thank you, sweetie."

He gazed up in wonder at the most beautiful woman he had ever known, the woman he'd married four years ago tonight, the woman he'd first seen seven Christmas Eves ago at a team cocktail party. He'd watched her work all night long, too shy to approach the beautiful caterer who smiled at everyone, had such a pretty laugh. He'd waited until the party ended and followed her to be sure she'd be safe.

She had pulled into a Gas-N-Go. He went to the next pump over and watched as she somehow managed to spew gasoline all over the side of her car. He came to her rescue, turning off the malfunctioning spigot and helping her out of her ruined coat.

Once he made sure she got home safely, she invited him in for a drink. She took a shower. He joined her.

And the rest was history.

He smiled at her now, still loving those wild, dark curls, the flushed cheeks, the large, tight nipples on those perfect breasts that he—*wait a second*.

Earl studied her closely and frowned. He raised a hand to trace her puffy areola and elongated nipple with a finger, then followed the blue vein that traveled outward across her left breast.

"Hey, babe? Could you—"

The doorbell rang in the annoying way perpetrated only by Mr. Hurley, the kook from next door.

"Mr. Hurley?" Valerie's eyes were wide with shock. "Now?"

"Just ignore him."

Valerie pushed up from Earl's body. "Honey, I can't do that. Maybe there's an emergency. You know his wife hasn't been doing so well since she broke her hip."

Earl sighed. He supposed Valerie's thoughtfulness was one of the things he loved most about her, but this was no time to be kind. There was a lot more sex to be had.

He watched her run across the living room, and enjoyed the view immensely.

"Just a second, Mr. Hurley!" She reached into the front hall closet and threw on her raincoat, tying the belt around her waist. She tossed his coat to him.

"Put this on, honey. And hide our costumes."

Earl sighed heavily, put on the coat and picked up the clothes strewn all over the floor. When he found her thong, he chuckled to himself and stuck it in the coat pocket. He threw everything else behind a chair.

Mr. Hurley burst in the front door bearing gifts. Earl

watched him kiss Valerie's cheeks and hug her tight, then shove about six packages in her arms.

"Merry Christmas and happy anniversary, kids—hope I didn't interrupt anything!" Mr. Hurley eyed Earl's coat, then Valerie's.

"Is it raining in here?" He burst out laughing. "I'll just show myself out."

"Thank you, Mr. Hurley, and Merry Christmas."

Valerie shut the door and turned to Earl, her arms laden with presents. At that instant, with her pink cheeks, bright eyes and rumpled hair, she was so beautiful that it hurt to look at her. He loved her more than he'd ever be able to tell her.

She put the gifts on the table and walked toward him, slowly untying the sash at her waist, then opening the raincoat to reveal the only Christmas present he'd ever need. The coat fell to the floor at her feet.

"It's gift-exchange time," she said, smiling.

"I was thinking the same thing," he said, peeling off his own coat.

Giggling, she bent down to retrieve a small box from under the tree. He joined her there, and grabbed the plain white envelope he'd topped with a gold bow.

They exchanged the items, and then sat down on the raincoat Earl spread before the hearth.

He studied the narrow oblong box in his hand. "Did you get me a pen?"

She laughed. "Nope. But before you open it, I have to ask you a question."

He took her hand in his, and bent down to kiss her knuckles. "Ask away."

"Do you really believe in everlasting love, Earl?"

He laughed. Damned if he could remember the last time he was forced to answer the same love question twice in one night. But he squeezed her hand in reassurance. "Yes, Val. I sure do."

Her smile spread wide. "Then open it."

He wasn't all that surprised when his eyes landed on the positive pregnancy test. He was thrilled, proud, and happy—and his heart felt like it would burst—but he wasn't shocked.

"You knew, didn't you?" Valerie was moving into his lap.

He held her tight, pressing his lips to her warm breasts, kissing her cleavage. "I suspected as much. Just a few sips of wine tonight. Two dinners." He licked her nipples. "And you looked just like this when you were pregnant with Molly, Val. You got fuller, and you got this beautiful vein right here—" He dragged his tongue across the swell of her breast.

"So you're okay with this?"

He looked up into her face. The tears welling in her eyes nearly did him in.

Earl dipped her back into his arms and cradled her, then kissed her for everything he was worth, which was quite a bit, now that he thought about it.

"I'm the luckiest man alive," he said. "It's the best present you could give me, Val." Then he kissed her some more and ran a hand down her belly. "How far along are we?"

She smiled. "Six weeks."

He laughed. "That's gonna be a busy time for us."

"I know it's in the middle of the season. And if your free agency—"

"Merry Christmas, Mrs. Matthews." He nodded at the envelope in her hand and watched with joy as she opened it, read the contract, and starting screaming.

"Everything we asked for, Val," he said, knowing he was smiling like a kid. "Papa's the newest relief pitcher for the Boston Red Sox."

Once Valerie had stopped whooping, bouncing in his lap, and hugging him so tight that he could barely breathe, he rolled onto his back and took her along.

Her hot, bare skin touched his from forehead to toes in one all-body kiss.

"How long till your mom comes back with Molly?"

"About two hours, Earl."

As she kissed him so soft and sweet, his need for her intensified, burned him up. "A lot can happen in two hours, babe."

"*Mmm, mmm*. I know." She rubbed her body all over his. "You know what I was thinking about for next year?"

Earl laughed. The idea that his lovely, pregnant wife had already thought about next Christmas Eve made him hard, real hard.

"Let me guess, your dishwasher is on the fritz?"

"No, silly. I would never do the appliance repair concept two years in a row." Her hand snaked down the front of his body and grabbed him. He groaned.

"I thought maybe my car could break down on a deserted country road, and I'll have to call for a tow."

"Ah-hah."

"And a big strong man with an extra-extra-large truck will come to my rescue."

"Earl's Emergency Tow Service?" He grabbed her ass, pulled her thighs apart and entered her. He felt her melt around him.

"Earl's Emergency Sex Service," she gasped.

"Open twenty-four hours a day," he added.

She breathed hot into his ear. "Even on Christmas."

BABY, IT'S COLD OUTSIDE

Donna Kauffman

Chapter One

Jace Morgan slammed the hood down on his father's old truck, then ducked his head against the driving snow as he trudged back around to the driver's door. At this rate both he and Suzanna would be stuck in town. For the first time since arriving back in Rogue's Hollow the day before, Jace felt like smiling.

Being stuck in the snow with Suzanna York was very probably the best thing that could ever happen to him. Or the worst, he conceded, as he rumbled on down the two-lane country road. He was still a good half hour away from the train station . . . and his reunion with the woman he'd given his virginity to the summer he turned seventeen. Then walked away from the summer he turned eighteen. Ten years. A lifetime ago. An eternity. So much had happened since that summer, when they'd both had scholarships clutched in their hands . . . and dreams held just as tightly in their hearts. Dreams only a college degree could provide. He'd gone west to Indiana State and a basketball career that had ended just shy of the pros, but provided him with the immense pleasure of teaching the stars of tomorrow . . . both in the classroom and on the court. Zan had left their country life in the foothills of the Blue Ridge in Virginia and headed south to Georgia on an academic scholarship.

They'd had plans. Such mature plans. They'd set each other

free during their college years, to experience life in and out of the classroom. But free or not, they'd vowed to maintain their close friendship, not really believing anyone would ever replace the other in their hearts. Their bond was special, ageless, timeless. Had been from the moment they'd laid eyes on each other, skating on Old Man Ramsay's pond when they were thirteen years old, days after Zan and her mom had moved into the guest house on the Sinclair property in the Hollow. Pretty much from that moment on, Jace couldn't imagine a world without Zanna York in it.

Suzanna, however, had apparently found a world without him a bit easier to conceive. Christmas hadn't even arrived before she'd stopped replying to his letters, was unavailable when he called. He'd realized the hard way that he wasn't as mature as he thought, because his heart had been shattered. And all these years later, he still hadn't figured out how to reclaim every last piece of it.

But he'd long ago assigned that broken heart to one of the many milestones a man had to pass on the way to adulthood. So what if he'd been an adult for some time now and still couldn't quite shake the feeling that the reason he couldn't give his whole heart to anyone else was because Zan York still held a small piece of it. The most vital piece.

Swearing under his breath now, he focused on keeping the damn truck on the road. He should have told Frances he'd book Suzanna a room in town, find some way to get her picked up and delivered home by Christmas Day. Seeing as it was only hours to Christmas Eve and the snow was coming down blizzard strength, with no signs of letting up anytime soon, he knew that was a promise he couldn't have kept. And why he should care was beyond him.

But Frances's phone call had caught him at a low point. Sitting alone in his father's big empty house, his past weighing so heavily on him he thought it might crush him completely, he'd begun having serious second thoughts about taking that job offer. About coming back to Marshall County for good. If only his brothers had made it in before the storm. All four of the Morgan siblings were finally coming home for Christmas. Not all that unusual for some families, but for the Morgan clan, it was downright miraculous. Flung to the four corners of the earth, mostly to get away from their tyrant of a father, they hadn't all been under the same roof in well over ten years.

Sentimentality and a warm holiday spirit had never been enough to draw the siblings back together. No, it had taken the death of their father, Taggart Morgan, to accomplish what love alone never would. In fact, only his oldest brother, Tag, had made it back for the funeral a month earlier, before heading back to the project he was overseeing in some South American jungle. But with the old bastard finally gone, there was a hell of a lot to consider about what to do with the two hundred plus years of Rogue's Hollow legacy left behind.

The snowstorm had stranded his three brothers in various locations, none of them being the train station in Porterville. So he'd been the only one wandering the rooms, staring out across the fields, trying to answer the stable hands and major-domo's questions, when all he had was more questions himself. There were appointments set up for after the holidays, with the lawyers and such. He supposed it would all be settled then, after he and his brothers shared some time alone to come to some of their own decisions.

He stared through the windshield, as the wipers whipped back and forth, losing the battle to keep the windshield clear. Frances's phone call had surprised him. He hadn't spoken to her since he'd left for college. Had never, in fact, been back to Rogue's Hollow since. He and his brothers kept in touch via the wonders of e-mail and cell phones, but none of them discussed home and hearth. Probably because none of them considered it such. Home for the Morgan boys had become wherever they hung their hat. And it had been a long time since any of them had hung anything in Rogue's Hollow.

Jace didn't bother wondering how Frances knew he was back home. The Hollow, along with the little town of Highland Springs, was too closeknit a community to hide much of anything from anyone, but it wouldn't have mattered if it were a metropolis; Frances York was a one-woman telegraph system. Jace doubted that had changed much. She'd always been close with her only daughter, and Jace knew she'd be more than happy to share every detail of why Zan cut him off all those years ago, and every last thing she'd done since. Not that he'd ever ask her. Then or now. To say he hadn't thought of it, of her, especially at this time of year, and early summer, would be a lie. Hardly a Christmas or Memorial Day passed that he hadn't. But contacting Frances was also opening up a conduit to a whole lot of grief he could do without.

Frances had been bookkeeper to the Sinclair, Ramsay, and Morgan clans over the years. And it was a biological compulsion with her to share every last bit of news and goings on in the Hollow and Highland Springs with anyone who'd listen. He'd left that summer without ever intending to look back, and he hadn't. Not even for Suzanna.

Another dry smile creased his face. Odd how the one thing that had been his ticket out of there—basketball—was now the one thing that would bring him back for good. He shook off thoughts of the job offer he'd received hours after he'd been given the news of his father's death. The timing couldn't have been better, or worse, depending on how he looked at it. His program at the high school in Indiana had just been drastically cut, making him feel even more constrained than he'd already been feeling for some time. A feeler to a local small college in Missouri had dried up, and he'd been pondering his options, feeling restless. Rootless. Maybe even a bit homesick.

He hadn't told anyone he'd accepted the job, not his brothers, not even the school. The school officials knew he was coming back to settle his father's estate, and had simply asked that he give them his decision by mid-January. That would give him time enough to be sure. And to find out what Tag's, Austin's, and Burke's plans were as well.

Right now it was more pleasurable to focus on Zan. What would she look like now? Would he even recognize her? It hit him then. What if he climbed the railroad platform, only to find her standing there with a husband holding her hand, and a couple of tow-headed kids clinging to her coat?

Idiot! He swore under his breath. Sure, he'd thought about that over the years, but not once since Frances had called earlier this evening had it even occurred to him. He hadn't come home expecting to see her, had no idea where or how she spent her holidays. Not for the same reasons, but she hadn't been in any more of a hurry to return to the Hollow than he had all those years ago. She'd been hell-bent on seeing the world, conquering what part of it she could. He wondered if she had.

Moving back again, he figured he'd see her at some point but had also figured he'd have plenty of warning. Instead he'd gotten less than an hour to prepare. Prepare for something that, if he were honest, he'd been waiting for since the moment they parted at that very same train station. Married, he thought again. It was definitely possible. He sighed, trying to adjust his whole thought process to that possibility. He just couldn't manage it.

No. Surely Frances would have mentioned if he was picking up a whole family. But hadn't she been the one to suggest taking Taggart's old truck? He'd assumed at the time that she knew—as only the town gossip could—that he'd driven home in a small sports car, hardly the thing for crossing the county in blinding snow. But maybe— No, he resolutely refused to think it. And a second later he laughed at his own thoughts. Like it mattered. Yes, he wanted to see her again, wanted to bury some long-held demons. But surely he hadn't fooled himself into believing he was going to be burying anything else. Namely himself, as deep and hard into Zanna York as he could.

Of course not.

Which didn't remotely explain why, as the miles crunched beneath the half-bald tires, his heart began to pound, his palms grew a bit damp and sweaty, and his cock grew a whole lot hard.

He couldn't seem to find a way to stop picturing that long-ago Christmas Eve, when he'd had Zan beneath him, pushed up to the hilt inside her, all that wet, warm, softness surrounding him, holding him so tightly . . . just as he held onto her tightly. Like she was everything a man could ever want or hope to have. He'd thought so then. And he'd told her so that night. Had, in fact, told her everything that was in his heart.

Six months later they'd parted. And he'd never said those words to anyone ever again. Sure, over the years there had been women who were special. Women he'd wanted, desired. He'd given his body, his attentions, even his care and concern. But he'd never given up his heart.

By the time he parked in the station lot, his blood was pounding as hard as the snow. The wind cut into his skin as he walked to the platform, but his emotions were what felt ravaged. Filled with anxiety, anticipation, and not a little dread, he forced himself to walk slowly, steadily. Not take the platform by storm, as he found he wanted to do, and tear through the clusters of families and other holiday reunions until he found her. Until he could touch her, hold her, taste her. Claim her once again.

Sheer insanity, he told himself. More than once. It didn't seem to want to sink in. But with every step, the hunger increased. Until he wasn't entirely sure what he'd do if she had, indeed, arrived with family and spouse in tow. *Get a freaking grip, Morgan,* he schooled himself. But his hands were clenched into fists, small puffs of air exploded from his mouth as his breathing grew more rapid, and his strides grew longer and longer. People moved out of his way and he had to force himself not to shout her name. He really was losing his mind, he thought, wishing he could see the absurdity of his behavior and wrangle it back under control. The rate he was going, she'd take one look at him and scream for help.

Not that it was going to do her any good, some darker voice inside him immediately responded.

He wondered what everyone back in Indiana would think if they could see him now. For that matter, what everyone in the Hollow would think. Jace Morgan. The nice one. The quiet one. The calm one.

Yeah, that was him. Except where Suzanna York was concerned. It had always been that way. And, apparently, no amount of time was likely to change that.

Then the crowds suddenly parted, as if ordained by some higher purpose, and there she stood. There was no doubt it was her.

His heart simply stopped, and the kind of hope he knew damn well he had absolutely no right to feel sprang to life inside him anyway. Long thick blonde hair, eyes so dark brown he could drown in them, and a smile as wide as the sky. She hadn't changed at all. And yet, when she turned and spied him standing there, he realized that no matter what foolish ideas he might have, the reality was that she was a stranger to him now. He had no idea who this Suzanna York was, or what she had become.

The second thing he noticed was that there was no man holding her hand, no kids hanging on to her coat. She was alone.

And as he crossed the platform, reality didn't seem to matter. Rational thought even less. Crowds ebbed and flowed around them, pushing and shoving their way past, but he was completely unaware of it. It was as if the two of them were trapped inside one of those glass snow globes, set apart in their own little winter wonderland.

And Jace realized right then he was going to turn that globe upside down and shake hard. Ten years ago she'd turned his world upside down and shook his heart so hard it never fully recovered. So while he was home conquering the ghosts his father had left behind, he might as well work on getting this one taken care of, as well. One way or the other.

Chapter Two

Suzanna blinked the snow from her lashes. It was a mirage. A figment of her imagination. Okay, and maybe the result of a long train ride . . . and some very hot and wet dreams. She'd known he wouldn't be here. She'd come home several times a year over the past decade . . . and not once had he, or for a long time, any of the Morgan brothers, been home in the Hollow. It never stopped her from daydreaming. And night dreaming. And basically just plain fantasizing about him. And what might happen if he should suddenly show up back home.

And what he might do to her if he did.

She shivered, and not from the cold and damp seeping through her coat. It was part dread because things hadn't exactly ended well between them, for which she only had herself to blame. And she was dead certain he blamed her, too. The other part, however, was anticipation. Which no amount of dread could quash. After all, it had been ten years. Surely no one held a grudge that long.

If she could have laughed at that moment, she would have. The Morgan family was famous—or infamous, actually—for holding grudges. But Jace had always been the easygoing Morgan. He'd left the Hollow rather than confront his father. *And he'd let you go, too,* she thought now, rather than track her down and demand to know why she'd stopped writing and calling. Why she'd let what they had slip away so easily, so quickly. As if it hadn't been the most important thing in her life.

Only she knew that while her bad judgment, and the choices she'd made because of it, had happened quickly, her regret had lasted forever. Of course, his heart had probably mended ages ago. Hers most certainly should have. But it hadn't. Not entirely.

Actually, that spot in her heart still twinged when she thought about him, about their past together, about the future they might have had, had she not so callously tossed it away at the first glimmer of a new love, so dazzling and shiny. So much more mature and exciting, she'd been convinced, than a high school sweetheart from her country town could ever hope to be. Well, she figured the occasional painful tug at her heart was the least she deserved. It had certainly served her well enough as a reminder, because she'd never made the same mistake again.

Which is probably why you're alone at Christmas. Again.

She brushed at the snowflakes that gathered insistently on her lashes, watching, unable to tear her gaze away from the man presently moving through the crowd of holiday travelers.

"It's not him, Zan. Just stop it right now." It couldn't be him. It was simply the memories that this holiday always dredged up. Memories of the nights he'd made love to her, so fiercely tender, so possessive, she shivered a little even now, thinking about it. Yes, she'd probably romanticized it over the years, as only a woman could when thinking back to the first man who'd made love to her, who'd told her he loved her. Only there was a part of her who knew she hadn't embellished one whit.

Even as a young man, Jace Morgan had made love with such natural force and passion, had so completely made her body his own that, no matter how silly it sounded, he had totally ruined her for any other man. He was no fantasy. He was the real deal. How foolish she'd been to think she could so easily replace that. When, in fact, she'd never once come close.

No, whoever it was she'd glimpsed through the crowd couldn't be him. He'd never so much as set one foot in

Marshall County in ten years. But that didn't stop her heart from tripping over itself. Didn't stop her temperature from rising. Didn't stop her from thinking about what those lips, that tongue, those fingers, had done to every inch of her body—

"Oh, for God's sake," she muttered, ordering herself simply to turn away altogether, before she flung herself at a total stranger and begged him to take her right here on the platform. Snow, strangers, and all.

She knew she shouldn't have packed her vibrator in with all of her other household goods; wondered idly if her mom had ever fixed the head of the hand-held shower massager.

Jesus, she hated Christmas. Had for ten years. *Damn you, Jace Morgan,* she swore silently, then damned herself. After all, it wasn't his fault.

And then the crowds parted, as if by some greater will. And he was standing there. Right there. Every tall, rangy, muscled inch of him. Jace Morgan, in the flesh, not five yards in front of her. No other man had those dark, tousled bed-head curls, laser blue eyes that pierced her right down to her soul . . . and that mouth, a mouth made for seduction, a mouth that had seduced her on more occasions than she could count. With words, with deeds. And oh dear God, the deeds those lips had driven her to perform, to allow him to perform on her . . .

No, there was only one man who had that mouth.

Her lips trembled; her heart stumbled. And maybe her thighs quivered, just a little. Okay, a lot. "Jace? Is it really you?"

He didn't say anything for the longest time. An eternity of time. Long past the time when they could have skipped the awkward part, laughed like old friends, embraced in a warm reunion, told each other how much they'd changed or how much they hadn't. She could have found some way to douse the firestorm of want and need just seeing him had ignited, a firestorm of need that raged to life so quickly she knew it had never entirely gone out, but had merely been banked. For a long, long time. If only he'd said something, anything, surely she'd have found some way to smile and embrace whatever he was willing to give her, be it a chilly smile or a friendly hug without wanting to claw his clothes off and back him to the nearest wall, demanding he drive himself deep into her . . . and drive out those damn ghosts of Christmas past.

Of course, she should have known if this day ever came that it wouldn't be easy, or smooth, or even worse, anticlimactic. Well, it was definitely none of those things. The word *apocalyptic* came to mind.

And she wanted badly to take the first step; she knew it was her responsibility, given how things had ended. But her feet were suddenly weighted down like blocks of cement. She wanted desperately to say something that would make it all okay, or at the very least, get the conversation started. But her throat was dry as sand, and her lips wouldn't move.

Why was he here? To pick up one of his brothers? If she could have made herself look away from him, she would turn around and very likely spot Austin, Tag or Burke standing right behind her. Because surely he hadn't been pushing through the crowd to see her. Of course not, what had she been thinking? He had no way of knowing she was coming home. Nor would he care if he had. Certainly he wouldn't have come out in this awful snowstorm just to pick her up from the station—

She broke off in midthought. *Oh no. No, her mother wouldn't do this to her.* Or Jace. She couldn't have. Even though Suzanna never spoke of him, or any of the Morgans for that matter, her mother had to know Jace wouldn't have been thrilled with this particular little chore. Because of course he would say yes. Despite his father's raging temper, or maybe because of it, Jace had always been so polite, so well mannered, mindful of his elders. The respectable Morgan.

Only, of course, she had known differently.

She had known there was another side to Jace. The side that could only keep things pent up for so long before he needed to find an outlet. And pounding a ball up and down a court could only do so much. Only she saw that part of him that others only saw on a basketball court. Driven, committed, hungry.

She did tear her gaze away then, unable to face him one second longer, shame flooding her anew for how callously she'd treated him all those years ago, the one man who had never been anything but driven, committed, and hungry for her. And for her alone. The man who'd been willing to set her free, asking only that she be faithful to their friendship, to that special bond that went beyond hot sex, beyond infatuation. Beyond even love.

But rather than look behind her, to see who he was really here for, she looked past him, searching in vain for the face of her mother or someone, any familiar face. Someone, she was even more ashamed to admit, who would rescue her, because she couldn't seem to rescue herself. But Frances York did not materialize in the crowd. Nor did anyone else she recognized from the Hollow. No way would her mother have risked driving in this storm. She knew that. In fact, the closer she'd gotten to Porterville and the heavier the snow had begun to fall, she'd pretty much known she'd be staying at a hotel tonight.

As it was, she wasn't sure how Jace planned on making it back tonight either. Which bounced her thoughts back to that hotel . . . and her gaze back to Jace.

Her throat constricted as the silence continued to spin out, their gazes irrevocably locked. So closed off, she thought, and so damn still. That was how he'd learned to escape the wrath of Taggart Morgan. Become invisible. She'd once been the person who saw past that stillness, past the quiet intensity of his even blue-eyed gaze. She'd once been the person, the only person, who ignited the hunger behind it, drove him to be anything but still.

Her thighs locked against each other as memory upon memory pounded through her body. Unwanted, unheeded, but unavoidable. She wanted badly to cling to the thought that it had been a teenage fantasy. Perfection idealized from what could only have been immature lust. Staring at him now, she wanted desperately to believe it hadn't really been perfection, hadn't been as wonderful and satisfying as she remembered. They'd been hardly more than kids. Fumbling, pawing, panting—

Only they hadn't fumbled. They hadn't pawed. Panting they'd done plenty of. Heated gasps, long moans of ecstasy.

It was no dream. It had been real. She could see every second of it right now in his eyes. He'd taken all of her, possessed her, driven her beyond any point of return. And then had taken her further. It was as if her body had been created exclusively for him, to frolic and cavort with in total abandon, his own personal playground of delights. And he'd reveled in it, in her, all but drowned himself in her. How, in God's name had she ever, even for one split second, thought she could replace the boy he'd been then, with any man, at any other time?

And how, in God's name, did she think she was ever going to be able to explain, to the man he was now, why she'd done what she'd done? Why would he even want her to?

Something of her thoughts must have shown on her face, because his expression faltered, only for a moment, but long enough to give her a brief glimpse of—

Dear God, she murmured beneath her breath. Surely she was mistaken. She trembled, clenched her thighs almost convulsively tighter together, which only served to jack her up even higher. But surely he couldn't want—couldn't think that they would—that she would—after all this time— No, she couldn't even let herself think that. He couldn't harbor those same fantasies, about the two of them together . . . like they had been before. Could he? She lifted a shaky hand to her lips as he slowly closed the distance between them, his gaze locked firmly on hers.

The closer he got, the harder she trembled. And the more painful the ache grew between her legs. And damn if she could do anything to stop it, no matter how foolish she knew it was to think, even for a second, that he wanted what she wanted.

For all she knew he was going to shake her, wring her neck, or worse, push right past her and keep on walking without looking back. She knew she deserved any or all of that.

And yet every quivering part of her cried out for him to just grab her, take her, make it all go away. All the years, the pain, the shame and regret, the questions left unanswered for far too long.

She saw the fury, even the hollow edges of pain, in the tight brackets of his mouth, the pinched corners of his eyes, the tic in his clenched jaw. But it wasn't until he was right up in her personal space that she saw what else was there. The hunger, raw and palpable. The heat, as raging as her own. The desire that had pushed him to the edges of his control, just as it had hers.

And she let herself believe, no matter that she knew she had no right, that for now, for this moment, it was okay to give in to all those things she found roiling up inside him, inside herself. To believe that the one girl who had once ignited the need deep inside a lonely boy just might be the woman who, even for a moment or two, could unleash that hunger once again in the man. Only this time she vowed she wouldn't screw it up.

Her fingers, shaking badly, left her lips and lifted, seemingly of their own volition, toward his. Wanting to prove for certain that he wasn't a ghost of Christmas Past. Before she finished making a fool of herself by grabbing him . . . and begging him to be her Christmas Present.

Chapter Three

Sweet Jesus, he burned to simply take her. It was like time stood still, only it was a man's hunger he felt now. And she looked more than woman enough to handle it. Of course, throwing her down on the snow-covered platform and ramming every achingly hard inch of himself deep inside of her was probably not the best way to say hello after ten years.

But it didn't keep him from imagining it, just the same.

He managed to stop just shy of grabbing her and hauling her up against him, not entirely sure if he touched her in any way that he'd be able to let her go again until they were both naked, sweaty and very satisfied. He didn't dare let her touch him either.

He curled his fingers inward as he forced himself to take a step back, jerk his gaze from hers and nod at the bag at her feet. "Is that all the luggage you have?" The question sounded raw, forced, but his throat had dried up and it was the best he could manage. Given the surprised look on her face, it had probably come out a bit more gruffly than he'd planned, too. Well, too damn bad. She was looking at him like he was a four-course meal and she hadn't eaten in a month. And he was thinking that being her personal buffet was a damn fine idea.

So it was a testament to his well-schooled control that he wasn't tossing her over his shoulder and storming off across the snow-covered parking lot. He was doing the best he could just to maintain here. A thousand questions matched the thousand feelings rampaging through him, and she wasn't exactly helping matters any.

She jerked back from him, fumbled somewhat nervously with her bag and finally managed to click the handle up. "I—I can manage."

God, just hearing her voice all but leveled him. How many times had he heard that throaty voice in his dreams? Hundreds, thousands, he'd lost count. And right at the moment it was like pouring lighter fluid on an already lit fire.

She straightened, putting the bag between them, like some kind of a shield. He could have told her she'd need to do a damn sight better than that if she planned on him keeping his hands to himself. But then she was forcing a smile, through lips that trembled just slightly. That lower one was all but begging him to tug at it with his teeth, just enough so he could open her mouth, dip his tongue inside, tangle with hers and—

"I take it my mother rooked you into this little chore?" she managed.

He could have told her it was no chore. Keeping his hands off her, his mouth off her, his body from wanting to drive as deeply inside of her as it could possibly bury itself . . . now that was a chore. "She was worried about you."

Suzanna looked up at him, as if wondering if he'd been worried about her, too. Now or at any time over the past ten years. If he'd even thought about her at all. He waited a second, wondering if she'd finally ask him. Anything. Because he'd be damned if he was going to be the one to breach the giant dark hole that was the past ten years of life between them. It was hers to explain away. Not his to beg questions of.

She didn't.

And he wasn't sure if he were angry . . . or relieved. Because now that she was standing here, and he still wanted her so badly his teeth all but ached with it, he found himself thinking that maybe, just maybe, there were some answers he might not want to hear.

"We'd better get on the road if you want to get back to the Hollow tonight," he said. "Snow's not supposed to let up until sometime late tomorrow." He thought about the long drive ahead of them. Just the two of them, stuck in Taggart's old truck, alone save for the sound of the windshield wipers and the whistle in the heater fan. And wondered how in the hell he was going to make it back without hearing some of those answers or finding some other way to occupy her mouth.

He reached for the handle of her bag, which brought him close enough to smell the scent she wore. Something spicy. And it hit him right in the solar plexus. That scent, it was so Zanna. No flowers or fruity scents for her. No, she always went for the exotic, the darker scents. Apparently that hadn't changed. He tried not to pause, not to inhale so much as another whiff. Much less turn and bury his nose in all that long, thick hair of hers. *Jesus, he really needed to get a damn grip here*. And not on her. "I'll take this," he said, all but grunting the words. He looked at her shoes, wondering why in the hell she hadn't worn boots, or anything with more traction than the low heels she had on. He gritted his back teeth, and danced close to the edge of his control. "It's slippery; take hold of my elbow."

She didn't fight him for the bag, but she wasn't quick to take his offered arm, either. "Still the gentleman, even when you're obviously furious about all this."

That stopped him. He felt a fury all right, a fury of need, a fury of desire. A fury of confusion about everything she was making him feel. But he didn't think that's what she meant. She thought he was angry. At her, at this errand he'd been forced to run. "I didn't mind coming," he said, choosing his words with care. "I just want to get back." He tugged her bag to his side, but instead of moving out of her personal space and keeping his mouth shut, he stayed right where he was, and asked, "What makes you think I'm mad at you?"

She looked up at him then, into his eyes. And hers were so familiar, staring out at him from a face he'd once known better than his own. Every freckle, every quirk, every expression. How was it, right at that moment, he felt like she'd never even been gone?

"I don't blame you," she said quietly. "As much as I'd like to, I know we can't just pretend everything is okay." She broke off, looked down for a moment, then let out a long sigh before looking back into his eyes. "It's been a long, long time, Jace, I know that, too. And for all I know you forgot about me a blink after I stopped writing you—"

"Are you married?" he cut in abruptly. "Significantly involved with anyone?"

She blinked. "What? No, no I'm not. Why?"

"Because I don't want to piss anyone off when I do this." He dropped her bag and yanked her tightly into his arms, crushing his mouth to hers. He had to taste her, had to somehow get past this driving need he had to just have her. Possess her. Surely if he just got a taste of her, then he'd be able to look at her and think straight.

She stiffened, but only for the briefest moment. Then a long, soft moan vibrated somewhere deep inside her, and it was like a hot injection of pure need shot inside of him. She dove her fingers into his hair and pulled him even more tightly against her, even as he wrapped her more deeply into his arms.

It was ten years of longing, frustration, questions and, yes, maybe more than a little fury, all wrapped up in one primal, soul-searing kiss. He plunged his tongue into her mouth, took her, all but ravaged her, and then took some more. She accepted him, almost greedily. And for a moment he forgot where they were, forgot what had happened between them, forgot everything but how badly he'd missed her, how badly he'd wanted her back. And by damn he wasn't letting her go again until he'd had his fill.

Considering how long it had been, a week or two straight might begin to take the edge off. And then he could settle in and really feed his hunger. And, from the way she was devouring him as rampantly as he was devouring her . . . feed her hunger as well.

It was the need for air that had him finally breaking free. His chest was heaving, as was hers. Her mouth was puffy and red and damn if he didn't want to do all sorts of carnal things to it right then and there. Jesus Christ, he hadn't expected—hell, he didn't even know what he had expected. He hadn't exactly planned on doing that, not like that, not before they talked. He'd just—dammit. He still couldn't think straight. Hell, he was even more jumbled up now than he was before.

She lifted her fingers to those softly puffy lips and he groaned. His cock, so rigidly hard and aching, twitched hard as she looked at him, her doe eyes big and full of questions. He pushed one of her fingers, then another, between her lips, twitching again as her pupils drowned her irises. He tugged them back out, then slipped them deeply into his own mouth, sucked on them as he drew his lips slowly all the way down to her fingertips before freeing them. She swallowed hard, then gasped when he abruptly set her back from him, knowing if he didn't he wouldn't be held responsible for what else he plunged into between those lips.

"Why?" she whispered.

"I just needed you to know. I didn't forget, Zan. Not ever." Then he grabbed her bag, and what little he had left of his control, and turned away. He'd gone two steps when she called out.

"Wait!" She tugged on the sleeve of his coat a second later, pulling harder to stay upright when he stopped and she slid into him.

He tightened against the feel of her body pressed up against his again, clamped down hard on that control as he steadied her with his free hand. "We've got to get on the road," he said between gritted teeth. "Hold on to my coat." He started moving again.

She clutched at his elbow. "Jace—"

"We'll have plenty of time to talk in the truck."

Mercifully, she didn't push it any further. It was enough to feel her hand gripping his arm, to know she was right behind him and that she tasted a damn sight more fantastic than even his ten-year-old memory had done justice to.

They slipped and skidded their way to the truck, his control in ragged tatters by the time they finally reached it. Her bag stowed safely in the back, and Suzanna buckled safely in the front, Jace paused with his hand on the doorhandle. His emotions had veered pretty wildly over the past couple of hours—and that was before he'd seen her again. Right now he had no idea what was the best course of action. It was the understatement of the century to say there was obviously a great deal of unresolved emotion between them. He knew the best thing was for them to spend the next couple of hours talking everything out. While he kept his hands firmly on the wheel and off her.

He climbed in the front seat and buckled in, thanking the powers that be when the engine turned over on the very first try. He remained silent as he maneuvered out of the lot. The snow was really piling up on the roads in town, which meant the road home was going to be that much worse. The wind was already gusting, so drifting was going to be an issue, along with visibility. He rolled slowly down the main street, heading toward the rural route north, which took him right past Porterville's only hotel. He knew she was thinking the same thing he was. Well, maybe not the exact same thing. His involved a lot of bare, heated skin, maybe even some bared teeth, the way he felt at the moment. There'd be a great deal of moaning, too, maybe some growling, even some screaming while he drove them both wild. Then drove them there again.

"Do you think it would be better to find a room?" she asked.

He almost wrecked the truck. He fought the wheel, slowed down and pulled over toward the curb, into a spot recently vacated by another car and still free of snow. When he thought he could keep his libido from clawing its way free, he risked a look at her. But the suggestion didn't appear to be . . . suggestive. She was peering out the window at the snowfall, not looking at him like a potential bedwarmer. Was he disappointed? "Probably," he said, answering both their questions. "But if you want to see your mom by Christmas Day, then we need to make a run for it now. The drifting will keep the roads more closed than open, and that's only going to get worse by tomorrow. If we stay tonight, we're probably here for two nights at least. I know your mom is anxious to see you and—"

"She'll get to see plenty of me." Suzanna finally glanced over at him. "I'm moving back home for good."

Chapter Four

It was a good thing Jace had already pulled over or he might have swerved off the road again. He thought of the one piece of luggage in the back. She obviously tracked his thoughts.

"The rest of the stuff is on a truck somewhere between Atlanta and here," she said. "I just brought the bare essentials."

Bare essentials. Sweet Jesus. He resolutely refused to go there. And did anyway. He tightened his grip on the steering wheel, wishing it were as easy to get a grip on his rampaging desire to have her, consume her, possess her. Do whatever it took to make her his again, even if he had no clue if he wanted to keep her or walk away when it was done.

Except now things were doubly complicated. It was one thing to give in to this insanity that still seemed to exist when they got within three feet of each other, if they were going their separate ways once they'd exhausted whatever it was that needed exhausting. But to give in to this now, knowing they were both going to be living here, seeing each other every time they turned around, that complicated things beyond what even he could rationalize. No matter how badly he wanted not to.

"Jace, listen, I know things are—" She broke off, looked back out at the snow. "Difficult," she finally said. "Between us. And it's obvious from what happened back there on the platform that we have a lot to talk about." She looked at him.

"At least, I'd like to. I'd like to be given a chance to explain or to try to anyway, what happened all those years ago."

He appreciated her straight talk. And decided that maybe letting her continue might be the best way to wrestle his hunger back into submission. Or the most foolish thing he'd ever done in his life. "And you think, after what happened back there on the platform, that putting the two of us in a hotel for a couple of nights is going to make talking easier?"

She surprised him by laughing. "Probably not." Her grin was natural, unforced, and now his heart squeezed painfully. "But we might not care all that much after it's over."

He surprised himself by chuckling, nodding. He rubbed a hand over his face, sighed. The tiny bit of levity didn't jack the tension level down a single notch. If anything, it tightened up, brought a certain poignancy to the surface, something else to bear along with this all-consuming hunger.

She shifted in her seat, so she was facing him. Behind her, out the window, the hotel was less than half a block away. Her smile had faded now, her expression earnest, sincere. "I only suggested staying here in town for safety reasons. I already have a boatload of guilt where you're concerned, Jace Morgan, and I don't need to add your death or dismemberment on a snowy roadway to the pile."

He thought about that, about the guilt she claimed to feel, and wondered why all of a sudden it just didn't matter to him anymore. Not right at that moment anyway. Probably because he was a damn fool. A damn fool with a hard on.

He peered through the windshield at the blinking hotel light. At the VACANCY sign that was still lit. And thought, given the storm, and the number of travelers coming in on that last train, it likely wouldn't stay lit for long. And all he wanted was Zanna York up in one of those rooms—and it wasn't about safety, or to talk about her guilt. He looked back at her, wondering if she knew how foolish the two of them were about to be, treading on their past, bringing things into the present. Doing God knows what to their future.

"Do you need to call someone back at the Hollow?" she asked.

He looked at her. "No. There's no one there. Or anywhere else, if that's what you're asking."

"I wasn't asking that." She huffed out a little laugh. "Okay, maybe I was." She stared down at the knotted fingers in her lap. "I guess I hoped after you asked me the same thing back there on the platform that you wouldn't have done what you did if you were otherwise involved." She finally looked up at him. "You always were the honorable one, Jace. I'm glad to know that hasn't changed."

The words were out before he could think better of them. "If you knew even half of the thoughts I'm entertaining at the moment, about exactly what I'd like to do to you in that hotel room—and I'll warn you right now that even forty-eight hours straight will barely put a dent in it—you might revise that opinion of me."

She opened her mouth, the closed it again and he saw her visibly swallow, then finally nod as if she completely understood, maybe felt the same way. "It was such a shock," she finally managed, "seeing you in the crowd. Mom didn't tell me. I had no idea you were back home."

"Home." Now it was his turn for a dry laugh. "I'm not sure what it feels like, but it hasn't felt much like that." He reached over, needing to touch her just then and no longer questioning it. "Until I saw you standing on that train platform anyway."

Her breath caught, and she grabbed his fingers before he could pull them away. She opened her mouth to speak but ended up saying nothing as they got caught in each other's gazes once again.

"There's a whole lot we need to deal with here, Zan," he told her, told himself. "And not just with each other."

"I heard about your father," she said, throat tight. "I'm sorry."

He nodded an acceptance. "I don't know what I am. But I suppose that's one of the things I came back to find out."

"And your brothers? Are they coming back, too?"

"Yeah. Except this storm has them waylaid up and down the coast. I expect they'll be in a day or so after Christmas."

She fiddled with his fingers, and he remembered how she used to do that when there was something she wanted to talk about but wasn't sure how to broach the subject. He squeezed her hand, stilling her nervous gesture, making her look up at him and smile. "Some habits never die," she said.

His body tightened painfully. "I know. Even bad ones."

Her smile faded. "Is that what I was to you?"

"Honest to God, Zan, I'm not sure what in the hell you were to me. I only know what I wanted you to be."

She might have ducked her head, might have looked away, but she didn't. Her cheeks colored, but she held his gaze steadily enough, though her eyes were decidedly bright with tears. "I know what I wanted to be, too," she said hoarsely. "I've always thought it was the worst mistake of my life, not believing in what I already had. That I could still have it. Have you."

"Why in the hell would you ever think—"

She squeezed his hand tightly, cutting him off. "Why don't you go find out if we can get a couple of rooms? I'll find a phone and call my mom." She lifted their joined hands between them. "And then we'll talk this all out. We're both here, right now, and we might never have the chance to clear the air again. Once and for all."

He tugged her closer, until he could see her pupils shoot wide, feel the little gasp she took. "Just talk?"

She didn't respond, didn't nod, didn't shake her head no.

"Are you sure that's all you want from me? Ten years. And no way of knowing if we'll ever be like this again."

She began to nod but then slowly shook her head. "I won't lie. You've got me so stirred up right now I don't know if I'm coming or going."

His grin was instantaneous. "I can pretty much guarantee I'll clear up that little bit of confusion with no problem whatsoever."

She laughed shakily, even as her body shuddered at his promise.

"We're not teenagers anymore, Jace. It would be insane just to give in . . . to do anything before we talk. Surely we can control—"

He tugged her half into his lap, kissed her again. Hard, fast, deep. And she didn't hesitate this time. It was as if her body knew what it wanted and wasn't going to take the chance that her head might overrule that decision again.

It was hot, it was wild and if he didn't drag his mouth off of her, he was going to have her right here in the truck. It was still a moment or two later when he finally managed it. Both of them were panting, their breath making white puffs in the chilled air the ancient truck heater couldn't keep warm.

"I won't promise control," he said, somewhat raggedly. "Or that I'll keep my hands and mouth off you. Mistake or not, foolish or not, if we head into any room in that hotel together, I will have you. Hell, if we don't get out of this truck in the next ten minutes, I might yank you the rest of the way onto my lap and take what I know is wet and waiting for me right here and now."

She swallowed hard at his bold statements but didn't so much as flinch at his raw proclamations. If anything, he could have sworn he heard a soft moan. In the end, she said nothing.

He pulled her closer, framed her face with his hands, wove his fingers into her hair, lowered his mouth an inch away from hers. "So tell me right now, Zanna, tell me to drop you off at the lobby door, to drive away and find somewhere else to sleep off this hunger I've got for you. And we'll talk later. When we're better prepared to do it and not keep grabbing at each other. Tell me," he commanded, his voice dropping to a rough whisper. "And I'll leave this, leave you alone."

She stared at his lips, then up into his eyes and then wove her fingers into his hair. "I don't want you to go." She closed the distance, brushed her mouth against his. "And maybe I'm destined to make foolish mistakes where you are concerned, but I can't push you away. I don't want to push you away."

She brushed her mouth across his again, and now it was his turn to moan softly. "I did that once. I'll never willingly do it again."

She was killing him by inches. Some of them more painful than others. He gripped her head, lifted her mouth away from his. "We will talk. At some point anyway. And you will tell me. All of it. Everything."

"I promise."

His heart took a hit there, but it was a valid concern, probably the only one that mattered. "Can I trust you?"

She looked him dead in the eye, her own swimming, and nodded, tears tracking from the corners of her eyes as her breath came and went in a muffled sob. "I swear it. But they might not be answers you want to hear, and I don't want to hurt you. Not ever. Never again."

"I don't think we get to choose about that," he said. Then he very deliberately kissed each tear away, before taking her mouth hungrily once again, determinedly shoving all the rest of it away. For now.

And one thing Zanna York had taught him, and taught him well, was that now was all he'd ever be able to count on having. So he was damned well going to enjoy it.

Chapter Five

What in God's name had she just agreed to?

Suzanna tried to gather her scrambled thoughts, not to mention scattered hormones, as Jace assisted her across the slippery sidewalk, then all but dragged her across the small vestibule-size lobby. Both gentleman . . . and not so gentle, she thought, shivering in anticipation of just what kind of hungers the boy had only hinted at having that now the man would be fully prepared to feast on.

She stamped the snow from her low-heeled pumps, trying to get her heart to slow down a bit—in pounding pulse and in pounding emotion. She was all over the place, so hot for him she could barely stand to feel her clothes brush her skin, so emotional over seeing him again, hearing him again, touching, tasting, having him again, she could barely keep those emotions in check.

She struggled to get at least a minor grip on herself, wishing she'd at least worn a different pair of shoes this morning. But she'd gone straight from the office party earlier this morning—on her last day at the Atlanta accounting firm she'd spent the past six years working for—to the station, not stopping for anything, barely making the train on time. She'd been aware of the forecast for snow, but she was equally aware that for every dozen times they called for the "worst storm we've seen in years," it actually happened maybe once. Maybe. Naturally, with all her stuff on a truck somewhere, *probably in a ditch by now,* she thought with a sigh, she should have known *this* would be one of those times.

She tugged her purse off her shoulder and pulled her wallet out as she approached the desk. But Jace was already turning to face her, holding one room key. So he hadn't had a change of heart. Or of body, she thought as she looked him over. She looked from that body—which she'd only felt against her through way too many clothes, but that she knew was hard and wanting and an elevator ride away from being hers—to his eyes. And felt desire pour through her like liquid heat.

"Last chance" was all he said.

She smiled then, settled with her decision, not knowing if it was right, or the worst wrong she'd ever been about to commit, just no longer able to care all that much. They were here. And he wanted her. Now. And that was more than she'd ever hoped to have. She motioned him to the elevator. "No way am I letting you leave here," she motioned to the front of his jeans. "Not like that."

He raised one eyebrow, gave her a look as his lips twitched in a surprised twist of a smile. And for a second she had a flashback to what it had been like between them before. Lots of laughter, shared thoughts that required no talking; a look, a touch was often enough. They'd finished each other's sentences. Okay, so she finished more of his, than he'd finished of hers. She talked a lot more. He hadn't seemed to mind.

I know what I wanted you to be.

His words pounded through her, making her wonder what he wanted her to be to him now. A fantasy one-night stand? A little bit of revenge, when he walked away afterward, leaving her begging for more? She had no idea. And found she didn't much care about that either at the moment. It was too late to turn back now, and the truth was, she had absolutely no desire to do so.

A better question might be to ask herself what she wanted him to be now. She had no idea. But she suspected that any fantasy she might have of a one- or two-night stand, of burning him from her brain, from her body, would never happen. He was more than that. Always would be. No matter how animal the sex—and based on the way he'd taken her mouth, she could only imagine just how thoroughly he planned on claiming her body, couldn't seem to stop imagining it, in fact—it wouldn't be enough. For either of them.

"Then what are we standing around here for?" He tossed the room key at her and she had to think fast to catch it. He slid her bag with his foot, snagged the handle and began to walk to the elevator.

"Damn good question," she murmured, hurrying to catch up with him.

He punched the button on the single elevator, then looked at her as she came to stand beside him. "Are you hungry?"

A laugh spluttered from her. "You're kidding, right?"

His grin teased the corners of his mouth again. How had she ever walked away from that mouth, from all those things he'd said to her, done to her, with that mouth of his? "I was actually talking about food. Did you eat on the train? It's late and I don't know how long they have room service here."

How was it he could be so carnally determined and yet so damned thoughtful? She wasn't sure which was in more danger—her body, or her heart. And knew she'd already put both at high risk as she stepped into the empty car. "I don't think I could eat a thing," she finally responded. Her body was on fire, but her stomach was a knot of nerves and anticipation.

Now it was his turn to chuckle. "You're kidding, right?"

She looked up at him, mouth dropping open in surprise. And they both laughed. She smacked his chest. "I don't remember you being so wicked."

He spun her so fast she didn't see it coming, had her trapped in the corner of the elevator, between the walls and his body, before she could blink. "I'm a lot of things you don't remember," he told her, tracing his fingers along the side of her face, cupping her chin, moving her mouth to the exact angle he wanted, then very deliberately lowering his mouth and taking it. Exactly as he wanted.

His tongue was so hard and yet so teasing and soft, all at the same time. He took insistently, plunged repeatedly, and somehow seduced her into doing the same. His hand left her chin, and moved, open palmed, down her throat and chest, until he cupped the weight of her breast. Her nipples had long ago peaked and ached now for a more intimate, direct touch. He dragged his mouth from hers, left hot, wet kisses along her jaw, took her earlobe between his teeth and tugged. "I was going to tell you that nothing has to happen that you don't want to happen."

They both laughed even as she moaned when he tugged again. "I'm thinking that's a pretty short list at the moment," she managed, struggling to regain her breath.

He shifted, letting his forehead rest on hers as he braced his hands above her head. "We don't have to take it, you know. Just because we want to."

"I think we can safely admit we both want . . . a lot of things."

He said nothing, and she knew he understood she was talking about things that had nothing to do with sex. The tension between them arced . . . spiked . . . thrummed.

"Admitted," he said finally. "But I also don't get a lot of the things I want. I'll live if I don't this time either."

So, she thought, he was telling her it was all heat, no substance. It shouldn't have crushed her, shouldn't have rocked her so hard. After all, just what had she been expecting ten years and a whole lot of living later? That he'd profess undying love for her once again? Maybe this was some kind of revenge fantasy after all. Only, no matter that the man was edgier than the boy, she doubted he'd changed that much. Jace had a lot of things to be angry about in his life. A lot of things to want revenge for.

Losing his mother young. Having a bastard for a father, a man who thought the flat of his hand was a perfectly fine way to communicate but that a hug was unmanly and weak. And God forbid Taggart Morgan ever told any one of his kids how he really felt about them, that he was proud of their individual achievements, that he'd died alone and accepted in those final weeks that he deserved nothing less.

She wished now she hadn't let her mother tell her even that much. She'd always wondered if her mother didn't say much about Jace because she didn't know, or because she knew her daughter didn't want to know. She'd never been sure of the answer to that herself, so she'd never pushed.

Suzanna lifted her hands to his chest, cupped his face, pushing him back enough that she could look into his eyes, look at the man he'd become. Not a vengeful man, that she'd lay money on. But a man with pride, certainly. A man who'd left as soon as he was able rather than look for a way to get payback, just as each of his brothers had. Each had chosen to look forward, none had ever looked back. So why did she think he'd look toward her now? Someone who'd left him as soon as she was able, someone he thought had never once looked back. Though she had. Still did.

He'd once been a man not afraid to love, to shove his heart out there, despite the fact that he'd only ever had it shoved right back in his face. Including by her. She'd never forgive herself for that.

"Did you ever get married?" she asked quietly, having no idea where the question had come from, but once it was out there, she found she really wanted to know. Needed to know, needed to know that he'd loved someone else, that her stupidity and carelessness with what should have been most precious hadn't caused him to withdraw for good the one thing he had going for him, the thing that set him apart from his father. "That's none of my business," she said just as quickly. "I'm sorry." She swallowed a sigh and wondered who the hell she thought she was. *Placing a great deal of importance on yourself, aren't you Zanna?* For all she knew he'd found the real love of his life a week after she'd walked away. For all she knew, he'd loved dozens of women. Just because she'd been his first, and might very well be his next, that was no excuse to think she—

"You're right," he said, shifting his face away from her touch, levering his body away from hers. "It's not." He raked a hand through his hair, punched the button for their floor as if just realizing they'd been standing in an unmoving elevator car all this time, then shifted his weight from one foot to the other. "But the answer is no. Never even came close."

She nodded, taking that bit of information in, not knowing quite what to do with it. Had he just never met the right one? Or, she thought, unable to fight it, had he been like her, pretty damn sure he'd already met the one, and no one else had ever measured up?

"You?" he asked, like the question had been ripped from somewhere deep inside him, and it made her want to smile and cry at the same time. He never had been one for lengthy conversation, had never found it easy to open up, or ask when there was something he wanted to know. Jace Morgan was an "actions speak louder than words" kind of guy. And though he'd said some very forthright things to her tonight, when it came to asking her questions—well, apparently some things hadn't changed.

"No, no, I never have," she told him. But didn't add that she hadn't come close. Because she had. Closer than she wanted to admit. Especially to him. In fact she'd come as close as she could have without actually going through with it.

It had been six years ago, the summer after college graduation. With Dan Butler, the man she'd left her childhood friend and teenage lover for. A man who'd offered her the sun and the moon or would have if they were for sale. Anything she wanted was hers. Anything except, she discovered later—too late—his heart. She'd believed it was hers. After all, he'd told her he loved her. Asked her to marry him.

How naive, how stupid to think the size of the rock on her finger could be equated to the dedication of his heart, when it had, instead, been more an indicator of his ego. A mark of possession rather than commitment. She'd been too blinded by the glitz and glamour to see that behind the perfect face, the perfect smile, the perfect family, the perfect social standing, the perfect future—the perfect freaking everything—lay a man who'd ultimately only been true to himself.

No, that she'd had to find out the hard way. At least she'd had her illusions shattered before she'd said "I do." But by then it was far too late to go crawling back to Jace, to beg his forgiveness. And why should he forgive her? It had been almost four years later by then. Surely he'd moved on, given that beautiful heart of his to someone else. Someone mature enough not to toss it away on the first bright shiny object waved in front of her face.

She'd spent a lot of time thinking about what she'd say when she saw him again, always assuming that at some point she'd bump into him back in the Hollow. They'd catch up on old times, laugh over her silly ideals and immature assumptions . . . maybe become friends again, if she was lucky. Very, very lucky. Only he'd never come back to the Hollow. He'd gone on to play college ball, then left to go teach somewhere. She'd stayed in Georgia, gotten a degree in business accounting, then worked her way up in a prestigious Atlanta firm.

The elevator topped out, jarring to a stop, jarring her from her thoughts. Jace's hand shot out automatically, steadying her elbow. He didn't let go as the doors slid open.

"Why the move back home?" he asked. "Is your mother okay?"

"No, she's fine. But she wants to slow down some, turn some of her business over to me. The Hollow isn't much different than it was when your Morgan ancestor settled it a couple hundred years ago, probably never will be. But Highland Springs and the surrounding area is changing; more people are moving to the western part of the county, getting away from D.C. and the suburban sprawl. I can grow her business enough to make a decent living for me and a nice retirement for her."

Jace's lips curved a little, and the boyish sincerity behind the smile wobbled her control dangerously. "You think Frances York is capable of fully retiring?" he asked.

She laughed a little, shook her head. "I know you're probably right. She's one of those people who need to be needed. And there's nothing wrong with that."

Jace lifted his hand, touched her once more, a brief trace of a fingertip along her cheek, a stroke down a strand of her hair. It packed all the heat of his other caresses, but the punch was doubled by the tenderness she saw on his face for the first time. "No," he said, the smile fading from his face, the intensity back in his eyes. "There's absolutely nothing wrong with that."

She drew in a shaky breath, but didn't shift away from his touch. She'd ached for it for far too long. "I, uh, I think I needed to be back home, too. Around people who know me, people I care about."

"What happened to traveling the globe? Conquering the world of finance?"

"I've seen as much as I care to. Guess I'm not much of a big city warrior after all."

"Is that right? Did it take you this long to figure that out?"

The edge to his tone caught her off guard. "What do you mean?"

He shrugged. "Nothing that's any of my business, I guess. I just wondered if someone might have helped you along with that decision."

She shook her head. "If that were the case, I'd have been home right after graduation." She immediately realized her blunder.

He cocked his head. "Really." But instead of grilling her, instead of poking at the sore spot she knew damn well they'd be doing a lot more than poking at at some point, he said, "And you stayed on why? To prove something? To yourself? To someone else?"

She thought about it, and answered honestly. "Yes. To both."

"And did you?"

She didn't have to think about that one. "Yes. I proved it's wrong to do something because you think you're supposed to, because you think it matters to someone else that you do it, instead of because you want to, because it matters to you."

He said nothing, let his fingers drift back into her hair. The doors started to slide shut again. Jace casually jammed his booted foot between them, keeping them open. Never taking his eyes off hers.

"I've come to that realization myself," he said, shifting closer. His mouth was hovering just above hers. "I need to tell you something," he said, voice low, breath tickling the fine down of her skin. "Before we take this any further."

"This?" she managed.

He ran his thumb across her lip, and they both visibly shuddered. "Yeah. This," he said. "We always were combustible, Zan."

"Yes, we were that," she managed.

He tugged her tight up against him, against every last hard inch of him. "We still are that." He kept his arm around her waist, kept her body snug between his legs. "I just wanted you to know," he said, already lowering his mouth to hers. "You're not the only one who's back in town for good."

The news stunned her. Shook her. And didn't do a damn thing to stop her.

Her last thought as he took her mouth again, was the very same one she'd had when she'd walked into the lobby.

What in God's name had she just agreed to?

Chapter Six

Talk, he knew they had to talk. Had tried his damndest to let her do just that. But then when they'd finally gotten close to the subject that mattered most, she'd danced around it . . . and he'd let her. Almost happy to let it go, as long as he didn't have to let her go with it. In all the ways he'd dreamed of seeing her again—and there had been many—taking her directly to bed might have been a fantasy scenario, but he'd never believed it would happen. In fact, he wasn't entirely sure he believed it now.

And yet, that was definitely him, stumbling from the elevator with Zanna plastered all over him, their faces flushed, bodies humming, all but begging to finish what they kept starting. Somehow they managed to drag themselves and her suitcase three doors down, jam the key card in the door and make it inside before they began ripping at each other's clothes.

"This is total insanity," she murmured against his jaw, her fingers already busy tugging his coat off his shoulders. It wouldn't come all the way off, because his fingers were too busy unzipping her jacket.

"Complete and total," he murmured, unable to tear his mouth away from the tender skin along the side of her neck. "For all intents and purposes, we're strangers now, Zan."

Half panting, half grunting, they finally shoved free of their coats and started on each other's shirts. "Not strangers. You know me. You've always known me."

Jace stilled, his shirt gone, her sweater pulled halfway up her midriff. "I thought I did. Once upon a time."

She looked at him in disbelief, as if she couldn't imagine that after they'd made it this far, he was going to get into it now. Then she huffed out a sigh and dipped her chin. When he said nothing, not sure what in the hell to say—was he really sabotaging this?—she carefully disengaged from his grasp, tugged her sweater back down. "Is that what this is about then? Because I do know you, and up until five seconds ago, I'd have bet money that revenge would never factor into—"

He snagged her arm as she turned away, spun her back around. "What in the hell are you talking about?"

"I left you. It was wrong. Not only the leaving, but the way I did it." She was yelling suddenly, but Jace didn't stop her. "I should have at least told you why . . . and I didn't. By the time I realized how badly I'd screwed up, the damage was done. It seemed best to—" She trailed off, dipped her chin again.

He tipped her chin up. Goddamn but she was still the most beautiful thing he'd ever seen. Eyes hot like a pool of melted chocolate; whether they were filled with rage, with pain, with sadness, with desire. How had he ever let her go? "To what?" he asked softly. "To leave me wondering why? Forever?"

"I'm sorry," she whispered, eyes glassy now, lips trembling. "I didn't mean to hurt you. Or myself. And I managed to do a really great job at both. I wanted to believe you got over me, that I could get over you—"

"Did you?" he asked, his voice deceptively mild. "Did you forget?" He laughed harshly, and for the first time, a little unkindly. "Oh, wait a minute, that's right. It only took you a few weeks, a month tops, to forget."

"Never," she said, anger threading her voice again. "I never forgot, though God knows I've tried."

"Well, thanks. I feel so much better."

"After," she said, temper building. "When I knew I'd ruined it, ruined us, for good. Then I tried to forget."

"And?"

"Like I said," she responded, trying to pull free. He didn't let her. "Never. Not once."

"When did you think of me, Zan?" He kept her close, still gripping her arm, but using his free hand, he pushed the hair from her face, traced his fingers alongside her cheek. "When? Some sunny June afternoon, like the one when we said goodbye? Back there on that very train platform?" He started walking, backing her up to the wall. "Or maybe it was fall, September fourteenth to be exact. Does that date ring a bell? Spark any memories?"

"Of course it does," she said, her voice rough with emotion.

"Yeah, I guess it's not every day you lose your virginity, is it?" He kept walking, her back came up against the wall. "It sure as hell wasn't for me. And what about now? This time of year? Do you think about me on Christmas Eve, Zan? Do you remember what we said to each other all those many years ago? Did you know then that I didn't say those words to you lightly? Even as a kid, I knew how important they were. So important in fact, that I've never actually said them again."

Her breath caught, and a single tear tripped over the edge, tracked down the side of her face. "Oh, Jace—"

"Oh no," he said, already angry for revealing as much as he had. She made him stupid then; she made him stupid now. "Don't you dare feel sorry for me. I'm not some damaged—"

This time it was she who cut him off. She yanked free, grabbed his face and kissed him. Pouring more emotion, more pain, and more regret into that one kiss than he thought it possible to feel, to understand. He pushed her back against the wall, took the kiss on, gave her back all the emotion, all the pain, and even all the regret she'd given him.

He buried his hands in her hair, felt her heartbeat ram up against his as he pressed his body fully into hers. She whimpered his name, he took that, greedily and without regret, only wanting to hear it again. And again. "It's not about revenge, Zan," he whispered, as he moved his mouth along her jaw, toward that tender spot below her ear. "I don't want to go back. It happened. It's over."

Her fingers were buried in his hair. She pushed at his head, made him pull away so she could look into his eyes. "So what in the hell are we doing then?"

And just like that, it didn't matter. They'd been young, they'd made decisions, some smart, most stupid. They'd decided to act on some things and not on others, and paid for it. She could have tracked him down, but to be fair, he could have tracked her down, too. Fought for her, fought for the right to be the one who loved her best. But he didn't fight, did he? No. When the going got tough, Jace Morgan got out. Much easier to blame Zan. Much easier to blame his father. Much easier to blame everyone else for his pain, his problems, his isolation.

How was it that only now, when she was back in his arms, the taste of her wetting his lips, could he truly see his role in all this so clearly? They were both victims and they were both culprits. Only right now wasn't the time for regrets. For hashing out old pain. Or who'd wronged whom and why. That was simply more time wasted.

"We're beginning," he told her. "That's what we're doing." A smile curved his lips as he let his hands trail away from her face and put just enough room between them so he could lift his hand. "Hi. I'm Jace Morgan, new basketball coach and gym teacher at Marshall Valley High."

She looked at him like he was crazy, but when his gaze didn't waver, she took his hand, shook it firmly. "Hi, Jace Morgan. I'm Suzanna York, Marshall County's newest CPA."

He kept her hand clasped between them as he crowded her back against the wall. "I need to warn you, Ms. York. I grew up around these parts. And you're liable to hear a few stories about me and my brothers."

"Are you telling me they're not true?" she asked, blinking her eyes innocently, unable to wipe the wicked curve from her lips.

His smile spread to a grin. "No, I'm just telling you not to worry about them. I'm a grown man now, responsible, hard working."

She ran a finger down his face, across his lower lip. "And no longer trouble?"

He moved quick, nipped the tip of her finger, making her yelp in surprise and pull it away. He leaned over, pulled her finger back into his mouth, tongued the sore end, slowly let it slide back out again. "Well, maybe just a little." He shifted, took another finger into his mouth, made her gasp as he pulled tight, then let it slide free. "What about you? You look like a nice girl. Probably I shouldn't have you up in my hotel room, with your shirt half undone and your fingers wet from my mouth. I might not be able to stop from making the rest of you wet as well."

"You might be too late for that," she said, half-choking on the words as he ran the tip of his tongue down the center of her palm, then sunk his teeth lightly into the heel of her hand.

She gasped, squirmed against him, then moaned when he took two of her fingers into his mouth this time. Slid up, then down, then back up again. All the while his gaze never once left hers.

"Well," she managed, half-breathless, "you're liable to hear some stories about me, too. You see, I grew up around here, as well. Got mixed up with one of those Morgan boys as a girl. Never did seem to recover."

"Is that right?"

Her smile faded just a little. "Yeah, that's exactly right."

He kept his grin in place, but when he spoke, he'd never been more serious. "Well, let's just see if I can make you forget all about that boy." He took her hands and pushed them back against the wall on either side of her head. He laced his fingers between hers, then slid her hands up as he came up hard against her body. "I only want you to remember this. Remember me. Here. Now."

Her chest was rising and falling as he nipped at her lower lip, trailed hot, open mouth kisses along her jaw.

"I don't know if I can," she choked out between gasps. "I don't want to forget that boy."

Jace's head came up.

"He's part of what makes this man so special," she said.

"Zan," he said, half-broken by her heartfelt words. He'd been crazy to think they could separate past from present. Much less present from future. He pressed his forehead against hers, squeezing his eyes shut. "Maybe this is stupid after all. We're playing with fire here." He opened his eyes, lifted his head. "We've hurt each other enough."

"You don't want to hurt me, and I don't want to—"

"We're just coming back home. Neither of us is going anywhere. What happens here will have to be dealt with."

"Just like all the rest. We can't pretend it didn't happen."

"Well, I don't want to want to end up pretending this didn't happen either." He let her go, shoved away from the wall.

"So, what? We're going to stand across the room from each other? Talk casually like old friends? Maybe decide to, oh, I don't know, date?"

He spun around. "Is that so insane a thing to want to do?"

"For anyone else, no. But for us?" She raked a hand through her hair, paced to the window, turned to face him. "Look at us, Jace. We haven't seen each other in ten years, have little to no idea what or who we've become—and does it matter? No. We can't keep our hands off each other. And, you know what's really scary? I don't want to."

"You're right. And I'd be lying if I said I wanted to. But like I said earlier, we don't always get what we want. Just because we want to have at each other doesn't mean we should. I want to believe it doesn't matter. Trust me, my body wants me to believe nothing else matters right now except getting both of us naked and me inside of you as fast as possible. And for as long as possible. Maybe even longer."

She swallowed hard. Twice. "You seem to have outgrown your awkward shy stage with women," she said, trying for dry humor.

He managed to find a smile. "I'm not so sure about other

women. But I figure keeping quiet about what I want didn't help me much last time around. Throwing you on the bed might not be the smartest thing to do this go round. Not if we want to keep going around." He shook his head, shrugged a little. "So I'm trying to clear the fog a little. I feel like I'm on a freaking emotional seesaw here and I don't want to do anything stupid. Hell, maybe I already have. Maybe stopping this is the stupidest thing I've done yet. But some part of me thinks that maybe, just maybe, it would be smarter if we figured out who the hell we are to each other before we get naked. Decide if this is what we really want, or if it's just the past jangling us all up inside."

"And what if it is the past talking?" Now she stalked across the room right toward him. "We're adults. Consenting. Single. Willing adults."

"Adults who'll be living in the same town, seeing each other all the time."

"And? You've already had me, Jace, nothing can change that." She kept on coming, pushing his chest, shoving at him until the backs of his legs hit the foot of the bed. "And no amount of talking about our past is going to change the fact that you want me again. Now. It sure as hell isn't going to make me stop wanting you. So here's our chance. Maybe we'll both figure out we're chasing memories; that what was special before is no big deal now." She pushed hard and he fell back on the bed. She pulled her sweater over her head. "And we can both move on then, no fault, no blame." She threw her sweater in the corner, began to slide the straps of her soft pink silk bra off her shoulders.

Jace's heart had locked up. As had his throat. Otherwise he'd have surely stopped her, done something, said something, anything to let her know this was crazy. A mistake as sure as the one he'd made not tracking her down ten years ago. And hadn't they already made enough mistakes?

But then she was peeling off that bra and, sweet Mother of God she was as beautiful, more beautiful, than he'd ever remembered. And stupid or not, he wanted her more than he wanted his next breath, more than he had any right to. And he didn't care. He was dizzy from trying to get his emotions back on a level plane, from trying to do what was right, over what was the most damn fun.

She slid her trousers down legs that simply went on forever, then climbed right on top of him. And he knew without a shred of doubt what would be fun right now. In fact it would be sheer heaven. And though he might very well damn himself to hell later, he did nothing to stop her from introducing him to heaven right now. Any rationale, any fight he had left was gone when she tugged his flannel shirt free, then popped every button off the front with one ripping tug.

His hands came up, gripped her waist. Her skin was so warm, so damn soft. "Zanna—"

She leaned down, pressed a finger across his lips. "Eyes wide open. No promises, no commitments. Just what we both want, for as long as we want it." She leaned down, pressed a soft kiss to the center of his chest, then one to his chin, then a heartbreakingly sweet one on his lips, one that was completely at odds with the way that hot damp stretch of silk between her legs was pressed tight up against the strained fly of his jeans. "And I don't know about you, but until I've had this," she wiggled down on him, "I can't think about anything else."

"Nope," he said, his throat a dry knot, his body a live wire. "Not a damn thing."

"But I'm warning you now. I don't think we're going to want to walk away when we're done here. No matter how long we talk into the night." She sat up, reached for his belt. "Or the morning." She flipped the end free, squeezed her thighs to press herself down on him farther, making him arch his back and groan. She moaned, but slid the belt free of the loops anyway. "Or the next night." She hung his belt around her neck, and popped the button open on his jeans. "Because I do think this is the beginning of something more than a one-, or two-, or three-night stand." She slowly tugged the very strained zipper of his jeans down.

He held his breath, twitched hard when her fingers grazed

against his briefs. "Zanna," he warned, knowing he'd explode if she tortured him for another second. And he'd be damned if he'd explode anywhere except buried tightly inside of her.

She smiled and tugged at the waistband of his jeans, hooking his briefs with her fingertips as well. "And I think that's a risk worth taking."

Chapter Seven

"Wait—"

"I swear to God, Jace Morgan, if you don't just let us—"

"I was going to ask about protection," he said, far too riled up with a mostly naked Zan straddling his waist to give much of a damn about much of anything. Except that. "But what, exactly, were you going to threaten me with if I didn't 'just let us?'"

A very adult, very wicked grin curved her lips as she took his belt from her neck, doubled it up and snapped it.

His eyes grew wide. "A lot has changed, but me not being into pain isn't one of them," he said warily.

She laughed and uncurled the soft worn strip of leather. "Oh, I wasn't thinking of using it that way."

His body twitched hard, oblivious to any concerns his brain might be registering. "Oh?" he choked out.

She slowly looped the belt through the open part of the buckle and pulled, then took one of his hands and circled the loop over it.

"Now wait just a minute," he said, though his body was clamoring full speed ahead.

She took his other hand and slid it through the loop, then slowly cinched the leather down snug on his wrists. And he didn't do a damn thing to stop her. Probably because she'd slid up a bit, until she was snug up against the one part of him screaming to be taken any way she saw fit, for as long and hard as she wanted it.

She tugged his wrists up over his head, scooting her body up as she did. He groaned, then sighed in disappointment as the sweet pressure of her body left the achingly hard part of his. But he was soon distracted by her leaning down as she tugged his hands up over his head. Those sweet breasts, tipped with perfect nipples so hard and begging for his tongue.

His mouth was on them before he realized what she was doing, not that he cared a great deal at the moment. She moaned, stilled for a second, then shifted slightly so he could give the same lavish attention to her other nipple.

"Oh, oh my . . . oh yes," she murmured, then finally redoubled her efforts as he continued with his own. "I'm not sure who is bound to whom," she said when she finally slid down his body.

Bound? He twisted beneath her. "What the hell?" He tugged his wrists, which were now secured to the wrought iron headboard—by his own belt! "Zanna," he said, tone full of warning.

She smiled, devilment and innocence all mixed up in a sea of blue. "Don't you trust me?"

"That's a very loaded question," he said darkly.

She didn't even blink. "Well, now I can earn my way back into your good graces." She slid down, shifting her weight *exactly* where he wanted it. And damn if he didn't groan, long and loud. The damp tips of her breasts drew an erotic path down his chest, tickling through the soft swirl of hair, making her catch her own breath. "And your conscience can't get the best of both of us."

"Oh, I'm thinking the best of both of us is going to have little to do with either of our consciences. Until tomorrow morning anyway."

She smiled. "Exactly." She pressed a kiss in the center of his chest, then swirled her tongue quickly around one nipple, then the other. He gasped, bucked despite himself. She leaned in and pressed a hot kiss to his mouth. "And hopefully when tomorrow morning comes, we'll have no regrets," she whispered against his lips.

"I hope not, Zan. I hope to God not."

She looked into his eyes, all teasing gone. "You know, as teenagers, we thought we were so smart, so mature. We took things slowly, each step in our relationship a monumental, well-planned-out move. The summer we went to college, we even walked away from each other calmly, rationally. My heart ached for you. I know yours did for me. And yet we did the *mature thing.*" She slid down and yanked his jeans and briefs over his hips. Never taking her gaze from his. "We were young and in lust, in love, and we never once did anything rash. Never did anything impulsively." She yanked at his jeans down farther, freeing him, every last hard, throbbing inch of him. To do with whatever she wanted. He wanted her to do with him whatever she wanted, certain he was not only going to not mind it . . . he might actually become addicted to it.

He was already toeing out of his boots even as she helped yank them the rest of the way off. Everything else followed, including her panties. And then she was climbing back up his body on her hands and knees, pushing his legs wide, sliding her hands up his thighs, cupping him, stroking him. Resting on her stomach, she slid her hands along the hard, veined shaft, making it jump. Making him groan.

"Well," she said, no longer looking at him, but eyeing what she so possessively had in her grasp. "Maybe this time we should be impulsive. Be more honest about what we want. More direct about going after it."

"I think I am in complete agreement about that at the moment," he said, then growled deep in his throat when she circled him with her tongue.

"You know," she said, oh-so-conversationally, while she was killing him by inches. Very specific inches. "And I'm not excusing the past," she went on, between swirls of what had become an incredibly talented tongue. "But maybe things happen for a reason. Maybe we did have some of it right back then." She slipped the head of his cock between her lips and he bucked hard. Only her arms pressing across his thighs kept him from pushing deep into her hot, wet mouth.

"Zanna, for God's sake," he said through gritted teeth.

She trailed the tip of her tongue along one rigid vein, then back up again. He thought he might actually climb out of his skin, the pleasure vibrated through him so intensely. Then she slipped him fully inside her mouth, or as fully as she was able, and his head slammed back against the bed, his arms straining tightly against the tether of his belt.

Before he could peel his eyes open again, she was moving up his body. Slowly. Brushing the full, twitchingly hard length of him, damp from her own mouth, along her body as she did. Between her breasts, down her belly, through the soft curls to—

"Sweet God," he sighed. Somewhere in the back of his mind he knew there was something they hadn't . . . something he hadn't—but she was pushing him inside and— "Protection," he mustered.

"Pill," she whispered against his ear, just before she nipped his earlobe this time.

He jerked hard, the tip of him just inside of her, unable to maneuver at all with her thighs clamped around his.

He forced his eyes open, forced his head to stop spinning, and looked at her. Goddamn but she was like some Amazon siren, hair wild and free, body his for the taking. "You're still the most beautiful thing I've ever seen, Zan," he managed, but was only looking into her eyes when he said it. Eyes that despite being drowsed with desire were looking at him the way no other woman ever had. He wondered if she saw that same need, that same bond, and yes, dammit, that same love, in his own.

"That's what I meant," she whispered, her own voice strained now with need that he was so close, that they were so close to finally being joined together again. She started to sink down onto him. "Maybe we had to go out and find our way in the world after all, be ready to come back home, ready to come back to each other." She pushed him deep inside with one thrust, screamed a little as she did, then fell over on top of him, taking his mouth as she did.

He kissed her almost savagely, hips bucking into hers as she took him and took him hard. He was frustrated by not being able to hold her, not being able to direct the path of their joining in any way, but that only lasted for an instant. Letting her control things had its own reward. And he knew he'd have his turn.

When she finally tore her mouth from his, they'd made it past the first furious thrusts and had settled into a slower, deeper, more gratifying pace. She kissed her way to his neck, around to his ear. "No matter what, I'm glad we're here together, like this, with you." She squeezed, he thrust hard, and she moaned deep and long.

"Like this," he rasped. "Do you know how often I've thought of you, of this, of us?" He no longer cared how vulnerable he'd become. God knows she had him coming and going at the moment. Literally.

"I'm guessing as often as I have. I'm sorry, Jace," she whispered, and he could hear the pain and emotion in her words. "Sorry I ever hurt you. Hurt myself. Hurt us both."

"You're not hurting me now," he said, and nudged her cheek with his nose, his chin, until she looked at him. "Cut me loose, Zanna," he told her, his gaze burning into hers. "I need to hold you. Take you the way I've needed to every night for the past ten years."

Her breath caught, and they both moaned a little in disappointment when she had to slide free of him in order to reach the belt buckle.

The instant he was free, he rolled her onto her back, pinned her neatly under his body, pinned her hands beside her head. "Maybe you were right, maybe we did need to find our own way back to each other. But now that we have, I sure as hell hope you don't plan on leaving me anytime soon." He grabbed the end of the belt, which was still tethered to the headboard. "Or I just might have to keep you here, naked, under me, like this—" He thrust into her, all the way, and she arched, gasped struggled to get free so she could hold him. "Any way I can," he finished through clenched teeth.

Chapter Eight

Zanna should have been nervous, and maybe she was, just a little. Jace Morgan was presently filling her to the hilt. Repeatedly, and with great determination. Pretty much that was all that mattered. He could tie her naked in public as long as he didn't stop, didn't leave her. Didn't ask her to leave him.

They bucked and arched, their bodies slapping together, grunting, groaning, even growling a little. And then he stopped, jaw tight, as if using a great deal of restraint. When he finally opened his eyes, they were glassy, shocking her.

"What's wrong?" she asked, alarmed.

"Not a damn thing," he said, his voice choked. He gentled his hold on her wrists, where he'd kept them pinned to the bed with his hands. Forced himself to relax his body, so tautly poised over hers, inside of hers. "Not a goddamn thing," he whispered again, sounding almost ravaged.

"Jace—"

"Shh," he said, letting her hands go. He pushed his fingers into her hair, spread wildly across the bed. His lips twitched at the corners a little, but the humor didn't quite reach his eyes. "We're having at each other like starving beasts here."

She tried a little smile, too, but still didn't understand what she was seeing in his eyes. "I guess we are, but can you blame us?"

He shook his head, tenderly stroking her hair now, her face. "A part of me is always going to be starved for you."

He made her breath catch in her throat. "Jace, I don't want you to—"

He hushed her with a kiss, a kiss so sweet and gentle she felt tears build behind her eyes.

"What's going on?" she whispered when he continued the trail of heartbreakingly sweet kisses along her jaw. "You're scaring me a little."

He lifted his head, surprise on his face. "Scaring you? I must really be losing my touch then."

She reached for his face, ran her fingers along every feature, stared hard into his fathomless blue eyes. "Don't say good-bye to me," she said, voicing her deepest fear. That now that he'd had her, now that he'd gotten what he'd dreamed of having for ten long years, he'd walk away. Not from revenge, just because it was the natural conclusion. Story over.

He smiled then. A smile as wide as the sky and as open. And every last thing he was feeling showed clearly on his face.

"Oh," she said, breath catching, body twitching as he settled his hips deeply into hers. "Oh, Jace."

"Put your arms around me, Zan. Hold me tight," he said, stopping to kiss her deeply, slowly. "I slowed us down because now that I'm inside of you, I know this isn't about slaking desire." He rained short kisses along her jaw. "And it's not about need, or fulfilling ten years of longing." He kissed her cheeks, her nose, her forehead.

Tears had already begun to track from the corners of her eyes. And when he lifted his head, looked down at her, she realized why his own were so glassy.

"This is about making love. To you. I've always loved you, can't imagine a world where that isn't possible. I want to take my time, do this right, fall in love with you all over again." He slid deep, pulled her legs up over his hips, until her body was wrapped completely around his. She already knew she was wrapped tightly inside his heart. "Make it last forever," he whispered against her neck.

"I don't know what I did to deserve you, Jace, but as God is my witness, I swear I will never underestimate the power of this . . . or you . . . or us, ever again." She pulled his head down to hers. "I never stopped loving you. I know I never will."

"Show me, Zanna. Show me. And don't stop showing me."

They moved together and it was as if their bodies had never been apart, as if they'd grown together, matured together. She supposed that was the way of it when you were meant for somebody.

He said her name as he came, held her possessively, fiercely tender as he poured himself into her. And that was all it took to meet him there. And then they could go even slower, rediscover each other, drive each other up and over the edge again. Long into the night, they turned to each other, took each other, loved each other.

And somewhere around dawn they finally began talking.

Tucked in a blanket on the couch they'd shoved over in front of the huge hotel room window, they watched the snow continue to fall in fat, heavy flakes while wrapped up in each other's arms. He told her about being a gym teacher, and coaching basketball. It was clear the honest enthusiasm and love he had for the kids he'd helped to learn the sport he loved. She told him about working her way up in the accounting firm in Atlanta, about feeling like she had to do something bigger and better with her college degree. That she'd told herself she was making her mother proud, but what she'd really been doing was trying to prove to herself that despite making a dreadful mistake in her personal life, that it hadn't all been an illusion, that she could get her own brass ring, that she didn't need someone to buy it for her. And then she told him about Dan.

How she'd been literally swept off her feet by his bigger than life world, how she'd let him make her believe that part of growing up was leaving all her childhood things behind. Make her feel childish for wanting to cling to the past. She'd learned, the hard way, that what he was doing by separating her from the things she'd loved was making her more dependant on him. Because he was insecure, jealous even, of the ties she'd had in her own life, ones he'd wanted but never gotten from his oh-so-perfect-looking family. He wanted her tied to him and him alone. She'd seen the real side of him the night before her wedding, when he'd come to her apartment, drunk from his bachelor party. He done things . . . painful things . . . said things even more painful, degrading . . . that despite his pleas for forgiveness later, she knew, in her heart, were merely proof of the niggling concerns she'd had all along. Her mother had voiced them often enough, but she wouldn't listen. But on the eve of what was supposed to be the happiest day of her life, she couldn't dare not to.

Jace held her tight as she told him all of it. He'd said nothing, just pressing his lips to her temple, letting her get it all out. And when she was done, rather than say anything, or pass any kind of judgment, he began talking about his father. About his guilt for not staying, for making a life somewhere else, for forsaking the life he had with his brothers in order to find some happiness for himself. About his restlessness of late, his thoughts of home, of his brothers, of making a mark where it mattered, and not where it was convenient. Then he'd told her that he'd always wondered what would have happened if he'd come after her. If he'd shown up on her doorstep and demanded to know why she'd let him, their friendship, their bond, slip away. And she told him she already knew that the what-ifs and maybes were the hardest things to live with.

"I know," he told her now, the sky still gray with snow. His lips were pressed against her hair as he held her cradled back against his chest. "We made some dumb decisions. I guess humans do that. You could wish you hadn't had your head turned around by that guy. I could wish I'd come after you anyway. We both have regrets. None of them will do us any good."

She shifted around, pulled his head down and kissed him. Their lips were soft and puffy from a night spent kissing, so she was as gentle as she could be. "Except maybe to make us more careful this time."

"All we can do is hope," he said. When she just looked at

him, he said, "We're going to make more mistakes, Zan. We're going to make more bad choices. We're still human." He grinned a little. "Although I was feeling rather super-powerful that last time this morning, in the shower."

She laughed, swatting him across the chest, but forced to nod in agreement. With a little sigh, she relaxed back against him. "Well, this time around, let's hope we make our mistakes together."

He squeezed her tight, eliciting a little squeal from her. "That's my plan." He rolled her over even as he slid down the couch, until she laid in a sprawled tangle of skin and blanket on top of him. "We weren't meant to be apart again."

She shook her head, the tears that never seemed more than a blink away of late, surfaced again. "Not unless we're really really stupid."

"I'd hunt you down this time," he said, nipping at her chin.

"Oh?" She nipped back, then began to slide down his body. "And just how do you plan on capturing me?"

He rolled her to the floor then landed in a crouch on top of her. "I have my ways."

Laughter bubbling up, along with the desire that seemed to have no end, she wiggled her eyebrows. "I don't suppose you'd be willing to show me?"

"Depends. How long do you think we've got until breakfast shows up?"

She caught him off guard with a quick shove. An even quicker roll later, she was astride him. "Depends," she shot back. "On how long it will take you to get free of my evil clutches."

He grinned, and her heart soared at the wide-open emotions he did nothing to hide now. "How do you know this isn't exactly how I planned to keep you enslaved?"

"Enslaved? My, my," she said, glancing about for his belt. "That conjures up all sorts of naughty images, now doesn't it?"

His expression turned more than a little wary and she couldn't help it, she laughed.

He rolled her to her back, pinned her neatly beneath him. "Why is it I think I'm going to have my hands full for the next, oh I don't know, half a century or so?"

She leaned up and nipped him right on the nipple. Making him jerk, and making his body twitch to life. With raised eyebrows, she looked back up at him. He just smiled and gave her an innocent little shrug. Then they both laughed and rolled together until they were fully entwined.

"I don't know," she finally answered, a bit breathlessly. "Are you interested in having your hands full?"

"Now there's a loaded question."

She merely continued looking at him, her heart so full to bursting, she didn't think she could survive such intense happiness.

"As long as they're full of you, yes," he said. Then with a sweet passion that still took her breath away, he kissed her tenderly. "I love you, Suzanna York."

"Boy," she said, her breath leaving her in a whoosh. "I'm just never going to get tired of hearing you say that."

He grinned. "I know the feeling."

"I do love you, Jace Morgan."

The jarring ring of the phone interrupted her, making them both jump.

"Don't forget where you left off," he told her with a quick kiss as he disentangled himself. "I'll need to hear that a couple more hundred times myself."

"Definitely. And that's probably my mother. Are you sure you want to answer—"

But he already had. "Hi, Frances. Yes, it's me, Jace." There was a pause, then he grinned and said, "Oh, she's perfectly fine."

Suzanna wrapped the blanket around herself and rolled to a sitting position. She pushed the hair from her eyes, and feasted on the vision of Jace Morgan, buck naked, talking quite casually on the phone—to her mother of all people! She had no doubts he understood the full ramifications of what he was doing. By noon today, blizzard or no blizzard, all of Marshall County would know they were back together.

She hugged her knees close, smiling, not remotely concerned.

Then Jace was hanging up the phone and her mouth fell open. "She didn't want to talk with me? It's Christmas Eve."

"I told her you'd call her back after we'd eaten breakfast."

Right on cue, there was a knock on the door.

"You do have superpowers," she said.

He winked at her, strolling to the door. "And don't you forget it. With a fortifying meal, there's no telling what feats of daring and death-defying excitement I might be able to accomplish."

She couldn't help it, she shivered in anticipation. Then she realized he was going to open the door and—"Jace! Shouldn't you put something on?"

"What?" He looked down. "Oh. Right." In two quick strides he was across the room. One yank and she was no longer wrapped up in the blanket. He wrapped it around his waist and strolled right back to the door, sending her squealing into the bathroom, shutting the door behind her just as he opened the door to the hall. She waited a few moments, until she heard the door close once again, and called out, "You're going to pay for that, you know."

He whipped the door open, tugged her out with one yank, right up against his once-again naked chest. "I figure we're even, since I have no shirt to wear home."

Her cheeks warmed. "Oh yeah. That."

He smiled, apparently unconcerned. "Yeah. That."

She turned to the cart with the food tray on it. If he could be casually naked, so could she. "You want to eat on the couch? Watch the snow fall?"

He tugged her back against him, nuzzled her neck. "You don't mind that your mother knows? Should I have let you tell her?"

She turned in his arms. "Oh, I'm pretty sure, knowing her, she had a good idea when we both got stuck here last night."

"But you didn't tell her how many rooms we had."

"I don't think I had to. Did it occur to you that she could have called on any number of other people to come get me from the station?"

He didn't have to answer. "We've been set up."

"By the best. Are you angry with her?"

"Are you?"

Suzanna shook her head, wrapped her arms around him. "How can I be? She gave me the bestest Christmas present of my life."

"The bestest, huh? I guess that's a lot to live up to."

She pumped her hips against his, noting he was already well on his way "up." "I think you'll manage just fine."

"Do you now?"

"I do."

His eyes darkened and his expression intensified. "Then I guess I should warn you, that I plan to hear those words from your lips again at some point in the future."

Her heart skipped a beat, then raced on, full steam ahead. She hugged him tightly. "As long as you plan on repeating them right back to me, I don't think we'll have a problem."

He kissed her, long and hard. "Thank you," he whispered against her lips.

"For?"

"For making me feel like I'm home. Really home. For the first time."

She could only nod, kissing him long and deep, until they were both so stirred up that breakfast was completely forgotten. "And thank you," she whispered.

"For?"

"Waiting for me. Not giving that beautiful heart to someone else."

"I couldn't give it to anyone else. It's always belonged to you."

She pressed her lips to his chest, right over his heart. "You were my Christmas past, you're my Christmas present . . ." She looked up into his eyes, her own shining with everything she felt inside. "And I want you to be my every Christmas future."

He pulled her up against him, taking her mouth in a kiss so hard and deep it literally lifted her off her feet. "Now that's what I call the bestest Christmas present ever," he said, spinning her around once before setting her back down.

She pressed a hand over her racing heart, laughing a little at his exuberance. He let her go and began taking lids off of their breakfast dishes. "Now, since my present is already unwrapped . . ." He turned with a bowl of strawberries and a little pot of honey. "I guess it's only fair that I get to do a little holiday decorating." With a grin as wicked as she'd ever seen it, he gave a little nod. "Couch or bed?"

She couldn't answer him, her gaze was going from the honey pot . . . to the wicked gleam in his eye. It was all she could do to remain upright.

"Okay then, right here." He juggled the bowl and pot into one hand, and lifted her arms out, one at a time with the other. "Hmm," he said, walking around her, dipping his finger into the honey.

She gasped when he let a drop of honey drizzle first on one nipple then the other. And tried not to squirm when he bit through a strawberry, and pressed each half firmly onto the dab of honey. "Now this is what I call trimming the tree."

She eyed him through a haze of pleasure. "Just be warned. I fully intend to deck your . . . halls. Later."

"Oh," he assured her, rolling another whole strawberry into the honey pot. "I'm counting on it." He pressed it into her navel, and when it wouldn't stay there . . . he pressed it somewhere else.

"Jace!"

He knelt in front of her, trailed the drizzle of honey dripping down her thighs with his tongue. "Hmm?"

"Nothing," she said, jerking with pleasure, grabbing on to his shoulders for balance. "Just . . . don't stop . . . what you're . . . oh my God."

She could feel his chuckle between her legs.

"Don't ever stop."

"Not until you beg me to." And he kept his promise.

Then again, Jace had always been the "dependable" Morgan. She'd just never known how much she could come to depend on him. But she was about to find out.

A Blue Christmas

Alison Kent

Chapter One

The last time Jessie Buchanan had seen Thomas "Blue" Miller he'd been walking out of her life.

He'd left her standing in the middle of a long graveled road, left her looking through watery eyes at shoulders too broad to belong to a boy of eighteen, at legs longer than she'd ever realized when she'd felt them heavy and warm, and tangled naked with her own.

For ten years now she'd revisited the mental image, wondering what Blue had been thinking, his head held so high after she'd told him that, no, love wasn't enough of a reason for her to stay, wasn't enough of a reason to spend her life in a town that, in eighteen years, had never felt like home.

He had felt like home, but he'd been bound to September, Texas, by ties she'd never been able to break.

Get over it, Jess. The ties were unbreakable. Blue never had any intention of living anywhere but in the one town you couldn't wait to put behind you.

And if that fundamental difference wasn't the foundation for a doomed relationship then she hadn't learned much since leaving. Of course, there was always the possibility she hadn't learned anything at all, considering here she was back in September and on her way to see Blue.

Approaching the railroad crossing at the city limits, Jessie slowed her low-slung sports car, remembering how many unsuspecting oil pans had met their fate on the seemingly mild-mannered bump in the road. The locals knew better than to take the lazy rise at face value because of its wicked backside drop.

Crawling up and over the tracks, she coasted to a stop at the first of the city's two traffic lights. The fact that she knew when and where to drive with caution didn't sit all that well. Taking the girl out of the country had apparently been more of a sure thing than wringing the country from the girl. Not that September was exactly a world away from Dallas, her home for six years now.

It just seemed that way, she thought, as the light changed and the car purred into town, what with Soup's Auto located immediately—and conveniently—between the tracks and the traffic signal, the Dime & Dollar on the far end of the next block, city hall on the near side, and the mayor's house smack-dab in between.

The town resembled so many of the other dots on the map she'd driven through since leaving her condo at noon. But subtle nuances still separated September from the others. Nuances noticeable only by a native. Or a long-lost daughter returning home.

No. Not returning. Never returning. Visiting. A short vacation and nothing more. Still, she could hardly deny that eighteen years spent in this town gave meaning to the places she drove past.

Places like Miller's Feed and Supply.

The white frame building sat alone at the far end of town, the location allowing for the constant flow of stock trailers and dual-axle pickups without getting in the way of folks needing to get to the post office or to Debbie Does Hair-Dooz or to the First Baptist Church Wednesday nights.

And behind the wooden structure loomed a thoroughly modern and huge barn red . . . barn.

Jessie knew from her Internet research that Blue was doing all right for himself. The addition to the original location now served as Miller's regional supply center, warehousing the stock for the extremely profitable chain of family-owned stores.

She had to admit a bit of a thrill, however, seeing that the business's first structure still stood, little changed since the days Blue had chased her up and down the aisles, letting her twist free when he caught her, until neither of them had the will to wait one minute more.

Jessie shivered, pushing the thought away. Or at least giving her best shot to turning her thoughts from the past.

But memories of Blue's naked body, memories of being as physically close to him as a woman could possibly be to a man—memories of her head on his chest, her hand deep between his legs, his arm wrapped around her with such desperation that their bodies seemed more one than two—were not easily buried. Especially when those very memories had brought her here.

It was late in the day, at least by September, Texas, standards, yet Jessie kept her sunglasses in place, deflecting both the final rays of the setting sun and the curious glances that had tracked her westward progress through town. Now nothing lay ahead but the highway that would take her to Blue . . . and his Christmas tree farm.

If anything in her snooping surprised her, the discovery of Blue's having converted twenty of the Miller homestead's sixty acres did—though, having read about the Virginia pine growing and harvesting timetable, she supposed he'd had his father's help in the venture's launch.

The year-old profile she'd searched out in the *Texas Monthly* online archives mentioned that Ann and Phil Miller, Blue's parents, had retired to the dry Arizona desert, leaving the family business in the very capable hands of their only son.

Blue Miller, CEO. Jessie smiled.

With September in her rearview mirror, she scanned the road ahead for the cutoff to the Miller place. When she'd left for her four years at Wellesley financed by her maternal grandmother's trust, Blue had been on his way to Stephen F. Austin

214 / Alison Kent

and a business degree. It was nice to see the proof of his success. She knew how much his parents had sacrificed to ensure their only son's future.

The most intriguing thing her research had uncovered, however, was the fact that Blue had never married. An online issue of the county newspaper featuring an article on his Christmas tree farm had labeled him one of the area's most eligible bachelors. But the issue had been five months old, and Jessie hadn't wanted to take a chance on showing up if his status had changed.

To that end, she'd bribed her marketing department's administrative assistant with a week's worth of lunches to give him a call. They'd concocted a story that the radio station where Jessie worked as an account executive was considering a Christmas promo involving a weekend stay at a local B&B topped off with the selection of a live Christmas tree.

Would he mind if they sent one of their people out to tour his place? Such a visit, of course, would be arranged not to interfere with his family life. Blue had obligingly let slip that he had no family locally and lived on his own, setting Jessie's plan into action.

As driven as she knew Blue to be, as passionate about life, she had a hard time believing he'd have chosen celibacy over a committed relationship. That left her believing—hoping—that his sexual involvements were casual. For her plan to work, she needed him to be open to her suggestion that they warm up the season by creating a few new Christmas memories.

Blue Miller had been the best sex she'd ever had. She'd come back to find out if he still was.

Chapter Two

One of these days, Blue decided, he really did need to learn to say no. Why the hell a Dallas radio station thought any of their listeners would want to make a trip to September for a Christmas tree was beyond him. But marketing wasn't his thing, and he'd agreed to meet with the rep from the radio station before thinking the idea all the way through. At least nothing legal or binding had been signed.

Turning onto his long, winding drive, he wondered again why he hadn't called this whole thing off days ago. Hell, it was barely a month until Christmas. The station's contact name and number were scratched right there on the chalkboard back in his store office. Yet when he'd finally looked up this afternoon from the tons of work still waiting, he'd realized the rep would've left Dallas hours before.

He'd had no choice but to save his spreadsheet, shut down his laptop, grab his coat and hit the road. And obviously it was even later than he'd thought, he grumbled, grunting as his pickup bounced through the gate and into the clearing surrounding the house.

An electric blue Mercedes Kompressor sat parked alongside the covered, wraparound porch. Feeling perversely inconvenienced, he parked directly behind, catching a flash of movement near the porch swing before climbing down from the cab.

He had a buttload of orders to see to for Miller's Annual New Year's Deals. He should be spending the evening at work, not making like the nice Christmas tree farmer at home. When his father asked about the delay in orders, Blue would remind the older man whose idea it was four years ago to plant all those damn pine seedlings. And who hadn't ended up sticking around to see the venture through.

With his work boots crunching on the crushed-shell drive, Blue headed for the porch steps, determined to send the station's rep packing and get his own butt back to the store.

"Sorry I'm late," he said, mounting the four steps in two strides. "I got caught up at the office." But that was all of his hit-the-road spiel he had time to get out before coming face-to-face with his past.

Jessie Buchanan had grown into a hell of a woman.

She wore black leather, black silk and black denim: a motorcycle jacket, a low-cut T-shirt and tight, skinny jeans. Her skin was as porcelain-pale as ever, her eyes brilliantly knowing. Her toenails were painted a deep lush red; she had on the strangest looking pair of heeled sandals he'd ever seen. Lace-up and velvet and black.

She looked nothing like the girl he remembered, the girl who'd turned his gut inside out when she'd licked her lips and begged. Not for what she wanted; it had never been about what she wanted. It had always been about what she wanted to do. For him. To him. He choked back the memory, took the last step onto the porch and stopped. He wondered what she was up to. He wondered if he wanted to know.

Fists shoved into jeans pockets and shoulders hunched forward against the cold, he acknowledged her with no more than the suggestion of a nod. "Jess."

"Hi, Blue." She walked toward him, her hips swaying in that same seductive walk he'd seen for years in his dreams. "You're looking good."

She looked better than good. She looked like the breakfast he craved when he rolled out of bed, the sinful dessert he never took time to savor. He lived on fast food and coffee, his life having become a series of quickies when his back had been turned.

And now here was Jessie Buchanan, looking like a bad girl who understood quickies well. The thought stirred the primitive heat seeing her had kindled deep between his legs.

"It's the air." He pulled in a huge breath. "The clean country living. It does a body good."

"You're full of shit," she said and moved even closer. "You always were."

"And I see you're still a mouthy little thing." Only she wasn't so little at all. She wasn't any taller; she just seemed so, her presence that of a lioness, confident, proud, where once she'd been more mousy and meek, skittish and easily cowed. Except with him. Never with him.

And then she was in his arms, saying hello with her body and smelling like the sunshine missing from these dreary winter days. His arms went around her waist; hers wrapped around his neck. He nuzzled his face to her hair and breathed deeply, remembering, reliving, aching from more than the press of her thighs to his, her belly to his, her breasts to his chest where his heart had started to thunder.

He stepped back and set her away, holding her upper arms because he didn't want her to bolt just yet and wasn't sure if she'd broken herself of the habit. And then he found himself shaking his head. This woman, this Jessie. Bolting looked to be the farthest thing from her mind. Long dark lashes swept down, swept up, her eyes as green as he remembered, as green as pine seedlings soaking up summer's sun, as green as winter's harvest of Christmas trees. The trees . . . Goddammit! She was here because of the Christmas trees.

He released her as if he'd been felled by an ax. The victorious look on her face confirmed his suspicion. "You're from the radio station, aren't you?" Her growing smile stirred the coals of his wariness. He moved back into her space, towering above her, glaring down. "What the hell's going on?"

She ran a hand through her silky black hair, shoving it back from her face. She licked her lips and started to turn away. He wasn't going to let it happen. They were separated now by ten inches, not ten years, and he held home-field advantage.

He reached out, ran his hand along the side of her neck, his fingers into the hair at her nape, and cupped the back of her skull. "I'm waiting here, Jess. I want an answer."

She nodded, a smile playing along the line of her lips slick from the touch of her tongue and tinted a dark winter rose. "You used to be more trusting."

He snorted. "I used to be eighteen."

"So did I," she said, turning her face to press her lips, the tip of her tongue, the barest edge of her teeth, to the inside of his forearm. "We're both older now, Blue. And hopefully more than a little bit wiser."

His pride ordered him to let her go. His cock that remembered that warm and wet mouth told him to pull her body to his. "Being wiser is the reason I don't trust you. If you set this up . . . if you set *me* up . . . so help me I'll—"

"You'll do what? Turn me over your knee?"

Why did she look like that's exactly what she wanted him to do? Not fifteen minutes ago he'd been working on a plan to get out of this deal with the radio station. Now the idea didn't seem like the same waste of time, except he knew that's exactly what it was.

He couldn't work with this woman. Fuck her, yeah. But deal with her professionally? Keep their contact strictly business when she was the last person on Earth he'd have invited back into his life?

He hated her even more now that she was standing here, her lips parted and her breathing labored, making him forget why he had never wanted to see her again. He needed to remember her leaving, the way she had given but half of the story, never telling him the whole truth. He tilted her head back, stared directly down into her eyes. His pulse roared in his ears—and in his pants, where his non-thinking head wanted a rough-and-raw pounding revenge.

"I think you'd better get back in that fancy import of yours and get the hell back to Dallas before you regret having come here."

"You haven't even heard my proposal yet." She caught at her lower lip with her teeth, once, twice.

The fog of breath she exhaled surrounded him, a warm cocoon in the rapidly frosting air. It was all Blue could do not to slide his hand into her panties and see if she was as slick and wet as the look in her eyes promised.

"I don't need to hear it. This Christmas tree thing isn't going to happen. There's only one thing that ever worked between us, Jess. And I don't think you're here to sleep with me."

"Think again."

Chapter Three

His eyes flared. That was the only way she knew to describe the flash of fire that consumed her where she stood.

His grip on her head tightened, and Jessie wondered if she would survive the force of his body when it finally slid into hers. When she'd made the decision to head for September, she'd never expected to find the boy she'd last seen.

But she sure as hell hadn't expected to find Blue Miller to be such a large, compelling and dangerous threat.

"Wait a minute. Are you saying the radio station promo story is bullshit?" He skipped right over the part about her being here to sleep with him. And he snorted. "You don't give a shit about the trees. You don't even work for the station, do you?"

"No. I mean yes, I do." *Deep breath, Jessie. Deep breath.* She'd never pull this off if she kept stumbling over her words, if he thought she was still the girl who'd run, who hadn't possessed the backbone to stay and bring her father up on charges of abuse. "And I *am* here because of the station's Christmas promo. It's just not . . ."

"Just not what?" He let her go then, took a step back and dragged a palm down his face before jamming both hands to his hips. "Just not a promo that has anything to do with my trees?"

"Do you mind if we go inside? I'll explain everything. I

swear." She shivered and told herself the night fog rolling in off the fields and surrounding the house was the cause. "It's too cold out here to talk."

"Oh, yeah, sure." He dug his keys from his front pocket and headed for the door. "Sorry, I wasn't thinking. I was waiting for you to take off your clothes."

She glared at his back. "Very funny."

"Hey." He shrugged. "You said you were here to sleep with me."

"Sleeping wasn't exactly what I had in mind, Blue, though I'd be more than happy to share your bed for the weekend."

She made the offer to his broad back. He froze, stiffened, then pushed open the door, letting off a muttered string of curses both raw and foul.

She ducked beneath his outstretched arm, dragging fingertips over his sculpted abs as she passed, amazed by the strength in his body, amazed by her own strength of will, the steadiness of her voice.

Hugging herself tightly against a case of the jitters that she hoped passed for cold, she walked to the center of the front room. The furniture had changed, as had the color scheme and the decor. But still she knew this house better than the one she'd grown up in. Never had she felt the same sense of things being right, and safe, as she had when here with the Millers.

Even now, tendrils of clinging nostalgia remained . . .

Blue shut the door and turned the deadbolt. The thud echoed from her jaw to her toes. "You're assuming a lot here, Jess. Like the fact that there may not be room in my bed."

"Why? Are you sleeping in a twin size these days?" She glanced toward the staircase that had once led to his room before turning to face him. "That never posed a problem before."

His pulse ticked in the vein at his temple. "I wasn't talking about the size of my bed."

"You live here alone, right?"

He nodded.

"Are you expecting company tonight?"

He shook his head.

"Then I'm not sure I see the problem. I'm talking about sex." Now to get the messy past out of the way so they could get down to business. "It's not like I'm asking you to marry me."

"No. You wouldn't. We both know how you feel about marrying me." Pushing away from the front door on which he'd been leaning, he shrugged out of his denim jacket and tossed it over the back of the sofa. Then he headed to the kitchen, leaving her with a look that made his feelings about her ten-year-old rejection quite clear.

Her eyes stinging, she watched him go, his shoulders as broad as she remembered, his legs as powerful and long. She'd hurt him, yes, but still her body responded. Her breasts swelled, her body quickened, yet hesitation crept in.

She'd told herself while concocting her plan that her motives were all about reliving the sex. She hadn't wanted to face or discover the truth—that Thomas Miller was the only man capable of making her body respond. But reality paced the tiled floor in the kitchen, banging cabinet doors, blasting water from the faucet, abruptly shutting off the flow.

Jessie waited, letting Blue steam and letting the coffee brew before she followed. She left her leather jacket on the couch next to his, brave enough now to face him wearing the low-cut and long-sleeved T-shirt she'd bought with this reunion in mind. She wore no bra, and five-percent Lycra gave a clingy *oomph* to the rich black silk.

Blue had loved her breasts more than any part of her body. She knew she wasn't playing fair, dressing to remind him of that fact, but she wanted him to remember what she couldn't forget. The way he'd buried his face against them, the way he'd suckled.

The way he'd straddled her chest, pressed her breasts together and repeatedly shoved his cock between. His face had grown strained, veins standing rigid along his neck with his effort to hold back, to wait. He'd failed, accepting the invitation of her open mouth every single time.

Oh boy, she thought and took a deep breath, wiping sweaty palms on her thighs before stepping from hardwood onto the kitchen floor tiled in colors of sienna and earth. Blue stood in profile, hands braced on the black marble countertop, shoulders hunched as he stared at the coffee streaming from basket to pot.

She wanted to go to him; she ached to hold him. The need to tell him again that she'd loved him wrapped vise-like fingers around her heart. But then he straightened, and he looked at her, and she thanked God that she hadn't said a word or made a move toward him. His eyes were cold and hurt, and he wasn't in the mood for sympathy or soothing.

He certainly wasn't in the mood for sex.

"One cup," he ground out. "One cup and you're gone. The caffeine will get you back to Dallas."

"I'm not going back to Dallas tonight."

"Fine. There's a Motel Six on the interstate. And the Kettle next door serves ham and sweet potatoes every night in December."

She clamped down on the need to tell him what she could easily show him instead. Her heels clicked against the smart Italian tile on her way across the room. She kept her gaze locked on his, looking away only long enough to reach up into the cupboard for a mug. The one she set next to the pot would easily hold a quart.

One of Blue's dark brows went up. "You drink that much; you'd better get a room. You'll be needing a bathroom every ten minutes, and between here and Dallas you're outta luck."

"So I'll get a room." Whatever. She wasn't going back to Dallas. Not with all the excuses she'd made, the begging off of parties and intimate dinners she'd done to free up this weekend.

"Suit yourself," he said with a shrug and poured.

Jessie wrapped both hands around her mug and brought it to her mouth, blowing across the surface before she sipped. The flavor was earthy and rich and, coffee-snob that she was, she knew it hadn't come prepackaged off the Maxi Mart shelf.

She wasn't completely successful keeping a smile from her face. "I didn't know you could get coffee like this in September."

"You can't." Blue sipped and grimaced at the burn. "I pick it up coming through Palestine or Tyler."

"Wow. I don't believe it. Thomas Miller admitting he can't get everything he wants living the good life in September." She backed across the width of the narrow kitchen and leaned against the counter opposite from Blue.

He refused to rise to her bait. "What gives, Jess? What's the story?"

She set her coffee aside and, hands on the counter's edge at her hips, boosted herself up on top. Leaning forward, she swung legs crossed at the ankles and stared at the floor beneath dangling feet. "The station *is* doing a Christmas promo. It's a Home for the Holidays contest. Several listeners will win airfare and lodging and rental car packages enabling them to visit family they don't have the funds to see."

"I don't get it. You don't have any family here," Blue said softly.

"I know. I wouldn't be here if I did." She wondered if the citizens of September knew where her father had gone. Or what he'd done to deserve the sentence that would keep him locked up for good.

She blinked and shuddered the thought away. "Anyway, I work for the station. I'm not eligible to win. But the promo got me to thinking about September. About you."

And about how the man she'd been dating left her cold when Blue had left her breathless. He was the only one who ever had.

"Can't be too popular a promo," he scoffed. "Sending people places they never wanted to see again."

She refused to let his sarcasm faze her. "I didn't want to see September. I wanted to see you. I wanted this Christmas to be one we would both remember."

She could've said more. She could've started taking off her clothes. But she didn't. She waited. And waited. Watching tendrils of steam curl upward from the mug he held at chest level.

He stood with his work boots crossed at the ankle, one palm heel-down on the countertop, fingers curled over the edge. The sleeves of his blue-and-green-plaid flannel were rolled back, those of his cream-colored thermal undershirt pushed up.

His forearms were thick and muscled, covered with hair a shade or two lighter than the dark brown strands caught up in the back by his shirt collar. She'd never known him to wear his hair long, and her fingers itched to feel the texture, to unbutton his shirt and pull the tails free from his worn denim jeans. To bare his skin slowly.

She wanted to taste his throat. To nuzzle the pit of his arm, his navel, the thatch of hair that cushioned his sex. She wanted to remind him how good they'd once been. And she wanted, needed, to prove that *once* was the operative word, that she'd inflated their connection beyond the simple sexual compatibility that it was. That Blue couldn't offer her anything more.

That she didn't love him anymore.

"Coffee's getting cold," he finally said.

She didn't even look down at her cup. "Can I get a refill?"

He shook his head. "Not part of the deal, Jess. Sorry."

The kitchen clock *tick-tick-ticked* through several long seconds before she sighed and picked up her mug. She wasn't ready to give up, not yet. Not when she hadn't accomplished what she'd come here to do. She had to know what was truth and what was fiction. She needed answers so she would know what to do with the rest of her life.

When Blue suddenly pushed away from the counter and walked out of the kitchen, she set down her mug without drinking. He returned seconds later carrying an antique oak bar stool with a curved spindle-back. He set it directly in front of her and sat, lifting both of her feet to his lap.

She took a deep breath and waited.

Chapter Four

He couldn't help himself. He was going to take her to bed. He was tired and hungry. He needed to work; he needed to sleep. But the only thing that mattered was taking care of his basest needs. The teeth of the zipper closing his fly were rapidly reaching their limits. He could get back to hating the both of them later.

Besides, he'd be seven kinds of stupid to waste a good hard-on when he had Jessie Buchanan sitting in his kitchen with her legs spread. Jessie, the girl who'd said yes to every single thing he'd asked her to do when she'd been naked and he'd been brick-busting hard. Her curiosity, her willingness, her uninhibited nature had never ceased to amaze him.

"Blue?"

"Hmm?"

"What're you doing?"

What he was doing was unlacing the strings to the funkiest pair of shoes he'd ever seen. That, and hoping when he stood up again his cock didn't break off at the root. Goddamn, but he was hard. "The way you're drinking, you're going to be a while finishing that cup."

"I see. So . . . you're playing the gracious host and seeing to your guest's comfort. Is that it?" She lifted her coffee with both hands, spreading her fingers to hold the mug's deep bowl, taking her time settling the rim at her mouth before she sipped.

Blue's hands stilled on her feet. He remembered too well the strength in her slender fingers, the pressure of her fingertips as she'd played between his legs, teasing the head of his cock, stroking the shaft, fondling his balls before reaching behind into territory no woman since had cared to explore.

He remembered, too, the temptation of her mouth, the way she held her lips slightly parted, the way she'd never been able to keep her tongue from flicking out for missed drops of whatever it was she'd been drinking. Her mouth was the mouth of his fantasies. And nothing about that had changed.

He turned his attention back to her feet, looking for the equilibrium he'd lost now that he'd given himself permission to indulge. She didn't make it easy on a man.

"No, Jess. That's not it. I'm actually seeing to my comfort," he said, wanting to add *to hell with yours* but knowing sex between them wasn't worth the effort if she wasn't having fun. Her enthusiasm was the bar by which he'd judged all others. And the reason he'd let his insistent cock win tonight. He hadn't had a good fuck in months.

"Oh," she finally said as she lowered her mug, slowly looking up and into his eyes as her tongue flicked at a drop of coffee on her mouth. Lower lip caught between her teeth, she sat up as straight as her spine allowed and poured the rest of the liquid into the sink. "What can I do to help?"

He finished unlacing and removing both of her shoes. And then he sat back, hands wrapped around her ankles holding her bare feet in place on his thighs. She looked like pleasing him right now was the only thing that mattered in her life. And he wondered how in the hell he was supposed to respond.

His heels hooked on the barstool's rung, he spread his legs; hers spread with the movement. He shifted his thighs farther apart, opening hers even wider. He wished she was wearing a skirt without panties. Or, better yet, nothing but a garter holding thigh-high stockings in place.

He wanted to sit here with her naked pussy at eye-level, the dark hair, the pink lips, the glistening juices he knew tasted of citrus and salt. The longer he watched, the wetter she'd get. Already he imagined her scent, imagined pushing her back on her elbows, pulling her bottom forward into his mouth.

His first impulse was to take his time, but he saw no need to wait, no need to hold back, no need to make nice and pretty pillow talk when he wasn't feeling the least bit nice and didn't plan to bother with a pillow. He wanted to be damn sure she knew where they stood. This was nothing but the sex she'd come here looking for.

He gave a slight nod. "You can take off your shirt and show me those fantastic tits you've been teasing me with."

He hadn't expected her to refuse; after all, she'd claimed she was here for this very reason. What he hadn't expected, however, was the triumphant gleam that came into her eyes or the calculated way that she stripped.

She took her sweet time reaching for her shirt hem, lifting it up to bare the bottom curves of her beautifully full breasts. He couldn't look away, as she obviously knew because she was damn sure putting on a show. He waited and waited, sweat gathering in the hollow of his throat as he continued to wait and to watch.

Higher and higher went the hem of her shirt, lifting the tits he so wanted to see until, suddenly, her shirt was over her head and off, her breasts bouncing, her hair whipping around her shoulders. Her coloring came straight from an artist's palette: inky black hair with blue highlights, china-doll porcelain skin, nipples as dark red as Merlot.

She moved her hands to her legs then, running her palms and spread fingers down her inner thighs. The movement of her arms pressed her breasts together; he knew exactly how sweet and how tight the fit between would be. Her nipples pebbled, begging him to drop his pants and thrust into the soft valley she'd made. It was all he could do not to come where he sat.

When she slid her feet up his legs until they met in a V on either side of his crotch, when she pushed down with her heels against his inner thighs in the exact spot she knew to apply pressure, he closed his eyes and groaned.

None of the things he wanted to do with her were going to happen if he didn't get up and get some air. Spending the rest of the night taking advantage of her offer had seemed like a good idea at the time. But things were moving too fast. At this rate, he'd go off in thirty seconds.

He wanted to blame his rapid response on the fact that he'd been celibate for too long. But the truth was he'd always been this way with Jessie. He pushed up from the barstool, dislodging her feet. She crossed her legs up beneath her, limber even in jeans. Yeah, he was about to be in big trouble.

Especially when Jessie's gaze lifted slowly to his from where she'd been staring at the bulge behind his fly. Her eyes widened and sparkled and spoke of a hunger he'd never known another woman to feel. A hunger he knew would consume them both in the sort of sexual feast he'd been starving for.

Take a break, Miller. Get some air. Easy for you to say, he grumbled to his pious inner voice. It was his outer self calling these shots. But even his cock knew when distance was called for.

"I want you to do something for me, Jess."

"What?" she asked, though she might as well have said, "Anything," because that's what his body heard.

"Take off your jeans, but leave on your panties. And"—he gestured toward the floor—"put your shoes back on. Then meet me on the back porch."

She unfolded herself from the countertop and slid to the floor as if she'd been waiting all this time for him to tell her what to do. Blue couldn't help it. He took two steps and backed her into the counter, pressing his erection into the soft give of her belly and covering her weighty breasts with his hands.

Her nipples pressed into his palms like gumdrops and she

tossed back her head. Eyes closed, she gave a long, throaty sigh of what sounded like joyful relief. Amazing. Absolutely amazing.

He dropped his hands as if he'd been burned, turned and left the kitchen, walking into the attached washroom and then pushing open the screen door leading to the back porch. He didn't want to witness her feeling anything resembling joy, or relief, or emotion of any kind.

It was hard enough seeing the way she wanted him.

With the cool, damp fog swirling round, he jerked his shirt-tails from his jeans, wincing as he unzipped his fly and reached into his tight cotton boxers for the source of his pleasure and pain.

And then he spit into his palm and began to stroke, getting rid of the intense initial rush of arousal so he could take the time he was going to need with Jessie.

Chapter Five

When Blue demanded she strip to her panties, Jessie never considered telling him no. It wasn't until he told her to add the shoes that she'd suffered a stirring of doubt. High heels and a thong were so not her thing.

Now, however, with her sandals laced and her thong covering only a little bit more than nothing, what she suffered wasn't doubt but a sharp anticipation, a biting sense of heightened nerves and need.

For the first time in her life, she got it—that *thing* she'd never before understood about the way a man saw a woman when she wore nothing but heels and lingerie.

It was a basic response, a primal reaction, the male of the species tempted by his female's posture, drawn to mate by the lift of her ass, the length of her legs, the thrust of her breasts, the arch of her back.

Standing in Blue's kitchen, in nothing but a black satin thong and three-inch heels of black velvet, Jessie had never been more aware of her body. And yet what she felt was truly unique to this moment, this man. Her man . . . who was waiting to see her with her feathers flaunted and spread.

Her imagination went wild, dreaming of Blue at her back, his erection pressed between the cheeks of her bottom, his hands cupping the heft of her breasts, rubbing down over her belly to the barely there strip of hair beneath the edge of her thong, his skin rough and callused on hers so pampered and soft.

She shivered at her body's response, the tightening of her nipples, the moisture that dampened her thighs . . . the beat of her heart, like hummingbird wings fluttering inside her ribs . . . the pulse of energy buzzing along the surface of her skin, raising the hair on her arms, tightening the coil of desire holding her belly taut.

Nothing in her life before this had ever seemed so right, so meant to be. No, she wasn't one-hundred percent comfortable with the idea of walking outside wearing nothing but a tiny scrap of fabric. At least he had no neighbors for miles. But she wanted Blue badly enough that she knew she'd comply.

Especially now that she was here, now that she'd seen him, been touched by him. Now that she was forced to accept that she needn't go any further for the answer to her question. The truth was she responded to Blue like no other man.

Understanding why would not change that reality. Accepting it, however, meant she had choices to make about any relationships in her future. Right now, however, she chose to give in to the mystery and the needs of both her body and Blue's.

She found him leaning both hands on the thigh-high porch railing. Fog swirled low on the ground, eclipsing the fields beyond the clearing. A touch of light spilled through the windows, and the security spotlight on the highest eave of the house cast a surreal halo over the whole of the landscape.

Jessie shivered because she was cold and because desire drove a powerful bargain. Her nipples pebbled into painful knots and she hugged herself tightly, running her hands up and down her goosefleshed arms for what warmth the friction provided.

Her heels clicked on the porch; Blue didn't so much as turn his head. She had no idea what was going on in his mind and decided she'd be better off not knowing. There was no need to involve heart and soul when all she wanted to do was prove nothing but the sex remained between them.

"Before we go any further, I need you to do something for me." She'd do it herself but, well, she wasn't exactly dressed for the hike to her car parked beneath the yard's security spotlight. "There's a bag in my front seat and a box of condoms in the bag. The car's unlocked."

She knew he'd heard her join him, but he didn't even look around when she made her request. All he did was blow out a snort and ask, "Covering all your bases?"

Actually, she was, though he sounded more put out than thrilled with the concept. What had he expected? That she announce her intentions to all of September? "I thought it best to come prepared. Buying condoms at Blossom Drugs never did remain a private affair."

To that, Blue had no comeback. He just walked off the back steps and headed for her car.

She listened, waiting for the crunch of his boots on the crushed-shell drive, the sound of her car door slamming shut. And then she listened for his return, for any sort of sound, his breathing, the scrape of denim against denim as he walked, even the winter-dead grass crushed beneath his feet as he passed. Standing in the shelter of the doorway onto the covered porch, she heard nothing beyond the beat of her heart.

When he rounded the corner, he kept walking, signaling for her to follow him out into the yard. She hesitated briefly, not exactly thrilled by the idea of walking naked into the yard but realizing she had no need to worry. She trusted Blue not to put her in an untenable situation. He might dislike her for the way she'd left him, but he was not a cruel man. No matter how the years had changed him, malice was beyond his nature.

Pulling in a steadying breath, she made her way carefully across the mat of brown grass carpeting the clearing behind the house. Blue waited at the cedar plank door to a structure he'd built since her last visit here. His gaze devoured her body as she drew closer to the dark corner of the yard.

She wanted him to look into her eyes and see her intention to meet boldly any challenge he issued. She was no violet, shrinking away to wither and wilt. Neither would she creep back in the direction she'd come, tail tucked between her legs because he'd widened his eyes and said, "Boo."

Facing him now was nothing compared to the day ten years ago when she'd gathered up what guts she'd managed to salvage and left him, setting out to rebuild her spirit crushed by her father's abuse and reclaim her right to live her own life fearlessly before involving herself in another's.

But instead of meeting her defiant gaze, he studied the shoes on her feet, shaking his head as she walked, his eyes moving upward the closer she came. His gaze took in her legs, lingered at her silky black thong, slid over her belly, stopped at her breasts.

She stopped as well, standing inches away beneath his outstretched arm that held open the door to what she realized was an outdoor sauna housing a shower and hot tub. The idea of having Blue wet and naked and warm, with the sky above clearing and the stars beginning to shine . . .

Her pulse doubled its already frantic pace. She stepped up onto the concrete floor and turned into the enclosure to find a light fixture matching the one from the porch, a cedar plank bench and a long row of clothes hooks. Thank goodness, because these shoes had cost an Yves St. Laurent fortune.

Blue followed her inside. The door shut behind him and he shoved the deadbolt home. She perched gingerly on the edge of the bench, crossed one leg over the other and leaned down to unlace her shoes. Her fingertips had barely grazed the laces before he ordered her to stop.

Slowly, she got back to her feet, feeling strangely lightheaded by how small the space seemed now that he'd locked them inside, feeling equally off balance by the hovering presence of the man for whom she'd shed both clothes and inhibitions. He loomed larger than her memories painted him as she looked up into his eyes. "These will ruin if they get wet."

"They won't get wet." Jaw clenched tight, Blue's hands went to the buttons on his shirt. "I'll take them off."

Nodding was all she was able to do while she watched him

shrug out of his flannel. He tossed it over a hook, then sat to remove his boots.

She wasn't sure what to do, but she was desperate to touch him, to run her hands across his shoulders, to slide her palms down his chest, to spread her fingers over his stomach, to stroke his penis, to cup his balls, to take him into her mouth—

"Dammit, Jessie," he said, shoving his boots up beneath the bench. He whipped his undershirt over his head and off, then looked at her and glared. "Don't look at me like that and expect me not to give you what you're asking for."

Shivers threatened to take her apart. He sat there half-naked, so beautiful in his anger and arousal, his muscles flexed, his jaw rigid, his pulse ticking in the vein at his temple. She had never wanted to feel him inside of her more than she did right now.

She moved directly in front of him and placed one heel gently onto the edge of the bench between his spread thighs. "All I'm asking is for you to take off my shoes."

His hands hovered over the laces at her ankle, but his gaze burned straight ahead. She felt the heat between her legs where the scrap of her thong revealed more than it covered now that she stood with her knee bent and leg raised.

Swearing under his breath, Blue tore his gaze away, deftly unlacing the wickedly expensive shoe, pulling it from her foot and tucking it safely into the far corner of the bench. When she made a move to step back and switch feet, he stopped her with a strong hand circling her ankle and held her there, saying nothing as his breathing grew ragged and rough.

She waited, expecting him to touch her intimately, wanting, aching, anticipating the slide of his finger into her sex. His hand began to move upward, over her calf to her knee and she trembled so violently she thought she would fall. Blue never said a word; he only continued his agonizingly slow upward progress.

Once past her knee, he spread his fingers, mapping a path along her inner thigh and then stopping, dammit, stopping.

Stopping with his fingertips barely brushing the dip where her leg ended and sensation began.

She closed her eyes and shuddered, opened them again and moved her bare foot to the floor, the other to the bench between Blue's spread legs. On these laces he wasted no time, and in seconds she was left wearing nothing but her thong.

"Turn around," Blue ordered, and she did. "Back up here," he added, and again she complied, holding her breath until she felt the brush of fingertips up the backs of her thighs to her bottom.

She held her clutched hands between her breasts, wondering how she would survive this night when she wanted to weep with the waiting. And when she knew this would not be the only night she would cry wanting Blue Miller's touch.

At the creak of the bench, she tensed further, then gasped at the feel of his mouth: his lips nibbling the fleshy cheeks of her bottom, his teeth taking tiny nips of her skin, his tongue slipping beneath the elastic band of her thong and following it down her crevice.

His hands gripped her hips and urged her to step closer before the palm he moved to the small of her back pressed her down. She bent at the waist; her hands on her thighs kept her steady as Blue wedged a knee between her legs and spread her apart.

She heard the click of a pocketknife, briefly felt the cold blade before he sliced through the silk, once, twice. The thong fell to her feet. And then his hands seemed to be everywhere at once, her spine, her thighs, her bottom, deep between her legs where one long index finger separated her labia.

She ached, she burned, and he did nothing but circle the tiny bud of hardened flesh before pulling away to spread the moisture that seeped from her core. He pushed into her then, the blunt tip of one finger seeking out and finding the soft pillow of her G-spot inside.

He rubbed and stroked, pulled out and pushed in, one finger first, then with two, until she whimpered and gasped. And then he withdrew, but only long enough to enter her with his thumb, holding her there and running the flat pad of two fingers up between her lips to find the hood of her clit.

He squeezed. She cried out, and he immediately let go, frustrating her further when he did nothing more than coat her with her own juices, sweeping the fluid back from her vagina to rub in circles over the button of her ass.

Anything. He could do anything. She ached with the need to come. She wanted him to take her, any way, every way. But he didn't take her at all. He pulled back, and she straightened, frustration growling loudly from her belly up her throat.

"Damn you, Thomas Miller," she whispered, emotion clogging her throat.

Behind her, Blue stood, nearly strangling on a desperate laugh. "Ah, Jess. You're still the whore all men want to find in their bed, do you know that?"

She bristled, and turned to face him, her breathing labored, her pulse racing. She looked up into his eyes, seeing the reflection of her own flashing as hotly as his, seeing a hunger that told her she could snap her fingers and bring him to his knees.

The power she held over him thrilled her. It equaled the power he held over her. "No, Blue. I'm only a whore in your bed. Never in anyone else's."

Chapter Six

He wanted to know what she meant.

He couldn't believe any woman who loved sex the way Jessie did wouldn't act on her urges, respond with the same fire, no matter the man. He didn't want to believe her. He couldn't believe her. Believing her meant falling into whatever trap she'd come here to set.

He'd never zipped up his fly after his earlier back porch fun, so he made quick work of skinning off his boxers and jeans. And then there he stood, naked in front of the only woman he'd ever wanted to marry. Anger warred with passion and lust, battled the sort of physical longing he hadn't experienced for years.

In the end, he said nothing. He simply took her hand and took the two short steps from the dressing alcove into the outdoor shower.

He turned on the water, adjusted the temperature until steam rose and billowed, backed up beneath the spray and drew Jessie close. Her hands went around his back to cup his shoulder blades; she rested her head in the center of his chest and sighed.

Gathering her hair into one hand, he slipped an arm around her, and then he stood there, afraid to move and hating himself for what felt like a monumental weakness. He was supposed to be long over this woman, but nothing had felt this right in years.

Though he'd hoped the heat from his body would warm her, still Jessie shivered. He took another step back and turned to the side, letting the water sluice over them both until the steam enveloped the enclosure, wrapping them in its fine mist.

He didn't remember her being so small or so thin, and that physical fragility bared the claws of his protective instincts. It didn't matter that a cold day in hell would dawn before she came to a man for protection. She'd always made him feel like she needed him.

And right now it was hard to separate those feelings from what was going on with him physically, what with her gorgeous breasts pressed to his chest and his cock throbbing where he'd shoved it against her belly, there where she wiggled and squirmed as if wanting to take him inside her however she could. The thought that she wanted him that much . . . he released a purely feral groan.

And then he felt her grin where her mouth met his chest, right before her shivers became a full-body shake. He reached over and upped the flow of hot water.

"The water's not going to help," she said.

"I thought you were cold."

She shook her head. "No. I'm wonderfully warm."

He stiffened and bit back a curse. "Don't tell me you're scared."

"No. Not scared." She snuggled in even closer. "Never scared."

He closed his eyes, unnaturally relieved and wanting nothing less than to examine the reason. "You're still shaking."

Her entire body trembled. And if her attempt at a laugh was intended to make him feel better, she failed. He felt as though he'd lost total control over the situation and what little was left of his mind.

"Believe me, I wish I could stop. This is not exactly the smooth seduction I'd planned." She lifted her head from his chest, tilted it back enough to look up into his eyes.

All he saw were stars . . . the reflection of the ones in the sky and those sparked by what Jessie was feeling. She'd never been good at keeping things from him, which was why he'd felt poleaxed when she'd told him good-bye.

He wished he had the strength to show her exactly how abandonment felt. Leaving her wet and trembling and naked in the dark would go a long way toward fulfilling the dream he'd once had of revenge.

But he didn't have it anymore. And he didn't resent her anymore for never telling him the truth of why she'd left him. This woman was not that girl. She was so very much more.

And only just now, with her breasts pressed to his body, her legs twined with his, only now with the way her hands massaged the very tired muscles in his back did he realize he'd let the past anger go. This moment was about nothing more than the here and the now.

He lowered his head and kissed her.

It was a fantasy kiss, a dream kiss, a kiss like so very few he'd shared in his life. It was a kiss of uncertain exploration, as if neither of them trusted anything about this moment or the rest of the night still to follow.

It was a soft kiss, gentle and tender, and his heartbeat roared in his ears.

What a fool, thinking making love with Jessie could be about revenge. She'd hurt him; he'd wanted to strike back. Now he wanted to do nothing more than make this night one neither of them would ever forget.

He pulled free from the kiss and moved his mouth to the soft skin of her neck, tasting her there beneath her chin, along the line of her jaw, to the spot below her ear that he remembered so well. She gasped as he'd expected, digging fingertips into his rib cage and tossing back her head.

Blood surged to his groin and he widened his stance, pressing his erection even harder into her belly's soft give. His hands slipped down to cup her bottom, his fingers reaching deep between her cheeks to tease her tender and intimate flesh.

He wanted nothing more than to drop to his knees, to feast on her gorgeously ripe breasts, to lap and eat at her sex, to shove his tongue into her as far as he could and love her with his mouth until she exploded all over his face.

But she stopped him before he could get his mouth anywhere near her luscious curves. Stopped him by doing no more than stepping away, putting a breath of space between their bodies and opening her mouth in the center of his chest.

His hands went to her waist while her tongue swirled through the wet hair on his chest to find his nipples, one then the other, teething and tonguing skin and muscle until his eyes rolled back in his head. His cock strained upward, reaching for his belly. He'd grown so fuckin' hard he could hardly move.

It was not until he smelled more than wet skin and damp cedar that he realized Jessie had squirted a ribbon of shower gel in a line across his chest. She pushed him back out of the spray, pinning him to the wall as she went to work massaging him with her fingertips, digging into the muscles of his chest and shoulders until he felt as if she'd nailed him in place.

He couldn't move; he didn't want to move, afraid he'd distract her from the incredible job she was doing of washing away the years of sexual encounters he'd pretended were enough. She opened her palms then, and spread the lather in ever widening circles, moving down his torso to his abs and lower, her hands slipping down either side of his package, into the crease of his thighs.

She forced his legs open, urged his hips forward, rinsing him clean. And then she dropped to her knees, raining kisses back and forth between his thighs as the water pummeled down on her back.

He damn sure didn't want her to choke before she got to where she was going and, then, oh, goddamn, but her hand was around his shaft, squeezing hard and stroking as her lips wrapped around his ripely swollen head.

He'd wanted to take care of her pleasure first, but she'd just made it impossible for him to think. All he could do was feel—her hand like a glove and all that sweet pressure, her lips working madly to suck him dry.

He thrust forward because he had to, thrust again before he could hold himself back. And when she urged his legs apart with her free hand, he gave up on anything resembling control and obeyed.

She teased him without mercy, fingering the seam separating his balls and slipping behind, pressing hard against the skin stretched as taut as that of his cock. He ached, and his ball sac drew up, tightening around the stones of his testicles as Jessie's exploration reached deeper.

And then nothing mattered anymore because he couldn't have stopped her or stopped himself. "Ah, Jess," he cried, his hands flat on the cedar wall at his sides, holding him upright as he filled her with his cock and his come.

Chapter Seven

Wrapped in the circle of his arms and cushioned by the pallet he'd made on the floor, Jessie lay curled against Blue's body. His nearness warmed her, as did the roaring fire at their feet, and she grinned. What a sight, his mad dash through the house, gathering quilts and pillows while still in the buff, his dangly bits swaying in the breeze.

While still in the backyard enclosure, she'd wanted more than anything to get into the hot tub with Blue, to straddle his body with jets of water pulsing all around. But once they stepped out of the shower's steam, Blue wasn't having any more of the water. He wanted her in bed.

Back at the house, he'd started the fire, dragging every piece of bedding he owned to the hearth. She adored his total lack of self-consciousness; she always had. She loved his comfort with his bare body, and the way his confidence put her equally at ease in her own state of undress. She was strangely satisfied, even without a single one of the orgasms she'd expected to have experienced by now. Tingly and frustrated, yes. But comfortable. And content.

For the moment, she couldn't imagine any other place she'd rather be. She was not being stupid; she was fully aware of the danger of deluding herself into thinking she and Blue had a future. As it was, when she left in the morning, she'd mourn losing him a second time. More than making Christmas memories, her time here had shown her that the sex between them was more than physical. It was the mating of souls she'd never know again.

She scooted even closer, hooking a knee over his thigh, moving her head to the center of his chest, walking her fingers from his breastbone down his abdomen to his penis that lay thick and soft on the pillow of his balls.

She held him in her hand, enjoying the flaccid weight and the way he stirred anew at her touch. Skating the flat of her palm from the base of his growing shaft to the head, she slipped down beneath to cup his testicles and marvel at the soft skin of his sac.

One arm bent and cradling his head, Blue growled low in his throat, tucking her even closer with the arm around her back. "My balls are going to be aching by the time you leave. They haven't had seen this much action since . . ."

Curious, Jessie picked up his trailing thought, blowing a stream of breath over a flat nipple before asking, "Since when?"

He hesitated for several seconds, then huffed out a snort. "Since that's none of your business, Ms. Buchanan. *Yeowch!*" he yelled when she tugged at a sprig of hair between his legs.

"Tell me," she demanded, knowing that the fantasy of Blue remembering the sex they'd shared as anything out of the ordinary was just that. A fantasy.

"Tell you what?" he asked gruffly. "How long it's been since I had sex?"

She thought about that for a moment before admitting to herself that she had no rights at all where he was concerned. "Stupid of me, I know. I don't know why I asked."

"Because you wanted to know?" He chuckled then, but the sound seemed to be more a case of laughing at her than with her or at any sort of shared joke. Then again, what did she expect, tramping off into territory beyond the physical terrain she'd come here to explore.

Laughter was the least she deserved, she thought, sighing as she moved her hand away from his groin back up to his belly. She'd barely reached his navel when he stopped her, grabbing hold of her fingers and wrapping them around his half-hard penis.

"It's been a while, Jess. And even longer since it's been any good." He took a deep breath, exhaled, thrust lightly into her closed fist. "When it got to the point where I did better by myself, I decided it wasn't worth the hassle."

She wanted to feel victorious. All she felt was sad. Sad for Blue, and bitter that things couldn't have been different, and angry with the other women who hadn't loved him the way he deserved to be loved. And now here she was, doing the very same thing. "I'm sorry."

"For what? The fact that I'm not getting any?" He turned his head toward her, forced hers up so her gaze met his. "Don't be. It's my choice. And it's not like I've been in any danger of becoming a monk."

She smiled at that, then cuddled her cheek back down on his chest. Tiny hairs tickled her lips and her nose. "I know. I just feel like I failed you somehow. If I'd been here for you . . . but I guess that's rather conceited of me, isn't it? Thinking I had any impact—"

"You had a lot of impact. More than I should've let you have," he added harshly. And then he shrugged. "But, what did I know? I was eighteen and apparently didn't know much of anything beyond what grass seed sold best in what month."

He cleared his throat and pulled her up onto his body, wrapping his arms around her back and twining his legs with hers. "One thing I didn't get, Jess . . . I was so wrapped up in school and football and the store . . ." He shook his head. "One thing I wanted to kick my own ass for not seeing was how bad things were with your dad."

"No one saw it. Or understood. You had to live it, to be there, to know what it was like." She trembled, not wanting to revisit the abuse that she'd suffered. She was beyond that now and she would never go back. "I missed my mother so much, but she was in a better place, not having to wonder when he'd go off, not having to bear the brunt of his tirades . . . or his fists."

Blue stroked his hands down her back, one then the other, as if his touch could soothe what was left of the pain. "You should've told me. That pissed me off more than anything, hearing the gossip in the store. I wanted to hear it from you."

"Why? So you could take care of things?" She shook her head; the vehemence of her conviction was impossible to hide. "I had to take care of things myself. Leaving September was the only way I would ever feel strong enough to live my life my way. Not his way. And"—God, she hated to say it—"not your way. I couldn't risk that you would ask that of me."

He held her tighter, saying nothing; she heard the click of his teeth as he ground his jaw. She felt his muscles tense along his neck, what with her head tucked up beneath his chin, and she wondered what he was thinking. His heartbeat thudded from his chest and into hers where she lay atop his body.

She raised her head, propped her chin on her laced hands resting on his collarbone. "I didn't want to leave you, but I had to get out. I had to go."

"I know you did, baby. I know." And then he held her quietly while they watched the fire, stroking her softly as if taking the past away.

She'd missed his tenderness so very, very much, missed the way he'd always had of making her feel so . . . special. As if she were the most precious thing in his busy life, the one part above all else that he needed to survive, that didn't have to be shared beyond the two of them, that required they meet no expectations but those that were their own.

She'd taken all of that away, no doubt hurting him in ways she couldn't imagine, and that one thing she would always regret. That, and the way coming back now had opened up those vulnerabilities again. Why had she selfishly not thought of what this weekend might do to Blue? How many mistakes could she possibly make when it came to this man?

Still, she knew—they both had to know—that things had

happened the only possible way for two eighteen-year-olds on divergent paths whose lives had reached that big fat fork in the road to adulthood. But here and now, she sighed, snuggling down into Blue's side. Those days belonged to another lifetime, and this one was so much better.

Finally he said, "You realize, don't you, that I've got you here naked and I'm still not gettin' any."

She looked up into his eyes, beyond the teasing glint to the hint of uncertainty lurking behind. "And I suppose you want me to do something about that?"

"Actually, yeah. That would be pretty damn great," he said, his smile growing wide enough to show off the dimples she'd missed seeing.

She pursed her lips, pretending to consider. "I'm not so sure I agree. It seems that things have been a bit one-sided around here in the way they've been going down."

He huffed. "Think so, huh?"

And then he was on his all-fours kneeling over her, straddling her and leaning down to kiss her full and hard on the lips. Before she could disentangle her arms or get more than a taste of the kiss she so wanted, he was drawing a line down the center of her body with his tongue.

She let her hands fall back beside her shoulders, let her eyes close and did nothing but feel. She felt the heaven of being naked beneath Blue's body and the magic of his mouth as he tickled and teased her with quick licks and nibbles, aroused her with long lingering open-mouthed kisses on her belly's soft swell.

Her nipples grew tight, her breasts swollen. She desperately wanted him—his mouth, his hands—to ease away the ache. To give her a taste of the pleasure her life had been missing for such a very long time.

But when she cupped her own hands to the sides of her breasts, kneading the fullness, pinching at her nipples with forefingers and thumbs until her breathing quickened and came in sharp, panting bursts, Blue suddenly stopped.

She opened her eyes to find him staring down at her with a fiery gaze. "What's wrong?"

He shook his head. "Christ, but you're beautiful."

"You don't have to flatter me to get laid, you know." It was so much easier to flirt and to tease than to be overtaken by the rush of emotion evoked by his words. An emotion she didn't want to feel, because in fewer than twenty-four hours she'd be on her way home.

"I thought you might've learned to accept a compliment by now," he said softly, reminding her of how many times and in how many ways he'd soothed her with nothing more than his voice.

She blinked back tears she didn't want to cry and gave him a wry smile instead. "I'm not sure that will ever happen."

He spent a long moment staring into her eyes, a moment during which Jessie had to force herself to remain still, to breathe slowly and calmly, to not reach for him the way she so wanted to do. She should've known she could never escape this weekend without involving more than her body. Now what?

She refused to buy into the hope that he was involving more, a hope that grew the longer he remained silent. Flippant and teasing she could handle. Mindless sex she could handle. A second round of broken hearts would be too much to bear.

"What are you looking at?" she finally asked when it seemed he had no intention of looking away.

"What?" He frowned. "You mean you don't want to know what I'm thinking? Contrary to popular women's magazines, men can use both heads at the same time."

She arched a brow. "Read a lot of *Cosmo,* do you?"

"Only the covers in checkout lines."

"Hmm. I didn't know the Maxi Mart was so progressive."

"What's with you, Jess? You used to take sex between us seriously. All this time I've been thinking that casual *Sex and the City* attitude was nothing but a ratings ploy. And, yes, I do get HBO."

She shook her head, frightened to death of admitting the truth but knowing a dose of honesty between them would give leaving more of a pleasant after taste. "I have a great life, Blue.

I love my job and have incredible friends. The money's great. If I want to travel, I do. If I want to shop, I don't think twice about my budget. There's only one thing I don't have."

"A man."

"No, actually I do have a man. A very nice man. Kind and stable and successful."

"Well, isn't that special." He rolled off of her and onto his back.

She shifted up to lean over him. "It would be, except when he kisses me I feel nothing."

"And when he fucks you?"

She shook her head. "I haven't slept with him yet. He's being very patient."

"Sounds like a saint."

"He is." This time Jessie was the one to roll away, to pull her uncertainties around her. "And he deserves a woman who can appreciate him, not one obsessed with sex."

"Doesn't appear to me as if you're obsessed at all."

"But I am. When we're out? All I can think about is what it would be like to sleep with him, to take him home to bed. How unfair is that when I fake even enjoying his kiss? He's everything I've ever wanted, and he leaves me totally cold."

Blue raised up, loomed over her, his expression burning with a possessive, primal heat. "So, you came to me to get off. Yeah, I'm really into being a sex surrogate."

"No, Blue. I can get myself off just fine. I've been doing it for years. I came to you to see if I'm as unresponsive as I seem to be. If it's me . . . or if it's them." And now for the big confession. "Or if you're the only one who will ever be able to make me come."

"Why don't we find out?" And then he lowered his head.

Chapter Eight

Her mouth was unbelievably giving and warm; she parried to every thrust of his tongue. And he couldn't believe she had any doubt about her sexuality. He'd never known a woman admit to loving sex the way Jessie Buchanan loved sex.

With her hands gripping his shoulders, he kissed her hard, ruthless in his intention to make her feel anything, everything. To figuratively tear her to pieces, to make her understand the truth of what they shared, the depth of their connection.

To make her feel what she did to him. He wanted her to know that he'd spent all these years hating her because no one else had ever delivered on the physical promises she'd made.

And he wanted to get that back.

When he tore his mouth from hers, she gasped, and gasped again when he moved down her body and curled his tongue around first one pebbled nipple then the other. Back and forth he suckled, drawing on her areolas with his lips, teething her gently until she cried out and writhed.

He took her breasts in his hands, pressing the plump orbs together, breathing in the scent of her arousal when he nuzzled and lapped at her skin. He wanted to straddle her chest, pump in and out of the soft valley until his balls retracted into his body and he shot his hot load.

He'd loved fucking her tits, and remembered too well the look in her eyes as she'd waited, as she'd watched, her lips parted in anticipation as if she wanted his cock in her mouth more than she wanted to breathe.

Even now blood surged and he thrust forward, the head of his cock sliding along her soft inner thigh. Her hands moved down his sides and she reached between their bodies. He backed up and away before she took him into her hand.

The fire behind him popped and crackled, bathing Jessie's skin in flickering light. He slid farther down her body, kissing his way around her navel and over the swell of her belly until he reached the patch of black hair neatly trimmed above the soft lips of her pussy.

Kneeling between her spread legs, he placed both hands on her thighs and opened her farther, loving the way her juices glistened in the flickering light, like clear crystal sugar coating pink silk.

And the sweetness was all his.

He moved closer, breathing deep of her scent that was salty and warm and caused the fire in his groin to surge hotter. He closed his eyes against the new pressure, opened them again once he found his control. And then he dipped his head, stuck out his tongue and pushed it into her gorgeous cunt.

She cursed loudly and cried out his name. He swirled his tongue inside her, pulling out to slide the flat from her hole, between her labia and up to her clit. Once there, he drew the hard knot between his lips, sucking her clitoris into his mouth to flick with the tip of his tongue.

She spread her legs wider, drawing up her knees and pushing up onto her elbows to watch. Her dark eyes reflected the flames from the fire and sparked with a consuming need. He couldn't wait for her to burn him alive.

He wet two fingers with his mouth and, as her eyes flared, pushed them inside her, lowering his head to lap and to suck, teasing her clit with soft touches and harder strokes while fingering her in the steady rhythm he knew she loved.

Christ, but she was wet. He couldn't help it; he reared back onto his knees and spread her juices over the head of his cock. She whimpered, watching as he gave himself pleasure, and he was almost unable to stop from coming. He closed his eyes and reached behind his balls, pressing upward against the surge.

And then he felt Jessie's fingers tangling with his as she took over applying the pressure he needed, wrapping her other hand tightly around his shaft while his breathing settled and he found his control. Of course, then it was all he could do to pry her hands away and push her down to her back.

"I love your body, Blue," she breathlessly whispered, clenching her hands into fists where he held her wrists to the floor. "I've barely had you, and already know I'll never get enough."

He gritted his teeth until his jaw ached from holding himself in check. And then he reached for a condom. He sat back, hooked his hands behind her knees and pulled her forward, draping the backs of her thighs over his.

She wiggled even closer, wide open and waiting, her hands reaching down to part her folds and invite him in. The invitation was impossible to resist.

He took hold of his cock with one hand, guiding himself forward, leaning his weight on his other hand spread flat on the floor at the side of her head. She sucked in a sharp breath as the head breached her opening, and then her eyes rolled back, her lids fluttered, and her lower body drove up to meet his.

The ride was wild. He kept his hand between their bodies, fingering her clit as he pumped to the rhythmic grip of her tight inner walls. Heaven. Pure heaven. She wrapped her legs high around his waist and forced him down. And then one hand was digging into his backside, the other holding his head and pulling him down for her kiss.

Her mouth devoured his even as her body demanded all he had to give. She was slick and hot, and she made it impossible for him to hold back. He couldn't hold back. Not when he was here, between her legs, where he'd never had a reason to deny the urges that drove them both equally.

He swallowed her whimpers and urgent cries, matching

each of her upward thrusts with his own downward motion, withdrawing until only the head of his cock remained clutched within her tight sheath. Christ, she was sweet. Unbelievably sweet. And hotter than he'd known a woman could be.

And then she burst, releasing her hold on his back and flinging her arms out to the side. Her upper body came off the floor; her head lolled back. Her heels dug into the backs of his thighs. He watched her come, caught unaware by her uninhibited exhibition, by the way she lost herself in the orgasm, the total and reckless abandon of her physical response.

That was all it took. He shoved forward into her body as far as he could, spilling his seed and flirting with the dark edge of consciousness with each shuddering stroke. She soothed her hands down his back, her body still with silent sobs that threatened to take him apart.

He finally pulled himself free from her body, pulled off the condom and tossed it into the fireside trash before wrapping Jessie in blankets and spooning her limp body with his. Once his breathing had settled and her pulse no longer raced, he tucked loose strands of hair behind her ear.

"Does that answer your question?" he asked, knowing he'd just been handed a mighty big truth, a truth ten years in coming. All this time come and gone and he'd been fooling himself into thinking he'd gotten over this woman.

Or that he ever would.

"Yes," she said with tears in her eyes. "It does."

Yet he had the feeling that neither one of them was the least bit happy with their answers. And that when she left a few hours from now, his shield of bitterness would return. He figured he was going to need it, or else he'd spend the rest of his life wondering why they could never get this right.

Chapter Nine

Wearing red flannel pajamas and wrapped in a soft woolen throw patterned with gaily wrapped presents and trees, Jessie peeled back the plastic wrap covering her popcorn ball and settled back with a DVD of Bill Murray's *Scrooged*.

Appropriate for Christmas Eve, she supposed, since she wasn't feeling the least bit ho-ho-ho jolly or gay. What she was feeling was simply impatient, wanting the holidays over and gone so she could get back to the wonderful life of which she'd bragged to Blue.

And it was wonderful. Just lacking in passion. And void of orgasms she didn't supply. She eyed the package she'd left for herself under the tree she'd spent hours decorating in white, pink and gold.

Surely Santa wouldn't mind if she opened that one early. There wasn't a thing wrong with a single one of the vibrators in her collection. But this was the first one she'd bought designed to look and feel like a penis. After making love with Blue, she'd been struck with the urge for more than hot pink plastic.

She missed him; she hated to admit it but saw no way around the truth. Blue Miller had grown into a hell of a man. The very man who would always hold a place in her heart. For now that put a relationship with anyone else out of the question. For how long, she couldn't say.

Definitely not until these feelings faded to a memory, if they ever did. One she'd be able to look back on fondly, instead of wishing circumstances had been different, and she'd been able to stay in September and live her life with Blue. He'd never said anything leading her to believe he wanted her there.

But then, when had she given him a chance? When had they talked over anything that mattered? Why hadn't she made the effort after she realized how much of what they'd shared still remained?

Easy enough answer. Because this time she was afraid of being the one rejected.

A light rap on her door caught her with her attention drifting between the movie and the tree. She closed her eyes, ground her jaw, determined to send her well-meaning friends on their way. She was alone; she was not lonely. And she did not need to be smothered in holiday cheer.

With her popcorn ball held in one hand and the other dragging the throw behind her, she readied her growling response and pulled open the door. And there stood the very present she would've begged for if she'd had a chance to sit on Santa's lap.

Blue stood in her doorway wearing boots and jeans, along with a Shearling coat and black cowboy hat that made him seem even larger than he already was, that made Jessie feel small and ridiculously feminine and protected and safe.

Her heart ached, beating so hard and so fast she thought her ribs would break. Tears welled in her eyes; joy made a fist in her throat. Her popcorn ball fell in crushed pieces to her feet.

He glanced down at the sugary pink and white mess. "I guess it's safe to assume you're speechless in a good way, and not that you're thinking up a way to tell me to get the hell out of here."

Why was he still standing in her doorway instead of holding her in his arms? "Yes. I mean, no. Don't leave. Come in. Please, come in."

He did, stepping over the threshold, shoving the door closed behind him and sweeping her up into a crushing bear hug. And then she was in his arms and in his lap on the sofa, staring into his face because she couldn't believe he was here. In Dallas. In her condo. On Christmas Eve, when she thought she'd be stuck spending the rest of the night with Bill Murray.

"What are you doing here?" she asked, cupping his face in both of her hands because she still didn't trust that she hadn't dozed off and was dreaming. But he was warm, except where he was cold, and he was bristly with needing to shave.

"You left without getting what you'd come for," he said, digging down into one of his coat pockets.

What was he talking about? Hadn't she learned exactly what she'd needed to know? That no man but Blue Miller would ever be able to make her feel this way because he was the only man she would ever be able to love.

He handed her a black velvet jewelry box. Her hands shook almost too hard to hold it. "What's this?"

"Why don't you open it?"

Because she was scared to death to know what it was? Frightened out of her mind that she'd never again experience this feeling of pure amazement? She lifted the lid of the hinged box and then looked into Blue's eyes as she worked to catch her breath between sobs.

"I was going to bring you a real one," he said, lifting the silver filigree chain from the box and fastening the catch beneath her hair at her nape. "But I didn't want to have to deal with decorations and lights all the rest of that crap."

"Wait. I can't see it." She tucked her chin to her chest, doing her best to peer down at the tiny emerald Christmas tree with a diamond star on top. "Oh, Blue. This is gorgeous. And so unexpected. And way too extravagant."

He shook his head. "Not extravagant at all."

"Maybe not for a wife or a girlfriend. But for an ex-lover or one-night-stand?" She gave him a tight smile. "Definitely too much."

"Well, that's the thing," he said, fingering the jeweled charm where it rested in the V of her pajama's lapels. "I thought maybe we could work something out to remedy that 'ex' part."

She blinked once, twice, a third time, uncertain that she was hearing him correctly. "You're asking me to be your lover?"

"That, yes. And . . ." He took a deep breath and she saw in his hesitation the hurt she'd inflicted all those years ago.

She opened his coat and laid her hands on his chest, over his heart, because it was all she knew to do. "Ask me, Blue. Please."

"We messed up somewhere, Jess. We were too young, I guess. I didn't understand shit about why you had to leave. Why you wouldn't let me be your protector." He brushed hair back from her face. "I wanted to be your protector. I wanted to be your lover. And I still do."

"Is that a proposal?"

"I know we have a lot to work out, and we might not be able to, anyway."

"Yes."

He frowned. "Yes, we have a lot to work out? Or yes we might not be able to? Or—"

"Yes. I want to try again. And, yes. I know it won't be easy and will mean a lot of work. But I really do like working on you, Blue Miller."

"Is that so?"

"Oh, yeah." And she got busy showing him exactly how much, shoving his jacket back off his shoulders and tackling his shirt buttons as he shrugged out of the thick Shearling and suede.

She went after his belt buckle next, feeling his erection rise beneath her fingers that weren't quite as nimble as she wished. Her body opened in response, shifting and swelling in sharp anticipation. A reaction that was solely connected to what she shared with Blue.

She remained in his lap, forced to catch her balance on the sofa arm when he raised his lower body and tugged jeans and drawers down his hips only far enough to free the goods tucked inside. She took hold of his thick shaft and lightly squeezed, her knuckles rubbing into the hair on his flat belly.

He scrunched up his abs behind her hand and shivered, releasing a bead of clear fluid from the tip of his plump ripe head. Jessie licked her lips. And Blue groaned like a dying man.

She caught the tip of her tongue with the edges of her teeth and raised her gaze to his, smearing his release in a circular motion over the flat of his cock's swollen head. "Blue?"

"Jess?" he ground out, his eyes flashing, his fingers unbuttoning her pajama top. Cool air brushed her bare skin and she trembled.

"Are we safe?" She closed her eyes, breathed, tried again. "I'm on the pill. I've had blood tests done annually for the last three years, since the last time I was intimate with a man." The admission hurt; she didn't want him to know anything in her past. But she was not a stupid woman. "I want to make love with you desperately, but I don't have single condom in the house."

Blood surged through his veins; his cock pulsed in her hand. "You haven't had sex for three years?"

She shook her head. "And until last weekend? I hadn't made love in ten."

"Lift up," he ordered, holding her balanced on one knee while she pulled the other leg free from her pants. And then he settled her back to straddle his lap, cupped her mound with one shaking hand.

"I'm safe, Jess. I've been tested. And I've never been without a condom. I have a pocketful of them now. We only used half of what you brought." Heat rose from her collarbone to infuse her face, deepening further when he cleared his throat and added, "I want to love you, to come inside you with nothing in the way. No latex. No secrets. No doubts."

When she raised up onto her knees, Blue pressed her breasts together and buried his face between. She rubbed the head of his cock the length of her slit, teasing the both of them mercilessly with their shared heat. And then she guided him to her opening and slid down, burying him to the hilt.

She sat there in his lap, unmoving, his cock so deep inside of her she felt as if they were one. And they were. One flesh. One heart. Exactly as they'd always been.

Blue threaded his hand into her hair and cupped the back of her head, his gaze red and watery as he pulled her to his kiss.

"Merry Christmas, Jessie Buchanan," he whispered against her lips. "I love you."

"Oh, Blue. I love you, too," she said, thinking Elvis didn't know a damn thing about the meaning of a Blue Christmas.

THE NUTCRACKER SWEET

Nancy Warren

Chapter One

"Ms. Ellison, since it *is* the season of goodwill and giving, could you *please* give me a break?" Daniel Jarvis almost shouted the words, looming across her desk, invading her personal space.

Tara Ellison shot him her coldest look, and she prided herself on them. "*Mister* Jarvis. As I've told you countless times, the miscellaneous column in your expense account should be used sparingly if at all." In fact, it was Tara's personal mission to do away with the pesky thing. If people—traveling sales managers, in particular—couldn't keep track of their receipts, they should lose the privilege of being reimbursed for them. Besides, she liked to scrutinize every one of Daniel Jarvis's expense items to be certain he wasn't charging the company for his out-of-town play girls. She was certain they littered the country; his reputation with women was legendary.

He glared at her. "Unlike you, we don't all count beans for fun and profit."

She glared right back. "Company policy clearly outlines that miscellaneous expenses without receipts are only allowable when the charge is less than twenty-five dollars. I will not authorize them for one penny more."

"But there's more than a thousand bucks there!" He pointed to his current expense report, the first he'd managed to complete in three months.

"Then I suggest you find those receipts and record them properly."

Frustration was etched in every line of his face. His deep blue eyes were hot with it, his jaw rigid. "I don't have time for this. I have to go sell more corporate jets to keep you in pencil sharpeners."

He stomped off and Tara allowed herself a moment to stare at his rapidly retreating back. His trouble was, he was too damn good looking, too accustomed to women falling at his feet when he turned on his charm.

She was proud to be built of sterner stuff; still, a girl could look, couldn't she?

As always after one of their encounters, Tara's blood pumped hot and fierce. How could he make her so angry and so . . . attracted at the same time?

And what was she going to do about it?

Since he hadn't bothered to pick up his unacceptably sloppy expense report, she decided to return it to him herself. In the last ten seconds she'd come up with a couple of annihilating insults she wished she'd thought of earlier. She rose and grabbed the report. She hadn't nearly finished arguing with him. It made her feel alive like nothing else.

She got to his office in time to hear him on the phone, his back to her while he tossed a Nerf ball into a basketball hoop. "Sorry. Had a run in with the Ballbuster." He laughed softly. "You got it buddy. Tara Ellison's problem is she needs to get laid."

Her strangled gasp of outrage had him spinning around, his eyes widening when he saw her. "I'll call you back," he said and slammed down the phone. He half-rose, then sank back into the chair.

Daniel knew trouble when he saw it, and wished he could think of something to say to wipe the utterly shocked expression off Tara's face. "Look, I—"

"Are you up for the job?"

"Pardon?" He expected rage, tears, a written complaint about him, not that coolly delivered question.

"You said I need to get laid." She propped a shoulder against his doorjamb and stared down her nose at him. "I'm asking if you're up for the job?"

"I . . . um . . . I'm . . ."

"Speechless. I like that in a man. See you at the party." And she turned on her heel and left.

Party? What party? Daniel couldn't get his brain to function properly, and watched a pair of slim hips twitch the skirt of a Christmas-red business suit as Tara strode away. Party? Oh, right. The secret Santa lunch thing was today. He smacked his forehead. If he'd thought his day had just hit rock bottom, he was wrong. In a sick twist of fate, he'd drawn Tara's name for the secret Santa gift exchange.

After this latest encounter, he wished he wasn't tied up with a sales meeting for the rest of the morning, or he'd run out and buy her a different present. He hadn't been able to resist the *nut*cracker, knowing it would give all the other men in the office untold amusement. But, since she'd walked in on him and overheard private guy talk, she already had his nuts in a vise, and it wasn't all that amusing.

And yet her challenge intrigued him. Could it be she was making a joke? Tara? A joke? About sex? He rubbed his chin as she disappeared from view. What if she wasn't joking?

She made him crazy with frustration, yet she was sexy in a bossy, pedantic way. But did he want to have sex with her? He thought about it for a second. Giving her mouth something better to do than berate him was definitely appealing. In fact, her mouth was luscious, along with the rest of her.

His musing came to an abrupt end as the obvious truth struck him. Hell, yes, he wanted to have sex with her.

Cheery holiday music wafted from the boardroom as Daniel strolled in for the annual staff lunch and secret Santa gift exchange.

The executive committee had decorated the boardroom and were doing the serving. As a sales manager, Daniel was neither upper echelon nor peon, and that suited him fine. He was top sales manager, which also suited him fine. He loved selling. He liked wooing the customer, putting the deal together, closing. It was kind of like seducing a woman. And he prided himself on his skill at both.

They were close enough to year-end that he knew he was tops in sales again this year, which carried a hefty bonus, and that put him in a particularly celebratory mood. The only cloud on his sunny horizon was already primly seated, her red suit jacket open to display a silk blouse.

He assumed Tara was wearing red because it was Christmas, but maybe she was literally waving a red flag in front of a bull. Himself being the poor wounded bull in this scenario. But the suit was sexy-woman red, and that made him pause. Her head was turned; she was talking to Gary from the mailroom. Poor kid was blushing so deeply you could hang him from the tree and call him an ornament.

From this angle, Daniel noticed the elegant curve of Tara's neck beneath the shiny dark brown cap of her hair. For some damn reason, his gaze followed that line to the V of her blouse.

When he realized he was trying to look down her shirt, he yanked his gaze back up, appalled at himself. He might not be a feminist, but he wasn't an office pervert, either.

At that precise moment she turned her head, as though she'd felt his stare. Their gazes connected and he blinked at the impact. How had he missed the obvious? His ballbuster was a babe.

He didn't know what to do. Usually animosity crackled between them. Every meeting was a confrontation. And damn it, he looked forward to every one. For the first time, he noticed the sexual hum that sizzled just beneath the hostility. Interesting.

"Come in and have a seat, Daniel," boomed Giles Monroe. The company president was resplendent in a bright red barbecue apron patterned with Santas in chef hats, which he wore over his usual three-piece banker's suit minus the jacket.

Of course, the lunch was catered, but Giles did make the eggnog himself. Since Daniel had discovered there were raw eggs in the recipe, he chose a beer. He liked Giles fine, but not enough to give himself salmonella.

There were forty or fifty people already in the room, and the fake tree in the corner was surrounded by gifts.

Daniel made his way over, placed his silver-wrapped present under the tree and found a seat across from Tara. If she was going to eviscerate him when she opened his gift, he wanted to make sure he was close to the door—so he could make a run for it.

The staff Christmas lunch followed the same pattern it had last year, but this one felt different. He was keenly aware of the subtle current of something new between him and Tara. Of course she was pissed at him; she had every right to be.

He still couldn't believe he'd been stupid enough to leave his office door open so she could overhear his comments. He felt a tiny twinge of remorse for making them in the first place, but they were guy comments, never meant to be shared with a woman.

He'd have felt a lot more comfortable if she'd done something predictable, such as stick her nose in the air and point out his behavior was rude and boorish and childish, *blah, blah, blah*. But for some inscrutable reason, she'd departed from the obvious script, and that left him unsettled.

Besides, what he felt sizzling in the air wasn't just anger, and his ability to read unspoken feelings was probably his greatest asset as a salesman. No, she was sending him vibes that in any other woman would be attraction. Strangest part of all was that he was pretty sure he was sending them straight back at her.

Odd.

When they'd finished the assorted sandwiches, the rum balls and Christmas cake, the music changed to "Here Comes Santa Claus" and the chiming of Salvation Army–type hand-held bells could be heard in the corridor. Giles, who'd swapped the apron for a Santa suit, soon appeared and the gift giving was underway.

As soon as his gift was deposited in front of Tara, Daniel

wished he could call it back. She glanced up at him as soon as it landed in front of her and he knew she'd seen it in his hand when he'd walked in. She'd nailed him like a missing dime in the quarterly financials.

"And here's one for Daniel." Santa, who'd obviously had a glass or two of his own eggnog plopped a flat red-wrapped gift in front of him. Looked like some kind of book.

When everyone had their gifts, Santa counted to three and wrapping started to rip.

There were groans at the gag gifts, laughter and cries of glee. The thing with the secret Santa was how easy it often was to figure out who your gift was from.

His was a perfect example. It was a book all right. A personal accounts ledger. A yellow sticky note was pasted to the front. *For keeping track of all those pesky receipts,* it said, in the neat and even handwriting he saw in his nightmares.

Tara.

Of course, since it was an open secret that he was more of a creative accounting type, and regularly sent suits with their pockets crammed with receipts to the dry cleaners, there was a big laugh when he displayed his gift. He opened the cover, and there was a pocket on one side—to hold receipts, he supposed.

There was something in the pocket. A folder from a downtown hotel. A small folder, the kind that holds a key card. Another yellow sticky note displayed a different message.

7 P.M. tonight. Do you dare?

He shut the book with a thud before anyone else could see what was inside and glanced up, his blood already pounding, to find Tara's gaze on him, taunting.

In her hand was his present to her.

A silver nutcracker.

In spite of the fact he'd figured the joke would go over her head, it hadn't. There'd been some muffled chuckles when she opened it, and, with a cool smile in his direction, she said, "Exactly what I needed."

She leaned across to the middle of the boardroom table where a centerpiece of poinsettia, pine boughs and holly sat.

Dotted amongst the branches were unshelled nuts. He recognized filberts, brazils and a few almonds, but her long-fingered hands, tipped with red to match her suit, reached for a walnut. The biggest of the bunch.

She put the walnut inside the nutcracker's jaw, put her hand to the mechanism and then, very deliberately, raised her gaze to his.

He crossed his legs instinctively as she twisted the handle and crushed the nut.

She shook the pieces into her palm then tossed them into her mouth and chewed. "Delicious," she announced.

Chapter Two

What did a man take to a sexual tryst with a woman with whom he'd never exchanged a civil word?

Daniel had no idea of the protocol; he frankly doubted there was one. This bizarre meeting had to be breaking new ground, if Tara had even been serious. For all he knew, he'd get to the hotel room and find all the women of the firm gathered together ready to have a good laugh at his gullibility.

His BMW cruised through the quiet December streets, throwing up slush in his wake as he rounded a corner a little fast.

Of course, the snow wouldn't last until Christmas. It never did in Seattle. Simply teased residents into enjoying a few days of the white stuff before the next good rain washed it all away.

He'd managed to get away from work with enough time for a quick shower, shave and change of clothes. She'd chosen the Westin downtown for their—whatever the hell it was. Rendezvous? Get together? Boinkathon? Hen party to make fun of the politically incorrect doofus?

The Westin added credibility somehow. It was big and anonymous, and enough holiday functions would be going on this time of year that if they bumped into anyone they knew, they could easily have an innocent reason for being there.

He might have blown the whole thing off as undoubtedly a

sick joke, except if he were planning a sexual assignation and he wanted to keep it a secret, he'd have picked one of the big hotels, too.

He could drive right past and spend the evening in a dozen different places, but he already knew he was going to the Westin. The decision had been made the minute he saw the key card and her dare.

A man didn't get to be a top salesman without taking risks. And the payoff on this one could be huge. Hell, he'd sleep with Tara Ellison simply to get her to lighten up on his expense reports.

He'd have sex with her to see what her face looked like when it wasn't glaring at him.

He grinned to himself. He'd make love with her because she'd surprised the hell out of him. He liked that.

Deciding he wouldn't look any more foolish showing up with wine and flowers, he stopped on his way and bought a couple of dozen red roses and a chilled bottle of vintage Dom Perignon.

After all, he figured that going from trading insults to trading body fluids in the space of twelve hours deserved some kind of celebration.

He entered the hotel lobby and did his best to keep his head down. He didn't remotely want to bump into anybody he knew. He didn't think he could fake a conversation right now, or explain the wine and flowers. All his energies were focused on what he hoped was awaiting him behind the door of the hotel room his key card unlocked.

His pulse pounded uncomfortably fast. He was anticipating this so keenly it was almost painful. When had he begun wanting Tara so badly? And how come he'd never known it before today?

The elevator carried him skyward with quiet efficiency, and then he was there. In a tastefully decorated impersonal corridor walking to . . . what?

He left the key card in his pocket and knocked, sliding the

flowers and champagne behind his back. If there was a hen party going in there, all ready to burst out laughing at his expense, he didn't want to give them any more ammunition.

A few tense seconds passed. Then he heard her voice, soft and low. "Who is it?"

For a second he wondered if she was thinking he might have brought a posse of yahoos with him, and he grinned. "It's Daniel."

The door opened and he stepped inside.

He knew immediately that this wasn't a sorority gag, but the real thing.

Music played softly, the lights were dim, and Tara, the woman he'd only ever seen in business attire, with a snarky attitude wrapped around her like a cloak, was standing in front of him in a robe.

Not a terry towel hotel robe, but obviously her own. It was soft, dusky rose and shimmered when the light hit it.

Lust shot through him.

Even though the robe covered her from chest to midcalf, he'd bet all next year's commissions that she was naked underneath.

He became aware of a stinging pain in his right palm and abruptly realized that as lust had gripped him, he in turn had gripped the rose stems so they bit him through the florist's cellophane wrapping.

Glad now he'd brought them, just to give him something to do in this awkward first moment, he pulled them from behind his back.

"For you."

"Flowers, how beautiful." She reached for them and it occurred to him that this was the first nice exchange they'd ever shared.

Instead of letting go when her hand closed around the wrapping, just below his, he brought his other hand from behind his back. "And champagne."

Her lips tilted in a smile. Was she thinking he didn't show much imagination? Probably. He didn't care. He used his imagination where it counted, as she was going to find out in the next few hours.

"I wasn't sure you'd come," she said. How had he never noticed before how soft and husky her voice was? Her hair was glossy as though she'd just brushed it and she smelled good, spicy and floral at the same time.

"I haven't turned down a dare since David Wilkerson bet me his Hot Wheels set I couldn't Rollerblade backward down the hill behind our house."

"Did you end up with his Hot Wheels?" She was gazing around the room, the flowers still clutched in her hand, and he realized she was looking for something to put them in.

With a shrug she picked up the ice bucket and headed for the bathroom.

"I ended up with a broken arm," he said to her back. Nice back. Filled out a silk kimono just right.

While she put water in the ice bucket and arranged the flowers, he crossed to the minibar and found a couple of wineglasses. He wondered how they were going to pull this off. Being polite to each other was a new experience and a pall of awkwardness cloaked the proceedings.

Well, he figured a woman wearing a silk robe intended to be eased out of it. He'd give them each the time it took to drink a glass of champagne and then he'd oblige her.

Truth was, he'd never received a present that he wanted to unwrap as much as his surprising secret Santa gift.

He eased the cork out of the bottle so it hiccupped rather than popped, and poured.

Tara was going to book herself into therapy first thing tomorrow. What had she been thinking?

All these months she'd sensed a potent animal attraction between them, but now Daniel was here in a hotel room with her, she had to wonder if she'd simply confused the crackle of anger with the sizzle of lust.

Now that they weren't exchanging insults, she didn't want to jump him. She wanted to transport herself to her own living room couch, with a cup of hot chocolate, her fuzzy bunny slippers and a chick flick in the VCR.

Instead, through her impetuous temper, she'd trapped them both into this horribly embarrassing situation.

She should have demanded an apology when she overheard his crude words. That's what the sane woman would have done, but she'd blurted out that crazy dare, and then had been so intrigued by the idea she'd followed it through. All the way here.

They sat by the window in the two armchairs flanking a rectangular table in some kind of dark wood. The roses graced the table. She'd offered to turf them so he could put the champagne on ice, but he'd tossed out all the soda from the minibar and managed to wedge the champagne bottle in there.

By craning her neck over her shoulder, she could look out the window at the lights of Seattle and the dark smudge of Puget Sound. If she sat normally, her view was of the king-size bed that dominated the room.

She sipped, wondering if politeness would take all the sizzle out of their relationship. Wondering if she should go ahead and admit this had been a stupid idea and let them both off the hook.

She sipped again, and took the time to savor the taste of champagne. Her favorite. Her gaze moved to the roses, looking elegant but casual in their ice-bucket vase. "You shouldn't have spent all that money," she said.

"Don't worry. I plan to sneak it into my expense account. Under miscellaneous."

Her ire sparked instantly, making her blood crackle like the champagne. She jerked her gaze to his, ready to really let him have it, then caught his expression and realized he was teasing. "Don't even think about it," she said, trying not to smile.

"What about the hotel room? I could put it on my corporate card. We get a special rate."

Impossible to believe that he was joking about the subject that usually had them at each other's throats.

She laughed, feeling a little of that sizzle make its way to her erogenous zones.

Then her laugh died in her throat.

Daniel rose and stepped in front of her. Frozen, she watched as though from outside her body as he reached for her drink, took it from her and placed it on the table. Then he took her hands and drew her to her feet.

His hands were warm and sure while hers suddenly felt cold and shaky.

Ohhhh. This was probably a terrible idea. If sex with Daniel was a monumental disaster and then she had to face him every day—well, this had been her ill-advised idea. She'd have to go get another job, that's all.

Daniel didn't seem to be sharing her doubts. He looked supremely confident. Keeping his gaze on hers, he let his fingertips travel over her palms to the soft, sensitive skin of her inner wrists under her silk robe. It was just a whisper of a touch, with both of them still clothed, yet it felt intimate and shiveringly arousing.

His lips came closer, brushed hers slowly, and, as her eyes fluttered closed, she knew monumental disaster was not going to be an issue.

Chapter Three

He deepened the kiss and she felt as though she had to hang on to him or risk slipping bonelessly to the pale green carpet.

Leaving her mouth, he kissed her jaw, found the sweet spot just behind her ear and made her gasp when he flicked his tongue, then kissed his way down her throat.

"You smell good," he said, his words rumbling against her skin.

She'd arrived at five-thirty, making sure she had time to bathe, pluck, shave, buff and scent herself. She didn't consider herself any more vain than the next woman, but she'd also dimmed the lights near the bed, so as to show herself—if it came to that—in the most flattering light.

"It's my body lotion." She sighed, tipping her chin to give him greater access, wondering how she'd ever exchanged an angry word with a man who could do *this* with his mouth. "It's imported from France."

Well, in the most intelligent remarks of her life, that one was going to go down as a list topper. While his mouth was busy with her throat, his hands moved slowly up her arms to her shoulders, then traced the V of her silk gown.

Her skin seemed to pulse with warmth where he touched her. He didn't pull the lapels apart but seemed content to discover her body's contours by touch rather than sight.

Fine by her.

His fingers traced the opening of her robe to where it crossed, and continued to the loose knot at her waist. Instead of undoing the sash, he took his hands back up her sides and feathered them across her breasts. She could barely keep still. The feel of silk sliding against her naked skin and the warmth of his hands through the fabric drove her crazy.

A quiet humming sound came from her throat as she played her hands over his shoulders, feeling muscle and bone. His neck was athletic and ropy, his hair thick and luscious when her fingers plunged into it.

But it was his mouth that most surprised and excited her. Based on what his kisses were doing to her, she couldn't wait to get on with the evening's program.

She could be naked at the pull of a sash, but he was still far too clothed.

Running her hands down his back, she took a moment to appreciate the fine wool of his shirt and the musculature of his back. Soon her hands were burrowing beneath to feel his skin.

No good. Needed more. She reached for his shirt hem again, to find him there before her, his own hands divesting himself of the shirt at top speed.

"I don't think I can take this slowly," he panted as he tossed the obviously expensive shirt to the floor. "I wanted to, but I can't."

"Me neither," she admitted.

He stepped back to give himself some room and went to work on his buckle.

With fire raging in her own body, Tara put a hand to her robe's silk tie.

"No!" He stopped her with a ragged half-shout. "I want to do that. I've been thinking about it since I got in here. You're part of my Christmas present and I want to unwrap you myself."

Since he'd just dragged his pants and briefs down in one jerky motion, and her gaze had eagerly followed the movement, her mouth was currently too dry to speak.

She was getting an inkling of where his legendary reputation with women originated.

Oh, my.

She didn't remember seeing him take off his shoes, but he wasn't wearing them now, and he snagged his socks with a practiced smoothness as he finished undressing.

"You are gorgeous," she heard herself say, then blushed at sounding such an idiot. So she scolded. "And it's not fair you get to undress me when I didn't get to undress you."

A purely carnal gleam lit his eyes. "I guess you're right," he said slowly. "Fair's fair."

He stepped to the end of the bed, giving her a mouthwatering view of his muscular back, adorably white butt and darker legs. He flipped the tasteful floral bed cover back, stacked a couple of pillows at the head and settled himself against them. She'd think he was settling in for a nap if it weren't for the straining impatience of his impressive erection.

"Okay," he said. "Your turn."

Why hadn't she kept her big mouth shut? Now he'd left her with two choices. She could act like a scared prude, which was exactly how she felt, dash to the bed, toss the robe and plunge under the covers, or she could bare herself to him as though she were one of those brazen perfect-bodied women who made exercise their life's work.

She grit her teeth. She'd be damned if she cowered. And her body wasn't going to attain perfection simply by standing here.

The hell with it. What could he do?

Apart from laugh at her and share the secrets of her nakedness with all the puerile juvenile men in the office.

She stood there, her hand hovering at the knot in her robe's sash.

"You look as though you're calculating the daily interest on the national debt," he said, with a crooked grin. "Come on. I showed you mine. You show me yours."

"If one word of this ever, ever gets out in the office, I will take you apart."

Instantly, he grew serious. "Some things are private," he said softly, and she found she believed him.

She pushed her shoulders back, took a deep breath. She undid the robe then shrugged it from her shoulders so it slid, raining silken kisses down her back.

For a long moment his gaze remained on her face and for that alone she wanted to kiss him.

Then his gaze took a slow, lazy tour of her body and instead of feeling self-conscious and imperfect, she felt like a goddess. There was no disguising the rapt adoration in his eyes.

When even her feet felt loved by his gaze, and her own feminine power was a high all its own, he said, "Come here." His voice was so husky she heard the barely leashed control.

All her womanly instincts responded.

She walked slowly toward him and let him look.

When she hit the bed, she reached for one of the condoms she'd placed on the bedside table and handed it to him. "Merry Christmas."

He reached as though to take it from her hand, then grasped her wrist instead and pulled so she tumbled across him with a squeak.

"Right back at you," he said and feasted on her mouth. His kiss was deep and hungry, drugging in its intensity.

Her blood pounded through her veins as need blossomed. Now that they were both naked and together, she wanted to touch as much of his body as possible with as much of her body as possible.

"Touch me," she sighed, even as she lay atop him giving him a full-body kiss.

He rolled her until she was underneath him, then trailed his fingers along the seam of her thighs until, with a moan, she opened for him.

When she'd said, "Touch me," she'd had more of a general touch in mind. But he'd obviously taken her request more specifically. When she felt his palm cup her mound, she was ill-inclined to clarify her words. This worked just fine.

"Oh, you feel good," he mumbled against her hair as she felt his fingers moving over her slick, intimate places.

"You have no idea," she said. His touch was masterful, as though he instinctively gauged just the right pressure and friction.

She felt wet, hot and womanly. While his fingers toyed with her hot button, his mouth stayed busy kissing her.

Knowing she was closing in on ecstasy way too fast, she tried to nudge him in the right direction so he'd be inside her when she climaxed.

"No," he said, kissing her softly. "I want to watch you come. I want to watch your face when it's not twisted with rage and hurling insults at me."

How could he? How could he caress her, naked and open to him, intimate and giving, and then bring up their less-than-harmonious work relationship?

"I should have known this wouldn't work," she panted. "Get up. Get off me."

He chuckled and slipped two fingers inside her body. "Are you sure you want me to stop?"

He was pressing . . . and rubbing . . . and she didn't want to give him the satisfaction, but she couldn't stop the swift slide into bliss.

"You bastard," she cried, even as he pushed her over the edge and she plunged into a noisy and satisfying orgasm.

Her climax left her barely sated, wanting more. She needed him inside her so fiercely, she burned. She also wanted to make sure she saw him at his most vulnerable, staring right into his eyes when he lost control.

Fortunately, he either sensed her desperation or shared it, for he sheathed himself with a minimum of fuss and before her breath was quite back in her body, parted her legs and settled between them.

She stared up into his eyes, feeling the strange disconnect between the business-clothed Daniel who drove her crazy and the naked on-the-brink-of-entering-her Daniel who drove her crazy in an entirely different way.

"I can't believe this is happening," she whispered, lifting her hand to touch his cheek, as though to prove to herself he was real.

"I can't believe how much I want you."

She felt the blunt, warm tip of his penis nudging her open and her hips tilted of their own accord as she felt her body softening, opening for him.

She could feel the tension in his muscles as he held himself in check and she waited for him to slip the leash and surge into her. Instead, he cupped her face in his hands and, eyes open, holding her gaze, he lowered his head slowly to kiss her.

It was a long, sweet kiss, so different from what she would have expected from him. As he slipped his tongue between her lips, he eased into her body.

The sound that emerged from her throat was part growl and part purr. He filled and stretched her deliciously, entering her so slowly that she felt the pull and clench of her own muscles sucking him deep.

Once he was fully inside her, she found she wanted to hold him there, even as she craved the friction. She wrapped her legs around his hips, taking him as deep as she could, then wrapping her arms around his shoulders.

He was big and solid and wonderful. Moving slowly at first, he sent warm currents scudding through her body. She was determined that this time he'd lose control first, and it wasn't long before she felt that happen. He thrust faster, up and hard, reaching a part of her she was certain had never been touched. Mindlessly, she arched against him, unable to hold herself in check, hearing their flesh slap at each mad joining, faster and faster until she was crying out once more, her lips plastered against his sweat-damp shoulder.

A couple more thrusts and she felt his body go rigid as he hit his own point of no return. She held him through his climax and then they collapsed in a tangled, exhausted heap.

She lay sprawled and spent across his chest. Her fingers played idly in his chest hair while she waited for their breathing to slow.

She'd never felt so blissfully and thoroughly loved, which made her uneasy. And that of course made her cranky.

Daniel's skin, she noted, was awfully bronzed for December in the rainy Pacific Northwest. His butt and crotch sported a paler, bathing suit–size patch. "Did you get that tan on company time?"

He rolled his eyes. "Was this whole thing a devious plan to check my body for illicit tan lines?"

She chuckled. "You didn't think I wanted you for sex, did you?"

With a shriek, she found herself flat on her back while Daniel bit—not all that gently—at her nipples.

"*Ow,*" she struggled, giggling. "*Ow,* stop it. All right, all right! I only wanted you for sex."

Immediately his mouth gentled, soothing her nipples with his tongue. "I spent a long weekend in Bermuda," he told her. "Between seeing customers on the East Coast. Okay?"

The way his tongue was curling around her nipple made everything okay.

There hadn't been a lot of foreplay before. They hadn't wanted it. Hadn't needed it. Both of them had been in too much of a hurry. Now it was nice to take the time simply to enjoy each other's bodies.

From her nipple, a tingling warmth began to radiate, and, amazingly, before her heart rate had entirely slowed from the last bout of sex, it started pounding again as desire flowed once more.

"How many condoms did you bring?" he murmured against her breast.

"A dozen."

He grinned up at her. "Me, too."

Soon he had number two on, and slipped into her body, which received him with quiet pleasure. Now that the desperate need was slaked, they took their time, touching, exploring, rolling around the bed until finally, she trapped him beneath her and took him at her own pace, sending them both over the edge once again.

"Hungry?" he asked later, when, sweaty and exhausted, they collapsed against the pillows again.

"Starving."

They ate room service sushi at the table by the window since Tara refused to eat in bed. She slipped back into her silk robe and he shrugged into the hotel's terry robe, and they drank the rest of the champagne.

They also talked. About traveling, which they both loved, and about sailing which he loved and she'd barely tried. "You live by the ocean and don't sail?" he asked, sounding astonished.

"Never had much opportunity, I guess."

"I'll take you out on my boat when the weather warms up," he said. And she wondered just how many women had heard those words, and how many of them had actually lasted through two seasons.

And then the bottle was empty and the food gone. There was a pause and Daniel assumed they were both thinking the same thing. Stay or go?

If they left now, or if only one of them left now, the whole affair remained casual. They could have sex again if they both so desired, or not.

But, if they climbed back into that big bed—after washing up and brushing their teeth if he knew Ms. Anal Compulsive—and spent the night, well, it catapulted them beyond the after-work quickie.

Did he want that?

He turned his head and found her gazing at him, and the answer was there. Hell, yes, he wanted more.

He plucked one of the roses out of the ice bucket and reached forward to trace the silky red petals down her cheek.

She smiled a little.

"We shouldn't drive after drinking that champagne," he said.

"No," she agreed solemnly. "You're right."

He shrugged. "We should probably sleep over then."

She grinned at him. "Don't plan on getting a lot of sleep."

She rose and stretched and, as he watched the silk contour her body, he felt like a guy who hasn't had any in months rather than one who'd spent all evening in bed with a sexy, responsive woman.

"Do you need a toothbrush?" she asked him. "I have a spare in my cosmetics case."

Why was he not surprised? "Don't worry about it. I stuck one in my pocket just in case."

"All right then. I think I'll take a shower before bed."

He thought about joining her but decided to give her some privacy. Besides, he needed to save his strength for later.

When she emerged, her body tingling and clean, Tara found he'd got rid of the room service stuff and tidied the bed.

His turn in the bathroom was predictably much shorter than hers, though she did hear the shower.

He wasn't wearing the robe when he came back out of the bathroom, his hair damp, and climbed into bed beside her.

He ran a hand across his jaw. "I borrowed your razor. Hope that's okay."

He'd shaved again. How considerate. "No. I don't mind."

He kissed her and she could feel where he'd missed a spot shaving.

He kissed his way down her body, parted her knees and settled between them. "I forgot dessert," he said, then proceeded to eat her as though she were a banquet.

Oh, what that tongue could do to a woman. He treated her clit like a lollipop he wanted to last a long time. But she was only human, and it had been months since she'd been with a man.

And he was too bloody good at what he was doing. When his tongue drove her up to bliss faster then either of them wanted, he simply gave her a minute and then started all over again.

Hours later, they fell asleep in each other's arms.

Chapter Four

"Ms. Ellison, what is this memo about?" Daniel slapped the offending paper on Ms. Decimal Point's obsessively, anally compulsive, neat-freak desk, on top of which sat one pencil sharpened to a perfect point—in her favorite shade of red. The only other item on the pristine surface was her nutcracker, which she'd turned into an ornament, he was certain, just to piss him off.

Not that she needed any props to do that.

She picked up her memo and pretended to read it, as though she didn't know perfectly well what had made him ballistic this morning.

"It seems fairly straightforward to me," she said. "Were there some big words you needed help with?"

"There's your big nose I'd like you to get out of my business."

"Accounting is my business. You can't give a discount that big to this customer. We could end up losing money on the deal."

He stuck his face close to hers and narrowed his eyes, doing his best to intimidate her with his size. "Selling planes is my business. Got it?"

The intimidation tactic didn't seem to work. She narrowed her eyes right back at him and he wished he didn't notice the extra sparkle in the glossy brown irises. "It's my job to vet those contracts, you know that."

"It's not your job to screw up a sale. I'm taking this up with Giles."

"Fine by me."

He stomped two steps to her door and turned back as though an invisible rope had yanked him. "My place. Friday night."

The sparkle in her eyes intensified and her breasts rose and fell on a jerky breath. She nodded sharply.

"Don't plan on getting any sleep."

Tara drew another jerky breath when Daniel left. They'd barely seen each other since waking, tangled together, two mornings ago. She'd imagined awkwardness and blushes at the office, but somehow, once she donned her suit and pumps, her liaison with one seriously sexy sales manager became a delicious secret.

She wouldn't reveal their afterhours relationship any more than she'd flip her skirt over her hips to show off her French cut silk-and-lace panties.

Daniel's anger almost made her smile. Was he really so egotistical as to assume she'd let flagrant abuses of their firm's accounting policies slip by her notice because she'd slept with him?

Well, if he'd thought so before, he no longer did.

Her intercom buzzed a few minutes later. "Tara," Giles's voice boomed, "could you come in here a minute?"

"Certainly," she replied coolly, while she seethed inside.

She swept into Giles's office all ready to do battle. From his belligerent stance over by the window, Daniel was in the same frame of mind. Angry sparks of fire shot from his gaze as he turned it on her.

"Ah, Tara," Giles said with his usual joviality. "We seem to have a problem."

"The problem is that Mr. Jarvis doesn't accept we have policies and he has to follow them."

"Ms. Ellison needs to understand that policies, like rules,

are made to be bent once in a while. It prevents them from be-coming *dry* and *rigid*."

She gasped. The way he'd narrowed his gaze at her while he said the words had her suspecting it was she he was talking about, not the company policies. Dry and rigid? She'd show him dry and rigid come Friday night. Why, she'd be so wet and . . . and pliant, he'd have trouble hanging on.

Giles shook his head at the pair of them. "You know I re-spect you both, but I wish you could respect each other a little more. Tara, Daniel's right. Sometimes we need to discount our prices a little deeper to hook a potentially valuable customer."

He held up a hand as she opened her mouth to argue.

"And Daniel, Tara's right. You can't take such a deep dis-count that we lose too much money. You're a gifted salesman. I think you can talk them up another five percent on the fleet cost. What do you think?"

"I can try," Daniel said stiffly.

"Good. Now, I'm going to insist you two go to lunch to-gether on the company. Get to know each other a bit. You might find out there's a lot to like."

"Hah," mumbled Tara.

What Daniel mumbled was a lot worse.

"I want to strangle you. And I want to sleep with you," Daniel said over antipasto at a trendy seafood restaurant that seemed to be constructed entirely of glass and cedar. "No, wait. I'm not into necrophilia. I want to sleep with you and strangle you."

Tara bit into a melt-in-your-mouth-perfect scallop. "Me, too. In our work hours I mostly want to hurt you."

"And outside work?"

She sighed, thinking of their magic night together. "Not."

"Me, too."

He ate another prawn. "You know, Giles has a point. We should try to work together better."

"But how can I work with you when you insist on dumping every other item in miscellaneous?"

"And how can I negotiate a deal if I have to worry about you hanging on to every nickel?"

They glared at each other.

"It's hopeless."

"Let's talk about something else."

She sipped ice water. There was something she'd been wondering about since the other night, but it had become particularly relevant since they'd booked a second night together. "Are you seeing anyone?"

He chewed slowly and she had a deep and disturbing desire to lick a speck of melted butter off his lower lip. "I'm seeing you Friday night."

"I mean—" She crinkled her forehead, feeling hideously uncomfortable and wishing it didn't matter, but it did. "Are you seeing other women? Besides me?" Before he could answer, she babbled on. "I know we're not exactly seeing each other—it's just sex, but I suppose what I'm asking is—"

"Am I having sex with anyone else."

"Yes."

"No."

She let out a relieved breath. "Okay."

A pause stretched into eternity. "What about you? Are you having sex with other men?"

"No!" What did he take her for? She was no saint, but she took her relationships one at a time. Not that they were having a relationship, exactly. At least not one that was like any she'd had before.

"Fine."

"Fine."

He helped himself from the bread basket. "So, about Friday."

"Yes?"

"Do you want to make it tonight?"

She felt suddenly confused and disoriented. "Do I want to have Friday tonight? It's Wednesday."

"Do you want to have *sex* tonight."

Oh, her body answered that one with a flood of desire so

intense she couldn't speak. So she nodded so enthusiastically her chin bashed her chest.

He dug a scrap of paper out of his pocket and scribbled. "Here's my address."

She pulled out her Palm Pilot and typed in the details then handed the paper back. "That's a Boston taxi receipt," she said, forcing her tone to remain pleasant. "You'll need it for your expense account."

"Right." He shoved it back in his pocket. "We should probably swap phone numbers, too."

"Why? It's the talking that gets us into trouble."

He rolled his eyes. "In case we want to have phone sex."

"Oh." That sounded interesting. "Okay."

She reached into her bag for a notebook and wrote her own address and phone number and handed the page to him. Daniel folded it and slipped it carefully into his breast pocket.

The bill came for lunch and he paid with his credit card and before her horrified gaze, crumpled the receipt and shoved it in his trouser pocket.

"Give me that," she cried, outraged.

He shot her a puzzled glance, then, with a reluctant grin, retrieved the thin piece of now-mangled paper. "Here."

She was relieved her address and phone number hadn't joined the crumpled bills headed for oblivion or—even worse—miscellaneous!

Chapter Five

Tara arrived at Daniel's apartment five minutes early, then dithered outside his door thinking she should have timed her arrival better. She'd rather show up fashionably late than appear too eager.

The trouble was she *felt* too eager. So juiced she couldn't stand still, but shifted from foot to foot, images and impressions of the last time they'd been together crowding her mind.

Oh, the hell with it. So she was a polite person who showed up on time. He could just get over himself if he liked unpunctual women.

Raising her chin a notch, she rapped firmly on the door.

It opened so fast he might have been standing on the other side of it waiting.

That impression was intensified when he grabbed her and yanked her to him. "What took you so long?"

She had time for a smug smile to half form before his mouth was on hers hot and hungry.

Oh, if she thought she'd been restless and turned on standing in the corridor, that was nothing to the scorching heat that now ignited within her body.

Opening her mouth to him, she began twisting and rubbing sinuously against him, not by design. She couldn't help herself. It was as though she were trying to climb right into his skin.

His hands were rubbing, tugging at her through her jacket,

both of them too mindless to take the thing off. With a groan of impatience, he tugged her navy DKNY casual skirt up and backed her against the door.

She was practically climbing his body, so it was an easy matter for him to hook one bent knee and drape it over his arm, then reach for her panties and shove them aside while fumbling with the zipper of his jeans.

She heard the ripping of a condom package and gave him extra points for having one so handy. Then his cock was nudging against her.

Except the crotch of her panties was once again in the way.

He made a growling sound in his throat, said, "I owe you one pair of panties," and then she felt the tug almost at the same time she heard the sound of ripping silk.

She was panting, desperate for him, her hips already rocking in anticipation. And then he was there, thrusting up and into her and she screamed with the overwhelming pleasure.

He thrust deep and hard and she met him thrust for thrust. Their hands were all over each other, mouths kissing, licking, biting every inch of skin they could reach.

She thought someone was knocking on the door, then realized the sound came from her purse, still hooked to her arm, banging in time to their passion.

The door was hard against the back of her head and her spine, but she didn't care. She used the leverage to grind her pelvis against his, driving them both even crazier. She climbed so high and so fast she thought her lungs might burst, then felt as though they did burst, along with the rest of her as she shattered.

Her cries and the instinctive tightening of her muscles around him were enough to provoke Daniel's explosion. His thrusts became frenzied, his muscles rigid, and, to her surprise, it was enough to set her off again so they came together in a panting rush.

There was no way she could speak. In fact, she was only remaining upright because she was sandwiched between Daniel and the door.

She leaned her forehead against the side of his neck and found it damp, felt his pulse pound, echoing her own.

He kissed the top of her head. "Hi. Can I take your coat?"

She chuckled. "I got what I came for," she said breezily. "I should be going now."

He rocked gently against her, his cock still deep inside causing aftershocks to ripple through her body. "We've barely started," he said.

"How's your account book working?" she asked him later, tucked up against him in bed. Evening had faded to night, but they'd barely noticed, so caught up in exploring each other's bodies, bringing each other pleasure. Just now, she felt that one more orgasm might kill her, but there was a quiet pleasure in lying here, his chest hair tickling her cheek, his heart rate slowing beneath her ear.

His hand, which had been idly tracing circles around her nipple, stilled. "Fine."

A certain defensiveness in his tone made her wonder just how much he was using his personal ledger. "Let's see."

"That's private," he said with a huffiness that sounded contrived. An interesting possibility occurred to her—that he wasn't merely disorganized. He didn't know how to do the most basic accounting.

"Daniel, I know how obscenely overpaid you are. We've seen each other naked, climaxed together—I think you could share your account ledger with me."

He shifted, his flesh sliding warmly against hers. "I haven't started using it yet."

She propped her head on her elbow and gazed down at his face, trying not to let her amusement show. "You don't have a clue how to keep your books, do you?"

His gaze narrowed and went steely on her, a lone gunfighter up against the posse. She didn't say a word, just raised her eyebrows.

He tried to pull her head down for a kiss, but she resisted. "Do you?"

When she refused his kiss, he must have figured out distraction was hopeless, and gave in. "No."

She kissed his nose and then rolled out of bed in one smooth motion. "Come on. I'll teach you."

"Are you one of those interfering women who no sooner gets in a man's pants than she wants to start improving him?"

She grinned at him as she shrugged into the navy terry towel robe hanging on the back of the door. "Yep."

The robe smelled like Daniel, and wrapping herself in it was like getting a hug from him, which the real Daniel didn't look in any mood to give her right now.

He grumbled, but shrugged into the jeans he'd dumped on the floor. He must feel, as she did, that they were going to wear themselves out if they didn't take a break from the sex. She'd never been so insatiable before. She no sooner felt him slip out of her body, both of them sated and panting, than she wanted him again.

She forced down the desire that raised its sleepy head when she saw him walk toward her bare-chested, his jeans riding low.

Accounting wasn't sexy, not even to Tara, so it seemed the safest occupation while they recovered. Besides, her gift of an account book was useless if the man didn't know how to use it.

She flipped on a light switch and illuminated the glossy walnut dining table she'd coveted herself when she'd seen it in the Ethan Allen catalogue, and seated herself at one of the high-backed chairs. She'd snagged her purse along the way, and pulled out her calculator, then waited patiently while he reluctantly went to a drawer in the matching sideboard, obviously designed to store linens. He eased open the drawer and she saw, not tablecloths and napkins, but a sea of crumpled papers.

The cover of the accounting book was bulging when he dug it out, which gave her hope, but that hope was dashed when she flipped it open to find more receipts stuffed into it and not a single notation in the ledger.

"Right," she said briskly, already sorting the receipts into piles, knowing she had to perform emergency financial CPR. "I'll need copies of your bank statements, mortgage, taxes, food bills, telephone, life insurance, charitable donations, the works."

She'd given him the book in the frail hope it might encourage him to turn in accurate expense reports, but somewhere along the way it had become her mission to teach him to organize his entire financial life. Including his personal finances.

"I knew sleeping with you was a terrible idea."

She might have been insulted at the gruff words had he not raised her hair and kissed the nape of her neck as he said them. Then, even more sneakily, he slipped a hand beneath his robe and found her breast. She let herself give in to pleasure but only for a moment. He might call her interfering, but she knew helping him get his books straight would do him a lot more good than another session of rolling around together on the bed, the floor, this dining room table even . . .

Resolutely she put the image away for now. "Later," she said. "You will feel so much better when your finances are organized. Trust me."

He grumbled some more, but went back to the drawer and started dumping all the bills, receipts and statements onto the dining table.

"Do you want some wine?"

"*Mmm,*" she said absently. Really, she just wanted to get hold of those receipts.

However, as he turned away and she simultaneously lunged for the heap of crumpled paper, he suddenly leaned over and stopped her with a hand on her wrist.

Startled, she glanced up to find him staring at her with a negotiator's impassive face. "You really want those receipts, don't you?"

She wanted them so bad her calculator hand was itching. It would be nice to act casual about this, but she was currently sprawled across his dining table, her breasts squished against his robe, one outstretched hand almost touching the papers.

"I only want to help you," she managed.

"I don't know." Not letting go of her wrist, he hoisted one hip onto the table, giving her a great view of his abdomen, tight with muscle and decorated with a sexy arrow of hair. "I'd say this is bringing the office home. Something we've never done."

"But you need—"

"I'm not saying you can't have a few, but there should be something in it for me." He shot her a teasing glance, which immediately made her squished nipples stir causing simultaneous pleasure and discomfort.

"Like what?" She tried to sound business-like and faintly annoyed, but her voice betrayed her, coming out in an excited whisper.

"Well, let's see. If I let you pound a calculator in our sex time, then the fairest exchange would be for us to have sex during worktime."

"You mean play hooky?" She was shocked. She never goofed off from work and she would have said Daniel didn't either.

"No. I mean have sex at the office."

"The office?" she squeaked.

He rubbed his chin with his free hand. "Yep. My office has no window and the door locks." He let her go and she sagged back into her seat feeling as though the bumpty cotton of his robe were imprinted on her flesh. "I'll check my schedule, but I think I'm free midafternoon tomorrow. How about you?"

"Midafternoon. For sex. In your office."

He picked up a handful of receipts and placed them within reach, but kept his hand over them. Damn the man, how could he torment her like this? She wanted to organize his finances the way a chef might crave a kitchen full of raw food, or a decorator might be compelled to fix beige walls and a shag rug.

Naturally, she'd refuse—if the very idea of having sex in his office tomorrow in the midafternoon didn't have her exhausted body perking up again. But she wasn't a pushover. She tried to mirror his negotiator face. "Two handfuls of receipts."

His eyes narrowed. "Okay, this better be done in half an hour, so we can get back to the real reason you're here."

"Agreed."

"And you'd better get out your electronic organizer and schedule our private meeting right now."

"All right." Ridiculous to feel so excited at the prospect, but she didn't think tomorrow afternoon could arrive fast enough. She pictured them having sex at Daniel's desk, in Daniel's chair, against the walls in his office, the filing cabinet. Oh, the possibilities were endless. She might have to stuff his Nerf ball in his mouth to keep the rest of the office from hearing. He had a way of roaring sometimes when he climaxed.

"Two o'clock all right?" she asked.

He checked his own schedule. "Yep."

"Fine." At last, she had her hands on those receipts. She wondered what she'd have to do to get to the rest of the pile, and licked her lips at a couple of the ideas that flickered through her imagination.

"We'll start with a simple system. Income. Expenses. Under expenses, you've got two sections. Essentials and nonessentials. It helps you budget." She glared at him. "Don't groan. Budget is not a dirty word. Essentials are things like heat and light."

He picked up a restaurant receipt and handed it to her. "Here's one for essential."

"Food is an essential, but restaurants are nonessential." She flattened out an old phone bill and scanned it, wishing she had a pencil sharpener with her. "The telephone is essential, but all those long-distance calls to Chicago—" She raised her eyebrows in a question, knowing damn well that two-hour calls at midnight weren't about selling planes.

"That ended a couple of months ago."

She was ridiculously pleased the Chicago thing was over. She imagined nights of phone sex with some woman in Illinois, and knew the only woman she wanted him having phone sex with was her. Besides, Tara thought piously, phone sex with her only involved local calls, he'd save a bunch of money.

After the allotted half hour, when her body was telling her

it was time to put away the calculator and get on with tonight's program, she asked him, "Do you think you can work with this?"

"Yes. I think so." He leaned over her shoulder, pausing to nibble her neck, and stared at her neat columns of figures. "Hey, where's the Miscellaneous column?"

Her lips tilted. "There isn't one."

Chapter Six

Were she and Daniel an item? As Christmas closed in, Tara began to wonder.

On the outside, nothing had changed. Every day she went to work as she always had, even if she stumbled out of bed verging on late, not because she'd slept in, oh no. She was waking up plenty early, but because Daniel had kept her in bed with his wiles and his clever moves, and she had to scramble to get to work on time.

Once there, however, the man whose lip prints she could still feel all over her body, behaved just as he always did at work. As did she. No one who saw their frigidly polite battles by day could possibly imagine the scorching intimacy they attained each night.

Her dare to Daniel had backfired in the worst way. She was pretty sure it was no longer just the sex that had her longing for the day to be over and the night to begin.

What she was going to do about the foolish problem with her heart was one issue. The other, more urgent issue was what to do about a Christmas present. She could be practical and buy him a decent calculator, which he really needed now he was attempting to keep his accounts in order, but that was dull even by her standards.

Something goofy from the love shop, or a pair of silly boxer shorts with happy faces or hearts would be more in keeping with how their relationship had started. Frivolous and unattached.

But what she really wanted to buy him was a pair of gorgeous gold cufflinks from a Belltown jeweler she loved. However, cufflinks could be construed as symbolizing attachment and clinging, which was, unfortunately, exactly how she felt. Attached and clingy.

For all their intimacy, she and Daniel had never discussed their feelings. Well, the *affair*, for want of a better word, had only been going on for a couple of weeks, but she'd never experienced anything as physically and emotionally satisfying before. Likely never would.

She hovered outside the jeweler's window, her breath fogging in the cold air as the cufflinks winked at her through the glass.

Well, she'd taken a risk in the first place with Daniel and it had worked out okay. Amazing, in fact.

Deciding she'd give him the cufflinks and the hell with the consequences, she entered the store and quickly purchased them before she could change her mind.

She even had them gift-wrapped so she wouldn't keep lifting the lid and torturing herself by staring at them, wondering if she was messing with a perfectly good casual relationship by buying an expensive gift.

They both had family in town, and neither of them had mentioned including the other in their holiday plans.

They hadn't made a secret of their . . . whatever the hell it was, but they hadn't put a bulletin in the employee newsletter, either, and, while she'd told her close friends about her new guy, she hadn't introduced him to anyone yet.

She felt as though she were playing wait and see. But she was getting a bit tired of waiting. Was it possible that she was nothing but a sex toy to Daniel while he was the man she'd fallen in love with?

The admission, even to herself, had her staggering down the street.

Oh, Lord. She'd gone and broken all the rules. First, she'd

started a steamy affair with a colleague. Now she'd done the ultimate no-brain move and fallen in love with the man.

Just what was she going to do about it?

"Not hungry?" Daniel asked.

"Hmm?" she gazed across the table at him, and realized he looked more appetizing than her dinner, even though they were in her favorite restaurant.

"You've barely touched your food."

"I was just thinking I'll miss you," she blurted, then wished she'd bitten her tongue. He was leaving the following day for a three-day business trip, and, she realized with a shock, it would be the first night in more than a week they'd spent apart.

Ever since the night she'd done his accounts, they'd gone to bed together every night. Woken up together, either in his apartment or hers. Her wardrobe now housed a couple of his shirts, her bathroom a toothbrush and some shaving stuff, while she kept a cosmetic bag and a stash of clean underwear at his place.

They didn't even bother with the pretense of asking anymore. Now he was going away for three days and she knew she'd hate every minute of it. He was going to Chicago. Home of the multiple-hour phone sex woman.

"I'm not hungry either," he said and signaled for the check.

She felt unaccountably nervous on the way back to his place. Her stomach felt kind of squishy and she knew she had to tell him at least a little of how she felt. The pretense that this was a casual fling was fine when he was in town and they saw each other every day, but if he was going to Chicago of all places, he had to understand he was taking her heart with him. And the thought of telling him that terrified her.

He seemed as disinclined to talk as she as they purred through town in his BMW, Mahalia Jackson belting out "Oh Holy Night."

A different kind of energy than the usual sexual desire sizzled between them. Oh, that was there too, but something else bubbled in the mix. Probably her own anxiety that if she admitted her feelings she'd find they weren't reciprocated and then the whole thing would become embarrassing. Worse than embarrassing. She could blow the entire wonderful relationship and lose him completely, then have to quit her job because it would hurt too much to see him.

What had she been *thinking?*

She shuddered.

When they got to his place, she knew she hadn't imagined the strange atmosphere. They pretty much always jumped each other the first second they were in the door, but tonight neither made a move.

Daniel took her coat and hung it along with his, then turned to her and rubbed the back of his neck as though he wanted to say something and didn't know how.

Her stomach felt like lead. He was going to Chicago for three days. Maybe he wanted to tell her their half-a-month affair was over.

She dropped her bag on the closest chair and decided she needed to know the worst.

"I get the feeling there's something you want to tell me," she said, crossing her arms as though giving herself a preparatory hug against bad news.

"No." He glanced at her, then down at the planked floor. "Something I want to show you."

His phone bill? she wondered sourly as he went to his accounting drawer. He pulled out his account book and flipped it open. "I wanted to show you that I've been keeping up the book."

"That's good," she said, feeling as though she were having an out-of-body experience. Her heart was about to shatter and he wanted to show her his household accounts?

She walked to the table where he'd laid open his book. There was her neat writing, where she'd started keeping his books for him, and there was his much messier writing. There were copious applications of White-Out she noticed as she scanned the columns with a professional eye.

Even in her emotional state, she realized something was wrong.

"What's this item under essentials?" She pointed to a five figure amount scrawled below his mortgage payment.

"That's my holiday."

"Holiday? Are you planning a world tour?"

She lifted her head to stare at him, and noticed an earnestness on his face she'd seen sometimes when they were making love. He'd gaze at her that way, as though she were the most important woman in the universe.

"I've booked one of those luxury resorts for couples. In the Caribbean. The dates are open. You can pick the time we go. I'll work my schedule around it."

She said the first thing that came into her head. "What is a holiday doing in your essentials column?"

He stepped closer and placed his hands on her shoulders, turning her so she looked up into his face. "You are essential in my life. It seemed the appropriate place."

Even though her vision was clouding with tears, she realized he was looking anxious.

She sniffed and blinked hard. "Yes. I think that's exactly the right place."

He pulled her against him. "I love you."

They kissed and, even though desire was there, strong and urgent, there was tenderness.

She sighed against his chest. "I love you, too." She rubbed her cheek against him, thinking how far they'd come in such a short time. "I thought you couldn't stand me."

"You are, without a doubt, the most stubborn, detail-obsessed, rule-oriented, hard-nosed woman I've ever met."

She pulled back slightly and glared up at him. So much for bended-knee declarations. "You forgot to mention ballbuster."

"Darling," he said. "You have me by the balls and you know it. What you do with them is up to you."

She grinned mistily up at him, letting her fingers trail down his belly. "I have some ideas and I promise they won't hurt a bit."

Please turn the page for an
exciting preview of
UNDER COVER by MaryJanice Davidson.
An October 2003 release from Brava!

Renee dashed into the middle of the busy street. Leaping like an ungainly brunette gazelle, she managed to avoid death three times before she got to the curb, taking the angry shriek of the bus's airbrakes as a musician takes applause. She didn't slow, but did take time to snatch a look over one shoulder . . . yep. Still about twenty yards behind her. They hadn't gotten a good look at her face.

She darted into the hotel and was momentarily dazzled by the brightly lit chandeliers and the ferocious grin of the concierge. The guy had a hundred teeth. Where to go where to go where-togo?

She heard the plaintive *ding!* of the elevator, and cruised in that direction. She had to get off the floor. After that . . . well, she'd worry about the rest later. Improvisation was her specialty. The bad news—like she needed more—the elevator was one of those glass cages. Everyone would see her going up.

She saw a few guests amble out, snug and smug in their dark autumn colors, with doubtless nothing more pressing on their minds than where to have dinner. She wanted to choke them and cry on their shoulders at the same time.

As the elevator emptied, a lone businessman walked in, his nose buried in a newspaper. A daring, reckless, and ultimately insane plan popped into her brain and, as usual, was approved by management.

They don't know my face very well, the picture they have is truly terrible, she reminded herself, putting on a burst of speed as the elevator doors started to close. *Plus, they're looking for a woman alone. So . . .*

Renee skidded along the tile and slid into the elevator, almost smashing into the far wall. Darned new shoes; she knew better than to wear unscuffed soles to work. Errr . . . on the run from work.

The businessman blinked at her over his *Wall Street Journal,* then raised his eyebrows as she snatched the paper out of his hands and flung her arms around his neck. "Sorry I'm late!" she panted, then mashed her lips down on his.

This was business, not pleasure. Or was it the other way around? The man was a stone fox, and that was a fact. Thick, wavy brown hair fell almost to his shoulders, an interesting contrast to the so-sober black suit, sky blue oxford shirt, and blue tie with black stripes. She saw that his eyes, in the moment before she sexually assaulted him, were the same blue as his shirt. His hair felt like coarse silk.

Far from shoving her away, or smacking her with his briefcase, the businessman kissed her back enthusiastically and hungrily. She felt her feet leave the ground and realized he'd picked her up, the better to snuggle her into his embrace. Oh, to be snuggled! It had been such a long time. Since—er—what year was it? She wrapped her legs around his waist and let him take her mouth again and again.

Ding!

Sure, she'd been having a rotten day. Week. Month. And yes, the bad guys . . . okay, good guys, *she* was the bad guy . . . were definitely hot on her trail. And she had no money and no place to stay. And if anyone figured out what she'd taken, her life wouldn't be worth spit on a sidewalk. At the very least, she'd never get a job in the industry again.

Ding!

But this man, this amazing man . . . his hands were all over her, big and warm, his mouth was kissing and nibbling, his aftershave smelled like a sunny apple orchard, and—

Ding!

The elevator had stopped.

With deep, *deep* regret, she managed to wrench herself free and put her feet on the floor. It was hard to get a deep breath. All that running, probably. Followed by the finest kiss of her life. Meanwhile, the businessman had thrust his hands in his pockets and was looking her over very carefully. He didn't smile.

"It's all right," he said at last, as she backed out of the elevator.

"What's all right?" She tried not to wheeze. What floor were they on? Who cared?

"Being late. You said, 'Sorry I'm late.'" His voice was a pleasant baritone. His gaze never left her face. To her surprise, he followed her out of the elevator, leaving his briefcase behind. "It's all right."

"Er . . . thanks. Gotta go."

His hand reached out and closed over her elbow. She briefly considered breaking his wrist, then decided against it. She had bigger things to worry about than assaulting Mr. Hottie. Again, anyway.

"Have lunch with me."

"I can't. I have to . . ." *Go. Run. Hide. Figure out what to do with PaceIC. Cry myself to sleep. Jump off a ledge. Kiss you again,* then *jump off a ledge.* "I have to go."

He chuckled, but still he didn't smile. "You misunderstand. I wasn't asking . . . Renee." She nearly fainted as he reached into his pocket and pulled out a badge. "You've got some explaining to do. And you can do it over lunch."

And we are proud to present
BAD BOYS TO GO,
with Lori Foster, Janelle Denison,
and Nancy Warren,
coming in November 2003 from Brava.
Here's a preview of Lori's story,
BRINGING UP BABY.

No two ways about it: Anabel just wasn't proper mother material. He thought of mothers as being like his own—no-nonsense, understated, ready with a hug and advice. His mother *looked* like a mother. Soft, a little rounded, casual and comfortable.

Anabel looked like . . . not a mother. He couldn't label her, but there was nothing comfortable about her. Exciting, yes. Hot, definitely. But not maternal.

Even while she had been pouring her heart out to him, a part of his mind kept thinking how sweet it'd be to push her to her back on his desk, to tug those threadbare jeans down her hips and thighs so he could . . .

Suddenly she slid off the desk and started toward him. "I know what you're thinking, Gil."

Along with the look in her eyes, that throaty tone brought him out of his reverie. "You haven't got a clue." If she did, she sure as hell wouldn't get so close to him.

"Wanna bet?" He caught his breath when she leaned into him, her hands sliding up his chest to rest on his shoulders. Her cool fingertips brushed the heated skin of his nape. Eyes direct, even challenging, she whispered, "You're thinking about sex. With me. I've seen that look on your face before."

He didn't back down. "What look?"

Her smile curled, lighting up her eyes, flushing her cheeks.

"Well, the look before you just went blank. It's this sort of heated expression, very direct and interested and naughty."

He caught her shoulders to hold her away—and instead, he just held her. His heart thundered and the muscles of his abdomen and thighs pulled tight. "You're mistaken."

"Oh really?" She went on tiptoe to brush her nose against his throat. "Mmm. You smell good, Gil."

Her breath whispered over his skin with the effect of a lick. Her breasts, shielded only by a clinging shirt, brushed his chest.

"Anabel." He meant his tone to be chastising, and instead it reeked of encouragement.

Her hand left his shoulder to glide down his chest, down, down to the waistband of his slacks, where she lingered, making him nuts, causing his lungs to constrict. Her lips moved nearer to his, and at close range she stared into his eyes.

"You want me, Gil. Admit it."

He wouldn't admit a damned thing. But neither could he deny it.

The darkening of her eyes should have given him warning. But when her slender fingers drifted lower, cupping his testicles through his slacks, he was taken completely off guard. To call her brazen would be an understatement. To call him unaffected would be an outright lie.

She held him, gently squeezed, expertly stroked. "You're already hard," she whispered.

Yeah, from his ears to his toes, but did she have to sound so pleased about it?

Still in that soft whisper, she purred, "Gil, I want you, too. I always have." As she said it, she moved her fingers up to his throbbing cock, teasing his length, deliberately arousing him further, pushing him. "We would be good together. I know you, know what you like and what you want. I'll do anything, Gil. Any time you want, any way you want."